FOGBOUND

Her hands groped behind her until they found the door latch. In a near panic, she shoved the heavy glass door aside, stumbled over the threshold and onto the terrace, and then managed to race down the steps without falling. The fog, a giant cauldron of bubbling wet smoke, swirled and shifted around her, blinding her.

At last she came to the steps leading down to the beach. One hand clutching the wooden banister, she felt with a cautious foot for each slick plank. During a pause to change her grip on the railing, she heard footsteps on the stairs above her.

"Jason?"

She waited, but she heard only the roar of the breakers and her own pulse thudding in her ears.

The noise sounded again. Closer. Like a shoe sliding softly, stealthily on wood.

"Jas—?"

Before Manda could turn, something struck the side of her head. After one brief second of searing pain, she crumpled to the ground.

DARK WINDOWS

MARY-BEN LOUIS

ZEBRA BOOKS
KENSINGTON PUBLISHING CORP.

For Micki Perry,
because she helped to make my lifelong dream come true;

For Debbie, Greg, and Kimberly Kifer,
because they let me call them "my kids"; and

For June, Francis, Larré, Sandy, Marylou, Donna and Paula.
They know *why.*

ZEBRA BOOKS

are published by

Kensington Publishing Corp.
475 Park Avenue South
New York, NY 10016

First printing: June, 1991

Printed in the United States of America

Chapter One

One minute the fog was hardly there at all. Like spiderwebs broken loose from their anchors, the thready wisps floated up from the ocean. They curled among the stunted junipers that clung to the walls of the ravines, angled steeply down to the beach. The next minute, or so it seemed to Manda Lethe, a threatening gray white mass pushed against her car. She slowed to a crawl.

Dammit! Before reaching the safety of the undulating coastal plain, she would have to negotiate nearly fifty miles of cliff-hanging curves. The two narrow asphalt lanes traversed a serpentine ledge, brushing mountain cutbanks on the left, and on the right rimming a two-hundred-foot drop to boulder-strewn surf. This was the most hazardous stretch of Highway 1, no simple driving feat even in good weather. For her to keep going, in pea soup fog with nightfall approaching, risked very possible disaster.

Through the swirling mists Manda spotted an overlook. Turning the brown Tempo onto the grassy parking area, she nosed it with care against the steel guardrail at the cliff's edge. She exhaled slowly and cut off the motor. Her faintly scarred hands ached from gripping the steering wheel. Grimacing at the needles of pain, she gingerly flexed her fingers and massaged her knuckles. The movements made her charm bracelet jingle, but she was so accustomed to its tinkle that she barely noticed.

Why on earth hadn't she chosen the safer valley route? More than once Dr. Nils had warned—no, ordered—her never to take the coast road if she were alone. Furthermore, when he learned the real purpose of her unsuccessful trip to San Francisco, she could imagine what he would say, his high-pitched voice incongruous in such a bear of a man.

"If I had suspected that you were seeking a job instead of attending the Western and Indian art exhibit—totally irresponsible behavior! My dear Manda, you simply cannot cope by yourself. Problems will arise that you are not able to handle. You must be with someone who understands your situation. I am the one who can protect you from the unkind curiosity of strangers."

Sometimes she thought he *wanted* her to feel inadequate and unreliable, but of course that was her rebellion speaking. She was truly grateful to Dr. Nils Johannsen, the psychiatrist on her case, for having invited her to live in his home when she had nowhere else to go. He had become almost like a father to her. However, his overly protective supervision had begun to smother her, to feed a determination to be on her own.

Manda knew that—except for her inability to remember anything that happened prior to two years ago—she was a perfectly normal and competent young woman!

But right now, trapped by the fog, she would have welcomed the doctor's advice. Should she backtrack to the inn at Big Sur, or creep ahead the forty-plus miles to San Simeon and the nearest hotel?

The stale air inside the car was stifling. She opened the window, eager to hear the waves pounding the shore, a sound that never failed to lift her spirits. But the fog muffled the roar of the surf, and the wetness rushed in, impatient to fill the one spot heretofore inaccessible.

A salty offshore breeze carried with it the acrid odor of rotting seaweed. Somewhere at sea a recent storm had torn the kelp from the ocean floor, and the ensuing high tides had deposited it far up on the beach, where it had soured in the past days' warm sunshine.

Manda swiped at the droplets settling on her left cheek and reached toward the yellow scarf on the seat beside her. Then, realizing it was too late, she put her hand back on the steering wheel. The dampness would already have caused the layered, feathery ends of her short hair to curl. Gone was the smooth, head-hugging style she had achieved at the expensive San Francisco salon, in the hope of making herself appear older during the job-hunting interviews. She hated her gamine face and petite, almost boyish figure, which made her look nearer sixteen than her actual age.

How old was she, really? She could not remember, of course, but the doctors who examined her in the hospital and the others who tested her at the mental clinic before she went to live with Dr. Nils—all those learned people—had concluded that she was in her early twenties. When Manda angrily demanded that she absolutely had to be one specific age, the psychologist had suggested, with no little amusement, that she consider twenty-one. Solemnly, she had agreed that twenty-one was a reasonably adult number.

Now, shivering in the chill, moisture-laden wind, Manda tugged her yellow sweater's shawl collar higher until it met the dark auburn ringlets at her nape. Hurriedly she rolled up the glass.

"Damn fog!" she said, expecting the sound of her voice to chase her feeling of aloneness. It didn't. Why was she so frightened of fog? Sometimes she had horrible nightmares about it. "Oh, I wish I were home!" Her throat muscles constricted with unshed tears. She swallowed hard. "I will not cry. I absolutely will not!" She squeezed shut her gray eyes and breathed deeply, deliberately, out and in. "I'll get through tonight okay, and tomorrow I'll see Emory."

Emory Wade, Dr. Nils's secretary. Behind closed eyelids Manda pictured his lopsided grin, his ice blue eyes with their dark, gold-tipped lashes, his wavy ash blond hair.

Was she in love with him? she wondered. All she knew for certain about being in love came from books she'd read, and dramas she'd seen on TV or at the movies. Was there a man out there somewhere, broken-hearted because she had suddenly and without reason vanished from his life two years ago? She hoped not. Emory would be sad if she left *him*.

Only three weeks after he met her and came to work and live in Dr. Nils's big pink stucco house, Emory had asked her to marry him. She hadn't known how to answer him then, and after two more months she still didn't know. His embraces made her feel warm and . . . nice. But she wished that love would come to her with the suddenness of fierce stormy winds, or like a skyrocket starbursting in a summer sky. Her relationship with Emory involved no heart-stopping surprises, just a deep affection growing out of friendly propinquity. Was she asking too much, wanting to experience the senses-rocking kind of love? Should she wait for it to happen, or give in to Emory's amorous demands?

His increasing impatience, plus a new tension between him and Dr. Nils—who at every opportunity hinted that Manda's amnesia precluded her forming a lasting personal attachment—had spurred her to look for a job in another city. She felt like a piece of property over which her two favorite persons waged a constant battle. She belonged to herself, and she intended to move her life forward in the direction *she* chose.

But why, she reprimanded herself as she stared at the wind-twisted wraiths outside the car, had she carelessly chosen the coast-hugging route when she knew full well that on an unseasonably warm November day like today, late afternoon fog was almost always inevitable? Why had she mosied along Seventeen Mile Drive and lingered in the stained glass shop in Carmel, instead of hurrying home? She supposed, to exercise her independence for a few more hours.

Well, I'm definitely on my own here! So why don't I conjure up a huge fan to blow the pesky white stuff back out to sea? Or arrange for a hotel to spring up like a mushroom around the next bend in the road?

Manda laughed at her impossible solutions.

Little by little, her grin changed to a frown of concentration. Something important hovered close beneath the plane of her awareness, a recent memory lying in wait. Fingers, still smarting from tightly clutching the steering wheel, plowed through her short mahogany-colored curls. Without realizing it, she'd held her breath. *Any moment now, I will remember,* she demanded of herself, as she gnawed on her lower lip. Her breathing resumed with a hiss through her teeth, and the shadowy worry in her gray eyes gave way to a merry twinkle.

"There *is* a hotel!" she shouted into the silence, jubilantly throwing up her hands.

Months ago Dr. Nils had been running late for an appointment in Monterey, and his silvery Continental whizzed by so rapidly, that only after they were several yards past it did what she had seen register with her.

"I never noticed that sign before," she said.

"What sign?"

"Back where the dirt lane led downhill through the woods. There's an inn. It must be right on the shore."

"Impossible," he proclaimed in his most authoritative manner. "There is no inn in this locale."

"I saw the sign," she insisted.

"You must be mistaken, my dear. As many times as I've traveled this highway, I have never seen a billboard advertising an inn."

"The billboard was barely two feet square," she told him, laughter bubbling in her throat. "And it was a faded gray green, the same color as the eucalyptus saplings growing up around it. Actually, the poor thing seemed to be saying, 'We really don't want to rent any rooms, after all.' Don't you think that's peculiar?"

"No. Now I understand. Since I last drove by here, some rundown beach house has been converted into a rendezvous for . . . ah . . . immoral behavior."

"You mean a cheap motel for adulterous one-night stands," she amended, a teasing lilt to her words.

"Manda!" He glowered at her. "If you please, we shall drop the subject."

"Yes, *sir.*" She grinned at him from across the expansive black leather seat.

But the sign's weather-beaten condition verified its having been there longer than Dr. Nils claimed. Manda knew she could have missed it on their previous trips along the coast highway because she was always looking ahead, anticipating the next breathtaking view of the sweep of the ocean. But Dr. Nils, with his keen eyes trained to observe every detail—How could *he* not have seen the sign before? Then Manda forgot about the whole thing as the Continental curled around another cliff-edged section of the road.

Now, parked on the mist-enshrouded turnoff, the sign's crudely printed words replayed themselves across the screen of her mind:

TANGLETREES
A Quiet Inn
By the Sea

The doctor's derogatory description of the inn bothered her somewhat. She shivered, only partly from the chill seeping into the car, as she reached for the ignition key with a trembling but determined hand. Better to spend one night in a brothel, she decided, than locked in a cold, damp car alongside a deserted road.

"One look at me, and the ladies of the evening will know I'm no competition," she murmured. "Who'd want to dally with a five-feet-two, uncurvy,"—she groaned—"wholesome-looking girl like me?"

With a firm resolve, she slowly backed onto the highway and headed south. Here, she noted with relief, the fog had thinned a bit. By switching the headlights to high beam, she could see a few feet beyond the right-hand edge of the asphalt. Her nerves twanged at the thought of bypassing the inn. Perspiration popped out on her forehead as she peered anxiously through the arcs cleared by the clicking windshield wipers. One at a time, she removed her hands from the wheel and dried each sweaty palm on her rust-colored corduroy jeans.

There . . . just ahead . . . the small green wooden object with darker green lettering on it . . . Was that the sign she sought? Yes! She could make out the word: TANGLETREES.

She blinked several times, glad she no longer had to stare so fixedly into the murky gloom.

Her ordeal was not over yet, however. There remained the lane from the highway to the inn to be dealt with, and its hairpin curves cut a steep downhill swath through a dense grove of trees and underbrush. In this poor visibility, the slightest error in judgment on her part could land her against a tree trunk or plunge her over a ridge top into a deep rock-filled canyon.

With a visible shudder, Manda acknowledged the eerie sensation of *dé jà vu.* How had she known the layout of the entrance road? Was she remembering another similar road locked in her yesterdays? She braked the car and waited, willing her brain to drop the right cogs into her wheel of recall. Because Dr. Nils believed her past could return someday, either all at once or in bits and pieces, she had schooled herself never to ignore anything that might prove to be a flash of memory. Like all the times before, her scorecard came up zero. Disappointed, she forced a yawn to ease the tension in her facial muscles.

The car responded to her foot's gradual pressure on the accelerator. At the place where the down-sloping trail disappeared into a scary veil of mist, she whispered, "Do it," and obeyed before her courage evaporated. For an instant the cornering auto balanced on the gravel shoulder like a seesaw, then inched forward. Manda felt as though she were moving out into a void of space. And of time. A vague premonition—of unhappiness? peril?—raised goose bumps on her arms.

Then she gasped with surprise and intense relief.

A ribbon of parallel amber lights, diffused by the fog, wound down the hillside. While she cautiously traveled the quarter mile of dangerous switchbacks, she silently thanked the electric eye, or whatever the magical device, for activating the glowing circles attached to trees lining both sides of the oiled clay roadway.

The smoky swirls lifted for a few minutes, and the large barnlike inn loomed bleakly in the twilight. Dusty green in color, it blended unobtrusively with the thickly wooded surroundings. From out at sea, Manda mused, the building should be practically invisible. Maybe Dr. Nils's assumption was correct; the inn certainly had the appearance of a business establishment that shunned publicity.

Regardless . . . Manda reminded herself of her goal: a reasonably clean, warm bed for tonight. In the morning, when the fog dispersed, she would go home. Any secrets pertaining to Tangletrees Inn, if indeed they did exist, were no concern of hers.

Where should she park? she wondered. Accumulated moisture on the outside of the windows blurred her view of the road. Lowering the glass so she could see better, she listened with quickening heartbeat to the nearby thrashing of the surf, and slowly breathed in the mingling tangy odors of salt and seaweed, pine and eucalyptus.

How she loved the oceanside! Even in her beforehand life, according to her therapy sessions with Dr. Nils. But where she'd once known an ocean, and why it was—as she discovered in Dr. Nils's pool—that she couldn't swim, those answers stubbornly remained shut away behind the loss-of-memory door. As were the more important facts, such as who she was, or how she had come to be wandering outside a hospital one cold, rainy dawn, bruised and filthy and hysterical.

Still looking for the inn's parking place, Manda took another deep invigorating breath and accepted with an unquestioned joy the sure knowledge that her soul belonged near the sea.

Turning right, she drove past the portico displaying a small, red neon *Enter Here,* because there was nowhere to stop without completely blocking the single lane. When she reached the north end of the inn, she spied four vehicles lined up on a distant, dimly lit rectangle of concrete.

"Why didn't they build the damn parking lot in *Ha-*

waii?" she fumed, as she continued on the downgrade trail.

Stopping her car beside an old Pontiac with an Arkansas license plate, Manda shut off the motor and stepped out onto the pavement.

"Whoever picked this spot for parking is a sadist!" she grumbled, stretching her aching spine and shoulders. "I have to walk back up the hill, around the corner, and all the way to the front door on the far end of the building. Carrying my luggage? No way! I'll sleep in my undies. From the looks of the place, that's more than most of the guests sleep in." She laughed, and her gray eyes glinted with mischief as she thought how she would shock Mrs. Hendricks with her tale of a night spent in what the sweet, old-fashioned housekeeper once had blushingly called "a house of ill repute."

Manda buttoned her bulky sweater against the increasing chill, and looked toward the path that led in the direction from whence she had come. Dusk had surrendered to night. In the wind-stirred, altering patterns of mist, the trees that huddled together on the perimeter of the parking area's illumination suddenly assumed ghostly shapes. While Manda watched, their branches seemed to sway in a slow ponderous dance, to reach out toward her, beckoning in malevolent fashion. Her feet, planted in a quicksand of terror, refused to move. Louder than the voice of the surf, her heartbeat thudded in her ears.

Then all the lights went out.

Chapter Two

Manda's scream, after clawing its way past paralyzed vocal cords, emerged as a weak kittenlike wail. Through the stygian darkness, tendrils of fog brushed her face, and in her suffocating fright she believed one of the menacing tree limbs had found her. Cold perspiration covered her body. Her flailing hands swatted the air in a feeble challenge against the unseen enemy; they touched nothing. She sucked in a ragged breath and tried to swallow the cotton in her mouth. Trees couldn't pull their roots out of the ground and come after her. Of course, they couldn't. Just the same, panic won out over reason. Like a wild thing, she raced up the hill. Once she stumbled over a brick or stone bordering the path, but she caught herself and rushed on.

The inn's neon-lit portico shone like the gateway to paradise. Manda took the two shallow steps with one leap, then staggered when a damp shoe sole slid sideways. Regaining her balance, she touched the doorknob, even as it was pulled from her grasp.

A tall, broad-shouldered man, his face in the

shadows, stood silhouetted in the open doorway.

"I heard your footsteps on the porch," he said. "Please, come in." He moved aside for her to enter.

Stepping inside the small lighted foyer, Manda gazed up into a pair of ebony eyes set widely spaced under thick, dark brows. The feeling that she had seen him somewhere gained credence when she realized that he was returning her stare with a puzzled frown of his own. Had they met prior to her memory loss? Her pulse rate quickened; she hopefully scanned his features.

High cheekbones above deeply hollowed cheeks dominated his craggy whiskerless face, the color of dark honey. Tiny furrows flared from his prominent nose to the corners of his wide, full-lipped mouth. His hair, straight and crow's wing black, lay close to the proudly held head in modishly cut layers.

He spoke again, his voice low and resonant like the notes of a skillfully bowed cello. "I'm Jason Tallfeather, the proprietor."

Tallfeather, her brain repeated. No wonder he looked familiar. His ruggedly chiseled countenance was a montage of the many fascinating portraits of American Indians on the walls of museums and art galleries she had visited.

"Manda Lethe," she said.

"An unusual name. How do you spell it?"

"M . . . a . . ."

"No, the other one."

She told him.

"Like the River of Forgetfulness in Hades," he remarked.

"Almost no one makes the connection." His perception surprised and oddly pleased her. It had taken a couple of weeks for Dr. Nils to associate the surname she chose for herself with the mythological stream of oblivion.

Manda's mind flew back to the afternoon almost a year and a half ago when, trying to relearn random facts, she had been leafing through an encyclopedia in the doctor's study. For no apparent reason, one paragraph riveted her attention:

> "*Lethe.* One of the five rivers of Hades. According to the Greek legend, a drink from the warm waters of this river made people forget everything."

Then and there, with the irony tasting bitter on her tongue, Manda decided. Lethe. The perfect last name for a young woman who three months previously had awakened in a hospital room, and remembered absolutely nothing that had ever happened to her.

Her thoughts returned to the man standing beside her as he said, "I did a research paper on *Dante's Inferno* in college, and I guess I never forgot it." He gave her a wry grin. "The poet's conception of hell scared me to death."

Somehow Manda couldn't imagine his ever being afraid of anything. Certainly not, like her, of fog or pitch black darkness or some silly old trees. She shuddered in retrospect.

"You're cold," he said, concern wrinkling his broad coppery forehead.

"Only a little. Mostly I was remembering how frightened *I* was down at your parking lot, when the lights went out."

"I'm sorry. I'll have to reset the timer."

"I should have been braver." She uttered a nervous little laugh.

His serious black gaze made her heart lurch, but not from fear, as he said, "At least you feel safe now."

Yes I do feel safe, she agreed silently. *With you.*

What was she thinking of? Jason Tallfeather was a complete stranger! She found him . . . compelling, because of his striking appearance and his Indian heritage. But his good looks didn't guarantee trustworthiness. Inasmuch as he was living—hiding—in this isolated, camouflaged inn, he could be some kind of criminal. Even a murderer. Tremors of apprehension vibrated through her.

"You are chilled," he insisted, and motioned her ahead of him.

Briskly she walked to the natural stone fireplace with its welcoming red and orange flames. Turning her back on the pleasant warmth, she surveyed the large room.

Instead of looking like the lobby of a shabby hotel with a questionable reputation, it might have been a clipping from *Better Homes and Gardens.* Tan carpeting and drapes afforded tasteful backdrops for the modern, seal brown and cream-colored furniture, in the corners of which glowed pillows that reminded Manda of the hues of a desert sunset—canary yellow, burnished gold, burnt orange, brick rust. Fleetingly she wished she'd have time to explore the built-in shelves stacked with books, and the glass-front cabinets containing bric-a-brac that filled the entire longest wall. On the sofa table, an arrangement of marigolds in a terra cotta Indian bowl brought the scene to life with a pungent fragrance, and the firelight moved over expensive accents of hammered copper—a lamp base, a pair of bookends, an ashtray—making them flicker and gleam, in contrast to the room's soft light.

Then Manda saw the handwoven reed basket, spilling khaki and rust yarns untidily over the edge of an end table. Pieces of an unfinished jigsaw puzzle lay scattered over the cocktail table and, near them, a book resting on its open pages and two tangerine pottery mugs still smelling of coffee. Those casual, lived-in touches dispelled the last vestige of her misgivings. There was nothing at Tangletrees Inn for her to be afraid of.

As though on cue, a woman's gravel-voiced statement added the final homey affirmation.

"Well, Jason, I finally got the bread dough set for tomorrow. So I'll say good night and—" She broke off when she entered the room and saw Manda.

She was immense, taller than Jason, and wider, without an ounce of fat on her sharp-angled frame. Her head, disproportionately small, appeared even smaller, because she wore her thin gray hair brushed severely back from an elongated face, to form a knot at the nape of her long, skinny neck. A smile, curving her too thick lips and repeating itself in heavy-lidded brown eyes, failed to detract from her homeliness, but Manda, understanding the humiliation and unhappiness of being different, felt a strong empathy with the newcomer.

"I thought I saw a car drive past the kitchen window," the woman said, "but when Jason didn't call me, I decided I was wrong. I'm Mrs. Meecher, the housekeeper."

Jason stepped to her side. "Bess, this is Manda Lethe."

"Have you had dinner, Miss Lethe? We've already eaten, but it won't be any trouble to fix you a plate."

"Please, don't bother," Manda told her. "I had a late lunch in Carmel."

"Humph!" Mrs. Meecher responded. While Manda tried to determine whether the utterance was a snort or a grunt, the housekeeper continued, "No Tangletrees guest goes to bed hungry. There's ham and potato salad and walnut pie in the refrigerator and, for something warm, how about a bowl of homemade tomato bisque soup? And coffee or tea?"

"The soup does sound tempting," Manda admitted, "and a ham sandwich and a glass of milk. I'm so tired, I'll pass up the dessert."

"You may have your dinner on a tray in your room, if you prefer," Jason said.

"I'd like that, thank you."

Mrs. Meecher nodded once in agreement and left the room.

"I'll go get your luggage," Jason offered, "if you'll give me your car keys."

"I forgot to lock the doors! I meant to do it, and then the trees were reach—" She stopped abruptly. He'd think her insane if she told him she had felt threatened by *trees!* Embarrassed, she hurried to fill the silence. "I don't know why I forgot. I'm usually more careful." Nervous fingers rummaged inside her handbag.

"Don't worry about it. You car's safe here, whether it's locked or not. That's just one of several benefits of our isolation." When she judiciously made no reply, he repeated, "I'll get your luggage."

"In the trunk of the Ford Tempo," she said, and dropped the keys into his outstretched palm. "The weekender and the cosmetic case. And while you're doing that, may I use the phone?"

"In the hall. Follow me."

He stopped at a hall closet to remove an orange windbreaker from a hook, then thrust his muscular arms into its sleeves. Sauntering down the corridor toward the brightly lit kitchen, he flashed a capricious grin over his shoulder.

"It's closer this way," he informed her, chuckling softly as if to say he was fully aware that the parking lot's location had inconvenienced her.

Manda smiled at his disappearing back. *I think I could like him,* she thought, reaching for the wall phone, *but I won't be here long enough to find out. Or . . . maybe I will!* Suddenly quite pleased with herself, she punched the appropriate eleven buttons on the telephone.

Mrs. Hendricks answered the second ring. Upon hearing Manda's "Hello, is Dr. Nils there?" she rattled off a string of agitated questions.

Finally Manda broke in. "I'm okay, Mrs. Hendricks. But, please, I want to speak to Dr. Nils."

"Of course, dear," came the meek response. "Why didn't you say so before? He's in his office. I'll buzz him."

Manda heard the intercom buzzer, then a click.

"Dr. Johannsen here."

"Dr. Nils, this is—"

"Manda, my dear! Where have you been? When I

contacted the St. Francis manager, he told me you checked out this morning. I expected you hours ago, even though you did neglect to advise me of your plans."

She ignored the rebuke. "I got caught in one of the worst fogs I ever saw, and—"

"You took the coastal highway? Alone? I have cautioned you again and again about—"

"I remembered," she interrupted testily. The doctor's singsong voice scraped her nerves. Or was she irritated because he treated her like an incompetent? "The sky was clear when I left Carmel," she added, gritting her teeth to bite back her temper.

"Where are you now? I trust you will not be so foolhardy as to start home before the fog dissipates." He paused, and in the interim Manda heard the kitchen door open and close, felt the cool rush of damp air in the hallway. "Are you calling from the Big Sur Inn, or did you have to drive back to Carmel to find lodging?"

"Neither. The strangest thing happened. I was miles from anywhere, and the fog was growing thicker by the second, and then I remembered seeing that sign one day when we came by here. Tangletrees Inn."

There was an odd stillness on the line, almost as if the doctor were holding his breath. Of course. He still believed the inn to be disreputable.

"Manda . . . you . . . *cannot* . . . stay . . . there!"

"You just told me to stay put till the fog lifts." Exasperation sharpened her voice. "This is a nice place. Not at all what you suspected." Hearing the proprietor's footsteps behind her, she was reluctant to say more on that subject. Ah! She knew what would please Dr. Nils. "There's a homebody-type housekeeper here, and the owner's name is Jason Tallfeather. He's—"

"Stop chattering!"

She gasped aloud at the grating, wrathful command.

At her outcry, Jason halted, throwing her a questioning glance, but he passed her without comment when she spoke crossly into the phone.

"I'm trying to tell you. I plan to stay here for a day or two."

"I'm sorry, but I fail to see how that will be possible. You must return home at once. You forget." She flinched at the cruelty, however unintentional, of the last two words. "Need I remind you?" he continued. "I am depending upon you to do much of the research for my upcoming lecture series."

"The tour doesn't begin for two months." She stiffened her emotional backbone against his attempt to keep her always under his thumb. "My mind is made up. Emory's your secretary. He can do whatever needs to be done before I come home. I'll let you know when to expect me."

She hung up before he could reply, but not before she heard his astonished intake of breath.

Manda had known, even before she told Dr. Nils her plans, that he'd be angry. Like the time last spring when, without consulting him, she'd taken a job as tourist guide at the Mission. After she skipped lunch three days in a row, the doctor had demanded an explanation from Mrs. Hendricks, his housekeeper and Manda's co-conspirator. Thirty minutes later Dr. Nils had marched into the Mission information office, denounced the lay hostess for hiring someone "much too ill to work," then led Manda, with a frightening kind of gentleness, to his car. She had felt like a puppy on a leash that had strayed too far from its master's heels and been jerked to a halt with a choke chain.

This past week Manda had dared again to venture beyond the periphery of Dr. Nils's control, and she'd savored every hour of her new freedom. Even the frustrating hours of futile job hunting. Because they had been filled with *her* decisions.

Although the doctor wasn't accustomed to her defying his wishes, he'd have to reconcile himself to it. Somehow she was going to break away from his unfair domination over her.

What better beginning than to stubbornly postpone her return for a few days? Meanwhile she could enjoy the seashore. And maybe get to know Jason Tallfeather.

He stood nearby, a disarming smile tugging at the corners of his mouth.

"I don't make a habit of eavesdropping," he said, "but this time I couldn't avoid it. I'm glad you're going to extend your stay with us." His dark gaze clung to her lips, almost like a kiss.

Manda tried to ignore the hot sensation in the pit of her stomach, and admonished herself that he was merely acting out the role of a gracious host.

"I need a brief holiday," she explained, as she avoided eye contact. She'd hate it if he thought she was lengthening her stay because of him.

Mrs. Meecher joined them, carrying a large food tray, and Jason led the way to the broad staircase. On the bottom step, he shifted both pieces of luggage to one hand and with the other took Manda's elbow as they ascended side by side. The housekeeper followed several steps behind.

"Which room, Bess?" the man asked.

"I'd like one with an ocean view if possible," Manda requested.

"Certainly," Mrs. Meecher said. "The blue room, then."

At the top of the stairs, Manda walked ahead of Jason to the first door on her left and grasped the knob. Before she could turn it, Jason's hand covered hers, his grip hurting her sensitive fingers.

"Wait." He spoke softly but imperatively. "Another guest is sleeping in there."

Confused and uneasy, Manda let go the doorknob and dropped her arm to her side. "Isn't this the blue room?"

Jason's obsidian eyes, glittering with pinpoints of silver, held her gray ones as though with a magnet.

"It used to be," he mumbled.

At his words Manda suddenly felt lightheaded . . . strange. Jason's features blurred, and his body seemed to sway, backward at first, then toward her. Gradually, as in slow motion, he receded farther into a hazy, distorted distance.

"Are you all right?" He sounded faraway and tinny. "You're so pale." He gripped her arm with his free hand.

Like a robot, mechanical and unfeeling, she permitted him to guide her to the last room at the end of the corridor. He released her, opened the door, and Mrs. Meecher, who had been lagging behind, hurried around them and through the doorway.

"That was getting heavy," she puffed, placing the

tray on the bedside table. "You'd best eat the soup while it's hot."

"Thank you," Manda responded dully. Her ears heard the woman's heavy departing footsteps, and the thuds when Jason set her luggage on the floor, but her mind gave no names to the noises.

She remained motionless, but, inside, an awful shivering assailed her. Except for where Jason had touched her, she was icy cold.

Worried, Jason scrutinized her pallid, expressionless face. The dead-looking smoky eyes focused on empty space behind him.

"Are you all right?" he asked again, once more clutching her arm. He feared she might faint.

"Yes, thank you," she recited woodenly.

He wrapped his fingers around her wrist for a few seconds to check her pulse. It was strong. Racing.

Manda blinked. Her gaze, now aware and clear, met his. The color rushed back into her cheeks as she realized she had very nearly marched uninvited into a sleeping stranger's bedroom. How could she justify such a rude and foolish act? It had seemed so right at the time.

"I must be more tired than I thought," she murmured, managing a feeble smile for his benefit. "I'll be good as new in the morning."

He nodded. "I'm sure. Sleep well, Miss Lethe. Breakfast is at eight."

As soon as the door closed behind him, Manda sank limply to the side of the bed, her knees weak and trembling. Her hand shook when she lifted the soup spoon. The attack of vertigo, or whatever it was, out in the hall, had taken its toll. Her appetite was gone.

After a half-dozen sips of the tart tomato liquid, she laid the spoon down and walked over to her luggage.

Was it her imagination, or were the padded blue leather handles still warm from Jason Tallfeather's grasp? The idea, although oddly comforting, she discarded with a stern denial.

"That's ridiculous. Exhaustion is making me crazy."

Crazy? No! To prove that she was as sane as the next person, she'd undergone at least a hundred tests and answered thousands of questions. There was a perfectly logical reason for what had just happened to her. At some time or another, she'd stayed in a place where her blue-decorated room was located on the left at the head of a staircase, and tonight her weary brain, not functioning alertly, had directed her to the same door. The fact that the room she almost entered had at one time been done in blue—well, that was pure coincidence. As for the weird floating sensation, she blamed that on fatigue and her embarrassment over the mix-up in rooms.

"What I need is a warm shower and a good night's rest."

Talking out loud to herself wasn't crazy either, because long ago she had figured out that sometimes it helped to fill the hollow echoes of yesterday.

Chapter Three

The sunshine, warm on Manda's face, woke her. She stretched, opened her slumber-lazy eyes, and sat up. A brinish aroma reminded her where she was, and the golden sunlight striating the room through the window panes told her the fog had burned away.

Last night she had been too weary to pay much attention to her room. Now, she deemed it pleasant and comfortably functional, with its powder blue walls, royal blue carpet, and plain driftwood-colored nightstand, bed, chest, dressing table, and bench. The blue-white-and-gray-striped bedspread that she had used for cover matched the thin tufted pillows tied to the seat and high back of the white-enameled rocker.

Manda donned her pink terry scuffs and knee-length robe and went to the partly open window. White unlined curtains floated inward on a westerly breeze. She waved the gauzy panels aside and inhaled every bit of the crisp salty air that her lungs could hold. Except for a purplish haze on the horizon, the last remnants of the fog, the ocean shimmered under a cloudless sky, and lacy whitecaps played tag with a gusty wind. Seagulls wheeled and soared high above, their plaintive cries barely audible. Although she couldn't see it, Manda heard the surf as it slapped at the beach and dissolved into a steady, liquid roar.

She would have liked to stand here for hours, looking and listening, but a faint rumble in her stomach put her in mind of the fact that she had eaten very little since early yesterday afternoon.

Jason Tallfeather had said breakfast would be served at eight. She wondered what time it was now.

She didn't own a wristwatch. She wore no jewelry except her charm bracelet, the one tangible link to her forgotten life. She had been wearing it the drizzly morning the nurse found her walking, half-staggering, near the employee entrance to the Paso Robles hospital.

Nursing supervisor Libby Devlin, arriving for duty on the seven-to-three shift, had noticed the girl because she wore no coat. How odd, she thought, on a cold, wet December dawn. As she drew closer, she saw that the girl's clothing was torn, caked with red clay, and streaked with blood. Ugly abrasions marked her bare arms, and her hands, clutched to her chest, were discolored and swollen to the point of uselessness. Her pewter gray eyes met Libby's pleadingly. Never in thirty-two years of nursing had Libby witnessed such mirrored depths of pain, and yes, absolute terror.

"Let me help you," the nurse offered. With compassion she reached out toward the shivering redheaded young woman, who at the gesture collapsed into a screaming heap on the rain-puddled sidewalk.

That was how Libby Devlin had described the encounter to Manda when she came to the hospital room late the following day. She removed the gold charm bracelet from her pocket and dangled it in front of the patient's wan heart-shaped face.

"They took this from your wrist when they prepped you for surgery," she said. "I hope it will help you remember who you are, where you came from, how you got here. Something."

Despair and confusion stared out at her from enormous gray eyes. Libby worked the dainty chain slowly over and around her hand, holding each charm immobile until the girl had time to examine it. When the nickel-sized disk with MANDA etched in Spencerian script slid into her palm, a fleeting almost imperceptible awareness flared in the young woman's gaze.

"Manda," she murmured. "That's somebody's name."

"Yes?" Libby held her breath.

"I—I think it—it's mine."

"Can you recall anything else?" the nurse asked softly, after a few tense moments of silence.

"No," the girl sighed. Suddenly a blinding rage at what she had lost—her past, her identity, her *self*—flared in her eyes. "No! I've already told the doctors! And I told the policeman. I told everybody! *I . . . can't remember!*

This morning Manda didn't want to dwell on those first bad days, when an empty existence of unknowns confronted her. Instead, she focused on the seascape panorama beyond the cliff.

The sun, changing rapidly from orange to brassy gold as it climbed, made her wonder once more about the time.

Turning away from the window, she spied a small

digital clock on the dressing table. Seven forty-five. Fifteen minutes till food.

She scurried to the bathroom, splashed cool water on her face, and brushed her teeth. From the weekender she pulled wrinkled jeans and a moss green blouse, all the while muttering under her breath because she hadn't hung her clothes neatly in the closet the evening before.

Downstairs, Manda's nose led her to the source of enticing aromas. Frying bacon and freshly brewed coffee!

Her footsteps on the dining room's bare wood floor announced her presence to the two people seated at a redwood trestle table.

Her handsome Amerindic host, rising, acknowledged her arrival with a cordial "Good morning." As he pulled Manda's chair away from the table, she stood behind him and watched his shoulder muscles bunch, a titillating hint of the strength and virility that lay beneath the loosely knit long-sleeved black shirt. She forced herself to concentrate on settling in her seat, and then for the first time she really looked at the person sitting opposite her.

The woman was a living, breathing golden Aphrodite. Heavy wheat-gold shoulder-length hair waved richly around an oval face, tanned to a soft amber and possessing the bone structure any aspiring model would kill for. Her bronze-glossed mouth formed a perfect social smile. The glint in her slanted yellow topaz eyes, and the way she curled well-manicured fingers around Jason Tallfeather's arm after he sat down, emitted a message proud and clear: This man is mine.

Until that instant, Manda hadn't considered the

possibility there might be a *Mrs.* Tallfeather. A peculiar twinge nudged the upper region of her abdomen. She tried to ignore it, not wanting, not daring to give the hurt a name. It couldn't be jealousy!

Feeling an awkwardness she hoped wasn't apparent, she smiled up at the homely woman who served her hot cakes and bacon and filled her mug with steaming black coffee.

"Thank you, Mrs. Meecher." The housekeeper nodded pleasantly.

"Miss Lethe," Jason said, "I'd like you to meet the only other guest in the inn at present. Sylvia Hathaway. Sylvia, Manda Lethe."

She wasn't his wife! Manda sucked in a slow breath, and the pain in her middle subsided.

"I'm delighted to meet you, Miss Hathaway." She smiled widely.

"Please, call me Sylvia." Even her voice was golden, like soft butter.

"Thank you." *Thank you for not being Mrs. Tallfeather.* "And I wish you both would call me Manda. When anyone calls me 'Miss Lethe,' I feel . . . ah . . . uncomfortable."

Probably because she hadn't been born with the name. But she wasn't going to explain that to them. Whenever circumstances compelled her to reveal to someone that she had amnesia, the person invariably gaped at her, first with shock, then pity and, finally, with embarrassment at not knowing what to say. Somehow she couldn't bear it if Jason Tallfeather felt sorry for her.

"And I'm Jason," he said, flashing a warm smile that heated every drop of blood in Manda's veins. "Tell me,

Manda, where do you live?"

"In San Luis Obispo."

"You're a college student there?"

"No, but my guardian—my benefactor—is a Cal Poly professor on sabbatical this year. You may have heard of him. He's written several popular books on parapsychology. Dr. Nils Johannsen."

"The psychiatrist," her host acknowledged.

"You know him?" On the phone last night, Dr. Nils hadn't picked up on her mention of Jason's name. But of course, he'd been too upset with her at the time.

"Not personally, but we share the same publisher."

"*You*—are a writer?" Dumfounded, she nearly dropped a bite of pancake off her fork. Her mind had categorized him as a restless man of action, outdoorsy, even adventurous. Definitely not a writer, tied to a desk for solitary tedious hours.

"*Sic transit* fame." Jason's hearty laughter rumbled throughout the room and beyond.

Manda silently applauded his attitude. Another writer's ego might have imploded because she had never heard of his work.

"I'm sorry," was the only thing she could think of to say.

Sylvia's smiling mouth seconded Jason's amusement, but her topaz eyes gently reproached the young woman across from her. "You must have been living on some other planet."

Her words had unwittingly flicked a raw nerve, and Manda shifted restively in her chair.

"Jason has written three best-sellers in four years," Sylvia went on to explain. "*Never Kill Again* and *Slow to Justice* and *A Rosary for Rosa*. Television made a movie out of the first one, and the female lead won an Emmy. Jason appeared on the 'Johnny Carson Show,' " she ended proudly.

"But, Sylvia, that was all of three years ago," Jason reminded her. "Manda wouldn't remember."

Manda's hands started to shake. Laying the fork on the plate with deliberate care, she willed her trembling to cease. She threw Jason a quick, inquiring glance. His piercing ebony eyes hinted at no special knowledge, but his last comment . . . Did he know who she really was? After a heart-stopping moment, she decided he surely would have said something before now. Wouldn't he?

Jason, observing her uneasiness, found it extremely puzzling. Manda's reaction had begun with Sylvia's remark about another planet. Then, even as he watched, Manda's nervousness had increased to the point of distress.

Manda fascinated him. In his thirty-three years, he'd known many kinds of women. Somehow Manda Lethe was different from all of them. And why did he have a haunting feeling that he'd seen her before? He prided himself on an uncanny memory for dates, names, faces. So how could the memory of her piquant face, those sad, incredible gray eyes, that delightful cap of russet curls, have slipped from his mind's grasp like smoke through his fingers?

"I'm sure your books are good," Manda said. "Probably the reason I never read one is that I'm not a whodunit fan."

"But Jason's books are not whodunits," Sylvia said, with a sweet surprised smile.

"They aren't? But the titles . . . I thought . . . I'm

sorry." Embarrassment flushed Manda's cheeks.

"No apology necessary," Jason's velvety low-pitched voice soothed. "My titles do suggest the murder mystery genre." The smile he directed at Manda was rueful. "Maybe I planned it that way originally, to capture the crime novel readers. Because my stories do deal with crimes. They're fictionalized fact. Or if you prefer, factual fiction. A crime I hear about kindles my curiosity, and I go interview the principals. The perpetrators as well as the victims, their families, their associates. I talk to local newspapermen, and when possible to the police officers who handled the case. If I believe the facts warrant my saying more on the subject, to clear up an injustice or to showcase a particular consequence of that type of crime, I come home and write a book."

"I suppose you use fictitious names of persons and places."

"Of course. The principals themselves would hardly recognize the story as the one that happened to them. Also, I add imaginary characters and events to protect the privacy of the real people involved." His rough-hewn visage tightened into a glowering fierceness not unlike that of his warrior ancestors. "If the tabloids ever discovered their true identities, details as private as their . . . ah . . . sleeping habits would be ferreted out, sensationalized, and exploited." Jason paused, grinning sheepishly. "I think I just made a speech."

Manda wasn't fooled by his levity. Ignoring his last sentence, she gravely capsuled his other disclosures. "You use fiction to wage a campaign against the truth of unfairness. I like that. Where did you get the idea? I mean—How did you get started?"

"I used to be an investigative reporter."

"The plots must be exciting. I don't mind typing Dr. Nils's manuscripts, but, to be honest, some parts are dull and tedious." She hastened to qualify the criticism. "Possibly because I don't know the meaning of the medical terms."

"Possibly."

Judging from Jason's terse reply and distracted expression, Manda thought he had lost interest, so she turned her attention to Sylvia.

"Are you here on vacation?" she asked the other woman.

"Partly. I came to get away from the pressures of work, but I'm also doing some sketching."

"You're an artist?" Manda's pulse stuttered. *Artist.* Why did the word suddenly take on a special, personal significance?

Before Manda had a chance to assay her reaction, Sylvia responded with a patient smile. "Not in the sense you mean. I own a small dress shop in Los Angeles and design most of the fashions myself. Currently I'm working on ideas for my spring line."

With newly informed eyes, Manda scrutinized Sylvia's simple buttercup-yellow sundress, and cringed at the thought of her own wrinkled off-the-rack apparel.

"And I really should get back to the drawing board." Sylvia rose to her feet, leaned over to place a proprietary kiss on Jason's cheek, and promised breathily, "I'll see you at lunch."

With envy Manda watched Sylvia's long legs carry her willowy but curvaceous body out of the room. "She's beautiful!"

"Yes." Jason sensed Manda's making of comparisons

and felt an inexplicable urge to buoy her self-esteem. Strange. Usually, Sylvia's devastating effect on other females amused him. "But you should have seen her when she was seventeen. All bones and angles, and as gawky as a baby bluejay right out of the nest."

"You knew her then?" Manda's heart plummeted to the soles of her grubby white sneakers. They must be very close, to have stayed in touch all those years.

"Yes, indeed. We were freshmen in college together."

Did his face momentarily cloud over and his black eyes lose their twinkle, or was it the unexpected change of lighting in the dining room?

Mrs. Meecher had opened the celery-colored drapes to expose a solid wall of glass overlooking the ocean.

Manda jumped up, almost overturning her redwood cane-bottom chair.

"Excuse me," she breathed, "but I have to see this."

Her rubber-soled shoes produced squeaky noises as she rushed across the waxed hardwood floor. No sooner had the housekeeper shoved aside the sliding glass panel, than Manda burst through the doorway.

A terrace, about ten feet wide, ran the full length of the inn. Ornamental iron tables and chairs, some painted white, some black, were grouped handily for conversation or snacking. Manda bumped her knee on a table leg as she hurried past. She hardly noticed. Only the beckoning view mattered. Looking out over a high drop to the ground, and across a rolling grassy meadow to the cliff, her thick-lashed gray eyes sparkled like the water beyond, and her small eager feet did a little dance step. One finger tapped the edge of the waist-high wall, then traced the warm slick pattern of the green mortar between the rough native stones.

Too engrossed in the emotional tug of the Pacific to hear Jason's approach, she jumped when he touched her arm. Then tiny seismic tremors rippled through her body.

"You like the seashore, too." That husky velvet voice again.

Manda glanced up, enchanted by his dazzling, empathetic smile.

"More than anyplace."

"Then why are you standing here?" Ever so lightly he placed a big hand on each of her shoulders and turned her to the right, until she faced the north end of the terrace. She trembled like a highstrung race horse locked in the starting gate. "The beach is included in the price of your room. Go!" he commanded blithely, and gave her a gentle push.

From the bottom of the terrace steps she hurried along the same path she'd traversed last night, down the slope and past the parking lot and then a few yards farther, straight to the sheer hundred-foot drop-off of the land. She paused to catch her breath and worship at Neptune's throne.

In long easy rollers, the sea marched toward the shore. Curling breakers, apple green where the sunlight shone through them, folded over with loud splashes and rushed up on the beach in a hissing, sudsy foam. The ocean's voice, like its surface, rose and fell and crescendoed again, a ceaseless mixture of noisy whispers and wet thunder.

Heaving a sigh, Manda tried not to think of the day she would have to leave this place and return to inland San Luis Obispo.

Because moisture from the fog still slicked the plank

treads, she held onto the rusty iron banister while she made her way down the steep steps to the beach.

Two strides, and both her shoes were full of sand. She plowed through the loose gray beige piles, to the strip firmed and smoothed by countless tides. There she sat down, heedless of the chilly dampness that seeped into the seat of her jeans. After removing her sneakers and rolling up her pants' legs, she scampered into the frothy surf. Bubbles tickled her ankles, and when she wriggled her toes, the sand filtered away from beneath her feet. Her laughter skittered through the clear, sunny atmosphere, and sounded for all the world like that of a gleeful child.

She soon quit wading, for the water was cold. Hanging her tied-together shoes across her shoulder, she sauntered along the hard-packed beach. Every now and then she paused to look back at her dull, pressed-dry footprints, or stopped to pick up a pretty shell and put it in her blouse pocket.

A swarm of pesky sandflies hovered over a decaying clump of giant bladder kelp, deposited at the edge of the hummocky dunes by a recent high tide. Wrinkling her nose at the offensive odor, she walked over to the whiplike plant. Uprooted seaweed, when tumbled by strong wave action, sometimes captured and held a rare shell from the ocean floor, but Manda quickly discovered that this batch had accumulated nothing except chucks of soggy wood and a couple of lost toys, a deflated red balloon and a green marble.

Absentmindedly she reached for the marble. As she moved the object around in her palm, she realized it didn't roll like a perfect sphere. One side was slightly flat, and the other side felt rough, marked by tiny ridges. Curious, she gave it more than a cursory glance.

Her heart pounded in her throat. She had to swallow twice before the words came out.

"Jade. It's jade!"

Wouldn't Dr. Nils be surprised!

Because of the doctor's zealous interest in the gemstone—he owned an impressive collection of jade artifacts—Manda had searched the city library for information regarding the precious mineral. She had read that somewhere along Highway 1 was a place called Jade Cove, where rockhounds discovered pieces of jade, presumably eroded from an undersea deposit and washed ashore during heavy storms. If amateur gemologists could find jade, why not Manda Lethe?

Laughing excitedly, she ran into the surf and dipped the stone into the water. Wetness, she knew, would make the raw specimen look as though it had been professionally polished.

"Dammit!" Manda exploded. The thing in her hand was an ordinary piece of emerald green glass! *Jade* of such a vivid vitreous green came from only one location in the entire world. Burma. Certainly not from the depths of the Pacific Ocean off the coast of California.

Only then did she recall that the atlas had described the Jade Cove gemstones as opaque, with a bluish tinge. Her very first glimpse should have ruled out its being jade.

Disappointed, and feeling a bit stupid, Manda dropped the glassy fragment. After taking three or four steps, she halted, then went back to retrieve it. Why, she didn't know. She simply could not bring herself to walk away and leave that shiny gewgaw lying on the ground. With her index finger she poked it deep into the hip pocket of her jeans, then slapped her damp hands together a couple of times to rid them of gritty grains of sand.

The clapping noise alarmed a nearby flock of gulls into flight. Screeching in protest, they rose up and up, wheeling in ever-widening circles. Manda dug one bare heel in the sand and with the toes of her other foot propelled herself around and around, her eyes following the birds' balletlike spirals until dizziness forced her to look down.

But the landscape continued to spin, and all at once she experienced the same sensation of displacement as last night outside the "wrong" bedroom.

"The trees are gone," she croaked.

Atop the cliff there should be visible a cluster of Monterey cypress, tangled by an eon of congested growth, tortured and misshapen by salty winds—a half-dozen or so of the endangered, beautiful-ugly trees projecting out over the edge of the ravine that drained into the ocean.

"The ravine's missing, too," she murmured, disbelieving.

Manda's eyes beheld only a solid, continuous embankment overhung with ice plant and dotted with spindly shrubs that clung tenaciously to gravelly outcroppings. No ravine. And no tangled trees.

The tips of her fingers tingled hotly. She massaged her hands with a wringing motion in an attempt to knead away their throbbing. Her jaws clenched so tight, her teeth hurt.

What was happening to her? Where was the other

site she had expected to see? And why had the strange feeling of disorientation struck her twice within a few hours . . . here, at Tangletrees Inn? Both times, in the upstairs hall last night and here just now, the uncanny sensate episodes had involved much more than her *remembrance* of a place. Her physical body had actually *been there.*

No, that was impossible. There had to be a reasonable explanation for the mystical occurrences. But what was it? Manda had no clue, but she did know her carefree rapport with the bright seashore morning was spoiled. Unable to throw off the somber mood, she ambled back to the beach steps, where she paused to jam salt-encrusted feet into her sneakers before climbing the steps and trudging up the long, red clay path to the house.

Chapter Four

Manda showered and slipped into her other pair of jeans. Grimacing at the salt-stiffened ones lying on the bathroom floor, she decided to leave them and ask Mrs. Meecher's permission to launder them that afternoon. For the job-hunting San Francisco trip, she hadn't packed many sports clothes. The white gauze blouse she had on, although tailored, might look too dressy with faded jeans, but it would have to do.

Ready to go downstairs, she remembered the piece of pseudo jade. Her short fingers dug deep into the hip pocket of the soiled pants, brought out the stone, and laid it on the dressing table tray beside the shells she'd already placed there.

Down in the living room a few minutes later, Manda wandered over to the wall units, where she hoped to find a Jason Tallfeather novel. In the center of each floor-level cabinet door was a six-inch-square carving. She stooped over and her fingertips traced one of the deeply cut designs. Overlapping, intertwining trees, some like ovals standing on end, some triangular, some resembling mushrooms, flat on top with rounded edges. How cleverly unique, she thought, as the meaning of the melange registered. Tangletrees.

Straightening, she walked past a hutch where a row of five authentic Hopi kachina dolls gave her pause. Next she spotted a grouping of driftwood animals, obviously whittled by someone with imagination and a sense of humor. The grinning upside-down frog augmented her own smile into a low chuckle.

Moving ahead to the book stacks, she would have missed the figurine except for the glint of metal that caught her eye as she passed. Instinctively turning her head, she saw the rearing bronze stallion, a masterful depiction of the wild, fierce pride of the equine monarch of the American West. Carefully lifting the statuette and drawing it slowly out of its niche into better light, she turned it this way and that, admiring it from every angle, until she spied the faintly scribed words on the mountain peak base.

"Blue Eagle," she quietly read aloud.

"Daniel Blue Eagle," Jason said from behind her, startling her for a moment. "The great-great-grandson of a famous Oglala Sioux chieftain. Most people know him as Daniel Edwards IV, Senator from South Dakota."

"The hours it must have taken him to create such perfection." Manda's unabashed awe permeated the words.

"Do you sculpt?" Jason asked.

"Goodness, no." Unexpectedly shy because he was standing so near, she tucked her chin and stared at the carpet. "I'm not a creative person," she added in a strangled murmur.

Then she must know one quite well, Jason conjectured, to have so readily identified with the sculptor's mental and physical pressures. Maybe she had a friend with an artistic bent, or, judging from her reaction to his question, more likely a lover. Had the young fool broken her heart? Could that explain the sadness that sometimes lurked in the depths of Manda's big gray eyes? Jason clenched his fists and tightened his jaw, furious with whoever or whatever had caused her unhappiness, strangely impelled to shield her from future hurts. He took a slow, ragged breath. He hadn't felt like this about a woman in a long, long time. Was that why, from the moment she'd rushed into this room last night from out of the fog, a sense of recognition had seized him and wouldn't let go?

As Manda preceded him to the nearest bookcase, an awareness of his piercing gaze on her back made her spine tingle. In the tense silence her eyes scanned the hardcover volumes, until she found what she sought. Although not noticeable when she reached for a *Rosary for Rosa,* the nervous tremor of her fingers when Jason came up close behind her again was enough to prevent her secure hold on the glossy jacket, and the book slipped from her grasp.

Simultaneously they grabbed for it. Jason's quicker reflexes won, but when he started to give it to her, her left arm moved in tandem with his right and got in the way, so that the novel tumbled to the floor.

Dumbfounded, Manda glanced up into Jason's bemused face, then followed his gaze to the arm that seemed not to belong to her anymore. Then she saw the reason.

"My bracelet is caught in your sleeve. I'm sorry."

"No problem." He gave his arm a sharp jerk.

"No!" she objected, deliberately pushing her attached arm along with his. "You'll pull the stitch and make a hole."

"It's an old shirt." He smiled in an attempt to mollify her apprehension, but the worried frown still squinted her eyes. "Come with me," he said, gently tugging her imprisoned arm.

"How can I do otherwise?" Irritation sharpened her response. But Jason looked back at her, his mouth quirking up in amusement, and she grinned at the ridiculous picture they must present, hooked together and scuttling like awkward crabs toward the sofa.

Once there, Manda painstakingly extracted the tiny gold link from the loosely woven threads of his sleeve.

"Good," she decreed after examining the fabric. "No harm done."

"What about your bracelet? If the link is sprung, maybe I can fix it." Without waiting for her reply, he slipped a long spatulate finger under the chain, catching it between finger and thumb. His touch was no more than the brushing of a feather on her skin, yet a heavy excitement trickled up her arm as he moved the dainty links around her wrist.

"Everything looks okay to me," he said.

The trio of charms, attached close together, bumped his fingers. One by one he examined them. The first was a tiny key, the size used to lock a young girl's diary. The handle of the little gold key formed an open loop ornately designed of interwoven vines and three minuscule mother-of-pearl flowers.

"Very unusual," Jason remarked. "I'd say quite old. Oriental would be my guess."

For perhaps the thousandth time, Manda wondered

what kind of drawer or case the key belonged to, and where that object was now, what its contents were, and if she had ever seen them before she lost her memory.

Jason was looking at the second charm, a small, rough-edged pebble, dark, bright green and pear-shaped, wrapped asymmetrically with braided gold wire no thicker than a human hair.

His quick indrawn breath moved the auburn curl that lay against her cheek as he opened his mouth to speak, then snapped it shut in a straight, hard line.

A chill wind—here, in the utter stillness of the living room—blew across the back of Manda's neck. She was perplexed, dismayed. And afraid. Afraid of what, or of whom? She tried to pull her hand away, but Jason clutched her wrist in a grip that would cause bruises tomorrow.

Then, although he released her arm, his fingers had captured the last charm. In her ear his breathing sounded fast and shallow, as he stared at the third ornament, a smooth gold disk with *Manda* scrawled across it in a Spencerian flourish.

"Oh," he said finally, as though only at that moment did he see what he had been looking at for a full ten seconds. "It's your name."

Before Manda realized what was happening, her basic honesty surfaced, and she heard herself saying, "I think it's my name. I don't remember."

Jason's expression froze into a blank mask.

Manda was appalled by what she had done. Now he would look at her in that far too familiar, unkind way that said, "You're not quite normal, are you, you poor thing?" But she knew she had gone too far to hold back now.

"I—I have amnesia," she murmured.

The words ricocheted again and again off the living room walls. *I have amnesia. I have amnesia.*

To people unaware of her situation, she had said those words with reluctance or embarrassment, sometimes even with a rebellion against Fate, but never with the weird sensation that overwhelmed her now. It was as though she became two Mandas. One hunched beside Jason, painfully involved in her personal little melodrama whose senseless plot consisted of innumerable loose ends. The other Manda sat immobile and numb, completely detached from the unhappy scene.

The two Mandas merged when Jason tenderly brushed a finger across her cheekbone, to wipe away the tear she had not known was there.

"I am *so* sorry," he told her huskily. "Is there some way I can help?"

"No, nobody can. I—didn't intend to tell you. It—just slipped out. I know it makes you uncomfortable, and—and I don't usually bother strangers with my—"

The back of his hand, laid with extreme gentleness against her quivering lips, put a stop to her stammering.

"I'm no stranger, Manda. Not to you."

The caressing velvet voice eased her pulsing anxiety. Through mist-beaded lashes she dared to look at him. Concern shadowed his deep-set eyes, compassion softened his mouth, and there was none of the dreaded, galling pity. *Oh, Jason, thank you!* Her spirits soared on wings of relief.

Then the import of his denying statement smote her. What had he meant, he was not a stranger?

Even as Jason watched the beatific glow on her

pixie face, she began to turn ghostly pale. He strode quickly to a hutch cabinet and took out a small glass and a crystal decanter. Hastily he poured some of the reddish brown liquid into the glass, and returned with it to her side.

"Sip this," he ordered, thrusting it toward her.

"But I don't drink."

"Today you drink. It's brandy to put some color back in your cheeks. Drink it, Manda. Now!"

She took a taste, choked, and sputtered. Jason nodded his head in approval, but pointed a commanding finger at the remaining liquid. She raised the snifter to her lips again and swallowed, this time managing to close her throat around the rising cough. When after a third sip the grimness faded from Jason's features, Manda resolutely plunked the glass onto the cocktail table.

"That tasted awful," she denounced breathily, resentment of his arbitrary ministration igniting silvery sparks in her stubborn gaze.

"But you do feel better." His grin refused to accept her annoyance.

She almost capitulated, her mouth beginning to curve upward at the corners, until she recalled his earlier upsetting comment.

"You said I'm no stranger. You've seen me somewhere. You know something about my past." His brows lowered in puzzling scrutiny, as her blunt defiance accused him. "You've looked at me like that before. It makes me feel like a bug under a microscope, and I don't like it one bit!"

"Of course, you don't." Jason's gaze grew warm, like the long, sinewy fingers that covered hers and squeezed lightly, creating a sensation both pleasant and disturbing. "Last night I had the feeling that I knew you from somewhere. Just now, I was trying again to think where I'd seen you."

"If only you could remember!" Manda's heart thudded against her ribs. She waited.

"No, I'm sorry." He shook his head with regret. Her whole body drooped as hope drained away. A sad thing to witness. The urge to protect her nudged him again.

"Maybe if I knew more about the circumstances of your . . . ah, handicap . . ." He stopped, having the good grace to be embarrassed. "No, that's wrong!" He rushed to atone for his unfortunate choice of words. "You definitely are not handicapped. You're a bright, lovely, normal young woman who can't remember some things."

Her shining eyes thanked him, as with a wistful smile she told him, "I can't remember *anything* except what has happened during the past two years."

The enormity of her predicament astounded him. "A total memory loss? What caused it? You say it's lasted two years? Isn't that a lot longer than usual?" He paused, striving for calm and control before he spoke again. "I'm asking too many questions."

Manda watched him lean forward, pick up the brandy snifter, and in one gulp down the remainder of its fiery contents. She had the amnesia; Jason required the drink. She very nearly giggled. The working of his jaw muscles as he gritted his teeth warned her against it.

"I don't mind," she said, amazed that this was so. His compassion made her confidences possible. "I know a little about my past, but I don't remember it. Therapy sessions brought out a few minor facts. Once Dr. Nils gave me an injection of sodium pentothal, and afterward he showed me his notes and explained what happened."

"Didn't he use a tape recorder?"

"Yes, he did. But he said I cried a lot and yelled and screamed. I know I woke up with tears streaming down my face. He didn't like upsetting me unnecessarily, so he let me read the notes, instead of listening to the more graphic tape."

"Perhaps that was best. What did you find out?"

"I grew up in a Phoenix convent. Apparently quite happily."

"Then why the hysteria on the tape?"

"That was when I relived something that happened to me when I was two or three years old. One day I appeared in a little Arizona town . . . somehow I remembered its name . . . Sandy Springs . . . stumbling and crawling out of the desert, dehydrated and half-starved, crying 'I want Mommy! Mommy went to sleep! Take me to my Mommy!' Someone sent for the State Highway Patrol, and they asked me who I was, how my mother and I came to be alone out there, where she was when I left her. I couldn't tell them anything; I was only a baby, after all. The only thing I knew was that she went to sleep and I couldn't wake her." Manda stopped, ran her fingers through her curls and gave her head a dismal shake. Today wasn't the first time she conceded that Dr. Nils had been wise to prevent her from hearing the truth drug tape.

Jason wanted to comfort her, to hold her small trembling hands, but instead he formed his own into fists and punched the sofa where it dipped under the weight of his hips. She sat so tense that he feared his sudden touch might make her come unglued.

"Couldn't the highway patrolmen locate your mother's car and find out who you were from the registration?" he asked softly, pulling her back into the present.

"Evidently not. Nobody ever came to get me. Dr. Nils thinks my mother may have been backpacking."

"Without at least one buddy along? And with a small child?" Incredulity wrinkled his brow. "What else did the truth drug session reveal?"

"Nothing important. At one point I babbled with joy about living near the sea and building beautiful sandcastles."

"But you grew up in Phoenix." None of the puzzle parts fit, and the few pieces he had were blurred by implausibility.

"Dr. Nils's theory is that my mother and I lived in some coastal city before we travelled to the desert."

Logical, Jason acceded, but still . . .

"How did Dr. Johannsen get involved with your case?" he asked. "If I'm prying, I apologize, and you must tell me only what you feel like sharing, but your story does help me know you better. And—I have to be honest with you, Manda—it lights a fire under my writer's imagination." His mouth stretched in a self-conscious grin.

"I can understand that." The answering smile she attempted for him felt pasted on, but she willingly answered his question. "Dr. Nils is consulting psychiatrist for several city hospitals, including Paso Robles. That's where I was. When the police couldn't identify me and my amnesia kept hanging on, the doctor in charge of my case sent for Dr. Nils."

Briefly she described waking, a stranger to herself, in a hospital room. The nurse's account of discovering her walking up and down in the dawn rain. The days and nights of pain and confusion that culminated in a demoralizing self-pity. And during it all, the physicians and policemen who demanded answers to questions that merely served to befuddle and torment her more.

"I truly wanted to die," she admitted, gulping a dry sob.

"Dear God in heaven," Jason murmured raggedly.

Manda took a slow, deep breath to reclaim her self-control. "That was the worst time," she said. "After Dr. Nils came, my state of mind began to improve. We had several long talks. He promised me he would do his best to help me regain my memory and that if all efforts failed, he would show me how to build a new life." She finally managed a rueful smile. "He kept that promise."

"And became your guardian."

"Not right away. I spent ten days in the hospital, and then he arranged for my admission to a private clinic for patients with mental disorders. I think he owns it. For more than a month, the doctors there gave me a lot of tests. Then they declared me sane." She laughed mirthlessly. "After that, I went to live with Dr. Nils."

"Why? I mean—why did he invite you?"

"I suppose because he wanted to help. I needed therapy, and had no place to stay, and he liked me. I know he sometimes seems pompous and overbearing, but he's essentially a very kind man."

"The authorities couldn't find out where you came from, or why you were in Paso Robles?" Jason asked. Manda shook her head. "And, of course, your fingerprints weren't on file. Someday a federal law will be passed forcing everyone to have his or her fingerprints recorded. Think how useful it would be in times of emergency or, the saints forbid, national disaster."

"That might be a good law," she agreed. "But no one ever took my fingerprints."

"No one took—? That's crazy! I mean—I didn't mean—" When he saw with relief that his use of the word *crazy* hadn't upset her, he began again. "During those first days in the hospital, after you failed to regain your memory, some police officer *had* to have fingerprinted you!"

"No, Jason. The doctors operated on me the morning Libby Devlin found me, and both hands were in casts, then heavily bandaged for many weeks. After all that time, I guess no one thought about fingerprints."

"What other injuries did you sustain?"

"Nothing except scrapes and bruises and scratches. One policewoman suggested they were caused by running through bushes and falling down, when she was trying to help me remember. She believed someone had been chasing me. Certainly something had frightened me, something so hideous that I shut it out of my mind, along with everything else. That's what retrograde amnesia is."

"Damn!" Jason's countenance was so grim, she looked away and went on with her narrative.

"Whatever happened, it was more than a bad scare. Several bones in my hands were broken. Some were crushed and had to be replaced with Teflon joints. There was some nerve damage, fortunately repairable. For months a physical therapist worked with me, massaging and whirlpooling my hands, teaching me exercises. I still do them sometimes, when my hands ache or get stiff. That's one reason I learned to type, to strengthen my fingers."

"What caused the injuries to your hands?"

"Who knows? One of the nurses told me she overheard the orthopedic surgeon telling Dr. Nils that it was as though someone had taped my hands to a cement block, and then pounded on them with a hammer."

Jason, his eyes narrow black slits, cringed at the horrendous scene she had described. "Oh, my God."

"If you look closely," she added, "you can still see the scars from the surgery." She held out her hands, palms down. Never before had she volunteered to display her hands in such a fashion, but for Jason it seemed the natural thing to do.

He placed his palms under hers. Aware now, he saw what he hadn't noticed when he'd looked at the charms on her bracelet. Tiny threadlike lines, faintly discernible in contrast to the light tan of her skin, ran along the inner edges of her fingers and tracked across the top of each hand.

"So many scars," he rasped, slowly pulling his hands away from hers.

"Well," she said and produced a shaky laugh, "my hands were a frightful mess."

He cleared his throat. When he spoke again, his voice was less brusque. "What were you wearing?"

"Wearing?" Sometimes she couldn't keep pace with

the mercurial shifts of his inquisitive mind.

"When the nurse saw you outside the hospital. I was thinking of store labels in your clothing."

"Oh, that." For the first time in minutes, a twinkle brightened Manda's eyes, and a genuine smile tilted the corners of her mouth. "For sure, I hadn't done my shopping at a salon like Sylvia's. My clothes furnished no clues. I had on a torn, cheap poplin wraparound skirt, a sweater that after they took it off looked like a tangled skein of red yarn, filthy navy blue sneakers and . . . ah . . . plain cotton undies. The only thing of value was my charm bracelet." A flash of sadness crossed her face.

"I see."

That I've-seen-you-somewhere gleam flickered in his eyes again, and Manda suddenly felt vulnerable. Exposed to some sort of danger. Did Jason know who she was but for some awful reason wasn't telling her the truth?

Chapter Five

Even as Manda teetered on the impulse of demanding an answer to the troubling question, Jason broke eye contact, rose from the sofa, and walked over to retrieve his novel from the floor. In an oddly strained silence, he placed the book on the cocktail table a few inches from her knees.

"I hope you enjoy a *Rosary for Rosa,*" he told her, his mouth a sardonic twist. "I think it's the best work I've done, and it may well be my last."

His glumness astonished her.

"You don't plan to write another?"

"Plan?" he snorted, dropping heavily in the chair across from her. "I've been struggling for months with a plot that won't gel. My editor is pressuring me for the first chapters, and I have nothing to send him. I may dump the whole project and look for a new set of crime facts to build a story on." Striving for control, his gaunt hawklike features assumed the stoicism of his native forefathers. Only his eyes, snapping orbs of black lightning, betrayed the magnitude of his frustration.

"Dr. Nils never has that problem," Manda said, "but I guess it's different writing nonfiction."

"I guess." He sounded preoccupied, and as suddenly as his eyes had blazed with thwarted objective, now they took on a steady look of purpose.

"Manda, do you have a job?" he blurted, the words a gusher of excitement.

Stunned, she stared at him until she found her voice. "I was looking for one in San Francisco this week, but—" She stopped, reluctant to talk about the still-smarting humiliations of the ineffectual trip. But she couldn't stop herself from recalling them . . .

Manda knocked on the door of Peggy Gant's San Francisco apartment. While she waited, her shoe tapped an impatient staccato on the bare, dirt-caked floor. She frowned. The corridor walls were dark and dingy, and a shadeless light bulb hung from the water-marked ceiling.

Well, she'd been warned not to expect too much, hadn't she? Peggy, Dr. Nils's secretary until four months ago, had answered Manda's letter: "You're welcome to stay at my place. It may disappoint you, but it's all I can afford on a beginning model's wishy-washy income. We can share everything, and the newspapers are full of want ads for typists." So here she was, standing outside what was to be her new home.

The door swung open on her dream.

It was a nightmare.

Peggy, it turned out, already had one other apartment-mate, an unkempt, unwashed middle-aged man, who undressed Manda with his wild eyes and made her feel sick to her stomach.

As graciously as haste would allow, Manda declined Peggy's offer to share and drove to the St. Francis Hotel, where Dr. Nils stayed whenever he came to town to do business with a local dealer in jade artifacts.

After checking in, Manda sat in her room and took stock of her alternatives. She could accept defeat and return to San Luis Obispo. She could attend the exhibit of Frederic Remington's sculpture and paintings, as she'd told Dr. Nils she planned to do, having deliberately picked a time when the doctor was conducting a seminar and unable to accompany her. Or she could look for a job, any job that would pay her enough to squeak by, living alone.

Actually, there was only one viable choice. Manda refused to go crawling back to Dr. Nils like some cowering little dog. She took the elevator to the lobby and bought a copy of the *Examiner.* Back in her room, she settled cross-legged on the bed, with the pages of the classified section spread out around her.

For six wearying days Manda trod the city's uphill, downhill sidewalks and stopped in at every office, every shop, every store that advertised in that morning's paper for a typist, a receptionist, a cashier, or a sales clerk.

She could give no references. Her total experience consisted of typing medical material and correspondence for her guardian and a few of his colleagues, and the prospective employers had only her word for that.

Furthermore, the simplest questions on the application forms gradually diminished what remaining confidence she carried into every new personnel office. *Give the year and date of your birth. Where were you born? List the full names of your parents. What is the last year of school you attended? If college, where, and what was your major?* When she left those spaces blank, the interviewers raised astonished eyebrows, shook their heads, and droned their unfeeling regrets.

Each unsuccessful job-seeking effort swelled her mortification, until the accumulated *no's* ballooned into one gigantic heartbreak.

Finally, footsore and dejected, Manda was forced to give up. Once again her hopes to gain her independence had been dashed. Holding back the tears, she paid her hotel bill and started home. True, the decision to return was hers alone, but she hated having to make it.

Now, sitting across from Jason, Manda hated the idea of repeating for him the discouraging details of her job search. So her sentence hung unfinished in the strained silence.

Surprisingly, Jason finished the sentence for her. "But because of your memory loss, you couldn't supply satisfactory answers to the employers' questions." Before she could speak, his hand made a silencing motion and his mouth shaped a triumphant smile. "Your worries are over, and so are mine. I need a secretary."

At first her heartbeat hurried with joy, but immediately her defenses rose like floodgates, to hold back the onrush of relief. Jason's offer reeked too much of coincidence. She wanted a job, and he needed a secretary. Just like that. Anger sparked her eyes and reddened her cheeks.

"I don't accept charity!" she stormed. "I can find my own job, thank you very much!" How wonderful it would have been to stay here and work for him, she thought, and the wish, a traitor to her pride, served to reinforce her antagonism. "I hate it when people feel sorry for me!"

"Why should I feel sorry for you?"

Manda gaped at him. However offhand his tone, there was no mistaking the exasperation that sharpened the planes of his face.

"Because you can't remember?" Impatience tinged his asking. "I get hives every time I eat shrimp, but that doesn't mean I shouldn't go to a seafood restaurant and enjoy broiled red salmon." A chuckled expletive gurgled deep in his throat. "What a lousy analogy! I'm trying to say too many things at once. First, each of us has characteristics that make us different. One of yours is amnesia. Your eyes are another; not only are they beautiful, but they're also singularly expressive of whatever you're feeling at the moment." The compliment earned from her a small, grudging smile. "Secondly, I don't hesitate before every bite of food and ask myself, 'Will this make me break out in itchy red bumps?' Manda, I do not want everything you and I say to each other, or feel for each other, to be sifted through a strainer called amnesia."

He paused, swallowing to ease an unbidden tightness in his throat. Then, carefully he emphasized the words: "And . . . I . . . do . . . not . . . feel . . . sorry . . . for . . . you." Tears of gratitude pooled in the gray eyes he admired. "Don't do that, Manda, don't cry. This is a happy day, because, if you want it, you finally have a job."

"You really do need a secretary?" She blinked, and with a fingertip waylaid the two teardrops sliding down her nose.

"Yes, I do. Temporarily, but for several weeks. My secretary flew to Kansas City ten days ago, to be with her daughter who was seriously injured in a private plane crash. Fortunately, Mrs. Burke's daughter is out of danger, but she'll require a second operation and extensive post-op therapy. There are three grandchildren below school age, and with their father remarried and living in Boston, Mrs. Burke will have to stay there, until the daughter is able to care for herself and her family."

"And you think I could fill in until she comes back?"

"I'm sure." Clearly he would brook no further uncertainty on her part. "You'll be organizing, cross-indexing files, and typing research notes, handling correspondence, retyping messy revised manuscript pages. The same tasks you've done for Dr. Johannsen. Ever since you spoke of helping him, I've had it in mind to offer you the job."

"Thank you. I feel very lucky." No longer could she suppress the radiant smile.

"Not too lucky," he teased, grinning at her delight. "The weekly salary is minimal."

He named a figure Manda considered more than adequate. Her first paying job! In her excitement her eyes shimmered like moonlit gray satin.

"Plus your room and board," Jason said.

"That's too much."

"Nonsense. For this isolated place, a good secretary is hard to find. The ad I put in the *Monterey Peninsula*

Herald hasn't had one response. Nobody wants to drive Highway 1 twice a day, and no one wants to take up residence here. The inn is too far from shops, theaters, and restaurants."

"That's why I like it. Right on the ocean, but without the noisy crowds of a resort beach."

"I know. After breakfast when we stood on the terrace, I watched your face light up, and then you took off toward the beach like a homing pigeon. I was fairly certain you'd accept the job."

"Job? What job?" Sylvia asked as she entered the room.

She seemed to float across the carpet to Jason's side. Her kiss deposited a lipstick smear at the corner of his mouth. Jason's easy smile gave no indication as to whether he'd intentionally turned his head just enough for Sylvia to miss his lips, or whether the movement had been accidental. Sylvia frowned, then shrugged a lovely bare shoulder and airily repeated the question.

"What job?"

"I'm Jason's new secretary," Manda told her.

"Amy Burke isn't coming back?" Sylvia's voice was as brittle as cornstalks in August.

"Of course, she is," Jason said. "But she'll be away for a number of weeks, so Manda has consented to stay and work with me."

"I see. Well, Manda, congratulations," Sylvia offered.

Manda, a bit unsure of her secretarial efficiency, was heartened by the way Jason had said *with* instead of *for.* He made her feel less of a lucky happenstance that Fate, or fog, had shoved into his front door. She resolved to do her utmost to justify his confidence in her.

Towering in the hall doorway, Mrs. Meecher noisily cleared her throat.

Jason acknowledged her presence with an enthusiastic "Bess! Manda will be our permanent guest. Temporarily."

Everyone smiled at the paradoxical announcement except Sylvia, who stretched her mouth in a polite facsimile.

"I'm glad, Miss Lethe," the housekeeper said, a merry twinkle in her brown eyes to bolster the words.

"I'd like it if you'd call me Manda, too."

"All right, if you call me Bess."

"Sounds fair to me," Manda assented.

Bess Meecher said, "I came to tell all of you lunch will be served on the terrace in about ten minutes."

"Then I'll have time to call home," Manda realized aloud, and left the room.

She phoned Emory person-to-person because she didn't want to chance getting Dr. Nils on the line. Sooner or later the doctor must be told about her job, but she wanted to avoid the inevitable argument for as long as possible.

When Emory heard Manda's voice, he cut into the operator's words.

"Manda! I've been so worried! When you didn't get here yesterday, after the hotel told us you'd checked out—"

"Didn't Dr. Nils explain?"

"He said you were staying overnight at some crummy motel because you got caught in the fog on Highway 1. He was furious." He chortled at the remembrance of the doctor's displeasure. "Whatever made you think you're the adventurous type?"

"Maybe I am," she bristled. "And what I told Dr. Nils was that Tangletrees is an excellent inn, and I intended to stay for a few more days. But now my plans have changed."

"You're coming home. Dr. Nils said you would, once you thought it over."

"He was wrong." She told Emory about the job, talking continuously to cover his sputtering attempts to break into her explanation.

"And what I called for," she concluded rather breathlessly, "is to ask you to drive up here over the weekend and bring some of my clothes. Mostly jeans, blouses, and T-shirts, comfortable walking shoes, some sweaters, and a raincoat. Mrs. Hendricks will know what to pack."

"I won't do it! You come on home. You *cannot* stay there!" he shouted.

How strange, she mused. Dr. Nils had spoken those identical protesting words to her last night, and in the same agitated manner. The two most important men in her life were entirely too bossy.

"Yes, I *can* stay here!" she stormed. "I'm a legal adult, and I'll be earning my own keep. This job will qualify as experience I can use for a creditable reference when I apply for another. If you won't bring my things, I'll ask Mrs. Hendricks to ship them. Greyhound comes by here every day. Please, Emory, call her to the phone."

While she waited, she seethed over Emory's refusal to help. She felt a keen disappointment, too, which she knew would linger long after her ire had cooled. For weeks Emory had been urging her to find the means to escape the doctor's domination, but she knew he expected her declaration of independence to be the decision to marry him. Now, because her new freedom meant being on her own without him, he was being stubborn and uncooperative.

Emory's voice, not Mrs. Hendricks's, took her by surprise.

"I'm sorry, Manda. I didn't mean to order you around," he said contritely. "Of course I'll bring whatever you want me to bring. I really need to see the girl I love." Soft as a caress, his words made Manda ashamed of her earlier outburst.

Emory could be so dear—and so exasperating—and she was never sure when he would be which. That was part of his appeal, but would she like living a roller coaster marriage?

Well, she didn't plan to marry Emory, or anyone else, any time soon.

Avoiding comment on his last statement, she reminded him of the cost of the person-to-person call. After a hasty good-bye, she added, "Don't forget to tell Dr. Nils about my job."

Congratulating herself on having delegated the unpleasant chore, she laughed at Emory's stammering protests and placed the phone on its hook.

After lunch, while Manda sat in the cheery yellow and white kitchen waiting for her jeans and blouses to wash and dry, she read Jason's latest novel. Mesmerized, she continued to read long after the dryer buzzer had sounded.

In a *Rosary for Rosa,* Rosa Chavez, an impoverished

naive girl in her late teens, fell in love with Paul Sawyer, the mayor's son, and lived with him for a few months before she discovered that he was a drug pusher. After threatening to report him to the police unless he stopped, she died suddenly of a heroin overdose—forcibly administered, her family and friends and the authorities believed, by her spoiled young lover. But the detective assigned to the case could obtain no proof of murder, and Paul—due to his father's clout—was not even indicted for dealing in narcotics. The epilogue portrayed a bittersweet if-only that might have happened if Rosa had survived.

When Manda finished the last page, she sat teary-eyed for a few moments, allowing the sadness to seep out of her heart. Then she found herself marveling at Jason's sorcery with words, his ability to look into his characters' very souls, and to make the reader look as well. Remembering what he'd told her about why he chose to write any particular story, Manda's thoughts flowed deeper into the undercurrents of Rosa's too impulsive love, the far from uncommon judicial travesty encompassing Paul's nonpunishment, and the lamentable consequences of such tragedies.

Bess, surprised to see Manda sitting at the breakfast table when she came in to start dinner preparations, queried, "You still here?" Then she noticed Manda's tear-streaked face. "What's wrong?"

Wordlessly Manda lifted the book so Bess could identify the jacket design, a curling strand of jet and silver rosary beads from which hung a plain onyx cross resting with an aura of finality on a backdrop of crimson satin.

"I cried, too, when I read it," the housekeeper confessed.

The two women exchanged self-conscious grins. Each knew that her pleasure and pride in Jason's talent had created a mutually satisfying bond between them.

Manda, extremely uncomfortable and annoyed during dinner, declined dessert and left Jason and Sylvia to continue their remember-when's. Once or twice Jason had tried to include Manda in the conversation, but Sylvia, in spite of a sugary-sweet politeness, somehow managed to make Manda feel like the unwanted third party.

Manda walked through the living room, opened the heavy door, and, stepping to the edge of the porch, gazed up at the sky. A million stars looked near enough to touch. As she watched, one of the "stars" became a cross-country jet slowly traversing the northeast quadrant of the midnight blue canopy. Eclipsing the full moon was one high dark cloud; the light from behind turned its broken outline into glimmering silver fringe. From the woods came the strident cry of a bird whose rest had been interrupted, probably by a venturesome owl. The air smelled of the briny sea and faintly of anise.

What a perfect evening, decided Manda, for a drive. The hazards of the coastal highway didn't worry her, not on a clear, bright night like this. Likely she'd have the road to herself, for the tourists would be checked into hotels miles away. Solitude was what she craved. Or, to be precise, she had no desire to spend more of this day in the company of Sylvia Hathaway.

Quietly she went inside, climbed the stairs, and from her room picked up a sweater, handbag, and her car keys. She left the inn by way of the kitchen, mumbling to Bess, who was loading the dishwasher, about needing some fresh air.

As Manda slowly maneuvered her car along the incline of the amber-lighted exit road, the headlights changed the blurred, ghostly shapes up ahead into harmless laurel, Spanish oaks, and pines. *Trees.* She could almost hear the switch click inside her head. She immediately forgot about Sylvia's rudeness, because the puzzling, unsettling occurrences and sensations of the past twenty-four hours began to nibble away at her self-confidence.

Braking once at the top of the final steep climb that opened onto the highway, and verifying that no other vehicle was in sight, Manda turned left toward Monterey. She had a strange compulsion to drive the strip of road that yesterday had been obscured by fog. Maybe tonight she would see something, feel something, that would provide a missing piece of the puzzle.

Whatever the puzzle was.

With both front car windows down, the crisp air, just short of being too cold, blew across her face. Evergreen boughs whispered sibilantly in the airflow of her passing; their pungency, freshened by the night's cool dampness, smelled fantastic. A hint of a smile lifted the corners of Manda's mouth.

A fat raccoon waddled along the gravelled shoulder of the roadway. When she drew alongside, it scrambled up the embankment, paws raising tiny puff-clouds of dust, and Manda laughed aloud at the animal's clumsiness.

In the moonlight the ocean's swells and troughs formed undulating stripes of dark and darker indigo. Where the cliff was low enough for Manda to see the breaking surf, it tiered in phosphorescent silver ruffles.

Soon she felt at one with the sea, and again at peace with her world.

When she reached the first overlook, she made a U-turn and headed back to the inn. The return trip being mostly downgrade, she quickly picked up speed. As she approached an especially dangerous curve, she sharply applied the brakes.

The car didn't respond.

She touched the pedal again. Encountering no resistance, her foot dropped all the way to the floorboard, and nothing happened to slow the onrushing automobile.

Manda's body stiffened in alarm, and, gasping, she reflexively pumped the brake pedal twice more before her mind assigned true words to the horror.

I have no brakes!

The momentum of the outswinging curve pushed the car straight toward the edge of the cliff. Her heart pounded. Confronting her was an endless, screaming fall, and if she survived that, the roiling surf would slam her body like a rag doll against the barnacle-covered rocks.

White-knuckled hands gripped the steering wheel tighter. She breathed rapidly, shallowly, through her open mouth. Her throat muscles ached with the strain.

Mustering every sinew and every nerve to hold the car steady, Manda pulled it gradually to the left. The Tempo slewed sideways, skidding so close to the rim of the precipice that she *felt* the oblivion only inches away.

At the last possible moment, her rear tires gained enough traction to hold onto the shoulder. Frantically she clutched the wheel, fighting the urge to jerk it in the opposite direction from the drop-off, realizing that if she went into a spin she would have absolutely no chance at all.

The car's path straightened, her death plunge averted. Temporarily. Because at the next outward curve . . .

Manda heard someone whimper. It took only a millisecond for her to realize that the soft, forlorn sound had come from her.

Now the car rushed toward the embankment. In the headlight beams, her terrified gaze could actually pick out individual stones partially imbedded in the sand. She was going to hit the solid wall head on.

Maybe it *would* be better to crash into an immovable object, rather than to hurtle two hundred feet through space and be cut into shreds by jagged boulders.

In the exact instant of Manda's giving up, a scene from an old movie flashed across her memory screen. A chase scene down a treacherous mountain road. Whether the recollection dated from before her amnesia or since, she didn't know or care, but she did know a way, however chancy, to slap at the hand of Fate so cruelly trying to snuff out her life.

Quickly, before she lost the minimal courage she had left, she steered the car with muscle-tense determination, so that for a few seconds it sped parallel to the embankment. Then, her blood racing cold, she spun the wheel to the left and sideswiped the overhanging bluff. Metal crunched and shrieked as it dragged along the resisting surfaces. Clods of dirt and tree roots torn from precarious footholds rained across the windshield. Gravel spat at the glass, cracking it in starred patterns, as Manda stared wide-eyed and added her screams to the doomsday cacophony.

Her attempt to stop the car had failed. She was going to die alone on this twisting deserted highway. And on such an incredibly lovely evening. The contrast was so obscene that she gave up the fight. She slackened her weakening grasp on the moonlit night and collapsed into a merciful blackness.

"Miss? Can you hear me, miss?"

An urgency in the voice compelled Manda to open her eyes. She stared at the upside-down dashboard. After a tentative hand explored the plushy cotton fabric and vinyl console beneath head and shoulder, her befuddled brain identified her car's front seat. Why on earth was she lying in this ridiculous uncomfortable position?

"Miss? I can see you moving. I'm a highway patrolman. You had an accident."

Suddenly she remembered. The brakes failing, her helplessness and fright, the last-hope decision to sideswipe the cutbank rather than tumble into the sea.

"Best you move slow and easy, miss." The concerned voice bore a trace of a Spanish accent. "Can you tell me, you hurt anywhere?"

To reassure him—and herself—she sat up. She closed her eyes for a few minutes to shut out a spinning world. But she felt no pain.

"I'm alive?" she muttered dazedly. Trembling hands pressed the sides of her head. "I'm alive!"

"That you are, miss," the man confirmed.

He was stooped over, watching her through the open right-hand window. In the glow of the flashlight he held under his chin, she discerned his round chocolate-colored face. White teeth flashed an encouraging smile below a neat mustache. She noted the blue seven-pointed star on the pocket of his uniform shirt.

"I'm Sgt. Pete Sandoval," he told her. "What are you called?"

"Manda Lethe."

"And where do you live?"

"3947 Oleander Drive, San Luis—" She stopped in mid-breath. The officer was testing her, to determine whether or not she was thinking clearly. "Right now I'm staying at Tangletrees Inn. Do you know it?"

"I do. Jason Tallfeather is my very good friend."

"Please, would you take me there?"

He ignored her plea and asked his own questions.

"How did this happen? We came over the rise and saw you scraping the hillside. Did you fall asleep? Don't you know you shouldn't drive if you're overtired?"

"No brakes," she murmured, momentarily intimidated by his gruffness.

"Pardon?"

"I had no brakes." She glared, daring him to scold her further. "That's why I ran into the bank. To make my car stop. It was all I could think of to do. And it worked, Sergeant! It worked."

Now that the danger had passed, she began to weep

silently.

"Holy Mother of—! You wrecked your car on purpose?"

Manda nodded, hiccuped a sob, and swiped at her unwanted tears with a small fist.

"You are one gutsy lady! That took a hell of a lot of moxie. I mean—" He stopped, lowered his gaze in abashment.

The unprofessional but admiring language brought a feeble smile to Manda's lips. "I know what you mean. But I really wasn't brave. Just desperate."

"I'll have my partner radio for a tow truck." He stepped back from the open window, and Manda noticed another uniformed man standing near the patrol car. "He'll stay with your car, and I'll drive you to the hospital. That'll be faster than waiting 'way out here for an ambulance."

"No, please! I—I hate hospitals." She looked more frightened than at any time since he'd first seen her. "Please, Sgt. Sandoval, I'm not hurt." To prove it, she slowly slid out the passenger side door, defying her shaky knees to buckle when her feet touched the pavement. "Nothing is broken." Manda, by way of confirming her diagnosis, took a couple of careful but steady steps, then turned to face the patrolman. "See?" she begged. "You can see I'm not hurt badly enough to go to a hospital."

"But you ought to have a doctor check you out." He sounded slightly less stern.

"I will, tomorrow, I promise, if I don't feel all right. Jason will take me. But not tonight, please?"

"Well . . . Mrs. Meecher is a nurse."

"She is?" The fear departed her big gray eyes and

her face brightened. "Then she'll know if I need a doctor—"

"Maybe. But the regulations say—"

"I doubt if regulations say anything about hospitalizing someone against her will," Manda stated with defiance. "Not if that person is rational and in control. I know I cried, Sergeant, but I'm okay now."

He capitulated with a wide grin. "Considering the brave thing you just did, I'd say you're more than okay."

Chapter Six

When Manda awoke the following morning, every inch of her felt as though it had either been jolted, stretched, or pummeled. The act of getting dressed turned the bedroom into a torture chamber. Hobbling down the stairs a few minutes later, she grunted in protest, and then with satisfaction, as she negotiated each successive step.

Bess Meecher, waiting in the hall below, watched with a quizzical smile. "It's only a little soreness," she said, "and that will go away in a day or two."

"A *little* soreness!" Manda wailed. "Even my hair aches."

Her feet at last touched level floor, and she expelled a hiss of accomplishment.

"Don't complain, young lady." The housekeeper's voice held none of the amusement of her earlier reproof. "You're very lucky, especially since you were not wearing your seat belt."

Guilt frowned across Manda's face. Bess had scolded last night, too, even as deft, gentle hands examined Manda for injuries and helped her into the satin nightshirt, cool and silky against an already hurting body. The nurse had discovered a curved red welt just beneath Manda's breasts, and an abraded, bruise-darkened streak on her upper left arm, both marks caused by impact with the steering wheel.

"I know, and I promise to buckle up from now on." A deep breath tweaked Manda's rib cage. She changed the subject. "I'm hungry."

"All right, but would you consider talking to Sgt. Sandoval first?"

"He's here already?"

"He's been here at least thirty minutes, but Jason wouldn't let me wake you. They're in the living room, working on my jigsaw puzzle. And arguing. Those two always argue." From the fondness in her tone, she obviously knew the sergeant well.

"I'd better not delay him any longer," Manda decided, wincing as she walked toward the front of the house. "But would you please bring me a cup of coffee?"

"Sure. Pete and Jason might like some, too."

As Manda entered the room, Jason jumped to his feet, jiggling the table and drawing a sharp invective from the uniformed man.

"Manda!" Jason, wearing a faded green Army surplus jumpsuit, hurried to her side, lightly touched her shoulder, and then gazed at her with tender warmth. "I'm glad you feel able to come downstairs."

"I'm all right. Just bruised and sore."

"Bess told me. Last night. Otherwise I'd have sent for our doctor. I'm sorry I wasn't here when Pete—Sgt. Sandoval—brought you home. After you left, Sylvia twisted my arm into taking her to a community playhouse down the coast."

Had it been a dream—Jason's drawn, grim face, peering at her through the blurred sleep induced by two of Bess's pain reliever pills?

He bent down, and his velvety breath brushed her ear as he spoke softly. "I came into your room around eleven."

So the remembered worry on his honey-colored face had been real.

"But you were sleeping," he added, "so I tiptoed out."

Jason's conscience still nagged. For a full three minutes he'd stood beside her bed, transfixed by the petite fetal-curled figure, childlike yet sensually evocative.

Sgt. Sandoval approached, flashing a white-toothed smile.

"Good morning, Miss Lethe. It pleases me to learn from Mrs. Meecher that your injuries are minor."

"Thank you."

"I must ask you a few questions. Jason, if you would leave us alone?"

"Why so damned official all of a sudden?" Jason grumbled.

"Because this, *amigo*, is official police business."

"And this is my inn," Jason countered. "And Manda is my guest."

Their half-playful bickering amused her. "It's all right with me if Jason stays," she said. "I have no secrets."

"Maybe I do." The sergeant tried to produce a menacing scowl, but his merry brown eyes negated the desired effect.

With a tray holding three yellow and orange thermal mugs, Bess edged past the trio. She pushed aside the unused puzzle pieces, deposited the coffee on the table's corner, and departed. The men settled on the sofa. Manda handed each a mug, took a hot bracing sip from her own, and dropped stiffly into the chair at the end of the long low table.

The sergeant drew a ballpoint pen and a small blue leather-bound notebook from his tan shirt pocket. His handsome brown face turned serious, and he cleared his throat to authenticate the interrogation. As Manda supplied it, he jotted down the usual information: her name, address, and phone number, car make and model, license number. Then he asked, "When and where was your car serviced last?"

"Two weeks ago, except for buying gas at self-service pumps. I had a mechanic in San Luis Obispo check everything, because I knew I'd be making this trip by myself, and I wanted to make sure the car was safe."

"It wasn't though, was it?"

"Pete," Jason interceded, "you sound like an old bear. In your job you see unexplained mechanical failures every—"

"Jason. Shut up or leave." The uniformed man inhaled slowly and almost imperceptibly squared his shoulders. Anxiety thickened his accent. "*Senorita,* I have much regret to tell you someone has tampered with your brakes."

"Damn!" Jason exploded.

The other man impaled him with a warning glare.

"That's impossible," Manda demurred, but her heart lurched nonetheless. "No one at Beall's Garage would do that."

"Not at the garage. Here. After you parked your car."

Jason sucked in a noisy breath, but closed his mouth over an instinctive protest.

"I don't understand," Manda said.

The coffee cups were forgotten.

"If the damage had been done *before* you arrived here two nights ago," the officer told her, "the accident would have happened sooner. You lost your brakes because the brake fluid drained out through some slits we found in the brake fluid line."

"But last night my brakes worked fine at first! I used them two or three times on the way to the overlook. They didn't fail until I turned around and started back."

"Yes, ma'am. Every time you applied the brakes, a little bit of the fluid leaked out. When you came to the steep downhill grade and hairpin curve, you pumped the pedal harder, several times, and the last of the fluid squirted out. That's how our patrol station mechanic who examined your car this morning thinks it happened, and I agree."

"I see." She accepted his explanation of the brakes' failure, but she could not, would not, accept his theory of malicious intent. "Normal wear caused the broken place in the line," she insisted. "I believe it's called metal fatigue?" Stubbornly she looked across the table at the sergeant in a manner inferring he was daft—in a perfectly nice way, but daft—to insinuate anyone would purposely sabotage her brakes, knowing she'd be driving on the treacherous curving rim of a precipice.

"No, Miss Lethe." Sandoval's countenance was

grim, his words brutally frank. "We have evidence to the contrary. Someone planned for your brakes to fail."

Manda stared at him, her bloodless face a mask of benumbing fear.

Jason could keep silent no longer. "Pete, you're scaring her! Her car sat twenty-four hours on my parking lot. During that time, no guests checked in. And the only car that left after Manda arrived belonged to an arthritic couple in their seventies, who couldn't possibly have crawled under her car, even if they'd known how to disable it. They didn't see Manda or hear her name. They left for Arkansas yesterday morning before she woke up. As for the Meechers, Sylvia, and me—none of us ever heard of a Manda Lethe until she arrived unexpectedly without a reservation. Not one of us has any reason to harm her. And who in the hell else is there? So tell me, how could the brake tampering have been done here?"

"Easy, *amigo*. Real easy. Your parking lot is not guarded. Nobody gives it a thought till you use a car. It's surrounded by trees and underbrush on two sides, and by the inn and ocean on the other two. Anyone could walk down the wooded slope from the highway, or climb up the cliff from the beach without being spotted. Especially if that someone was trying *not* to be seen."

"Evidence," Manda almost whispered. "You—you said you have evidence to . . . to show . . . what it shows." Unable to verbalize the awful words, she shuddered.

Although her anguished gaze begged the patrolman to refute the allegation, he knew an honest straightforward explanation would serve her best in the long run.

"Ordinarily, everything on the underside of a vehicle is coated with road oil and grime," he said, watching her sorrowfully and wishing he were anywhere but here. "Not so your brake fluid line. It has been wiped clean, and there are shiny scratches where someone held the line with pliers or a wrench while the file cuts were made."

"Then it's true." Manda's sigh emerged from low in her twinging chest.

The two men, temporarily at a loss for words, watched the emotions play across her pale face: acceptance, then shock, and finally a fury that colored her cheeks and blazed in her eyes.

"I could've run into a car full of people," she moaned, "a family with children! Dear heaven, whoever ruined my brakes could have killed others besides me. Who would do such a vile thing?"

"That was my next question." Sgt. Sandoval spoke in his most calming, professional tone. "Can you think of any reason why someone would want you—ah—out of the picture? Have you made anyone very angry recently? Or jealous? Any trouble with a gentleman friend?"

"No! I mean—I have a—a friend, but the problem is with me, not him! I—I'm not sure I'm ready to get married."

"I see." The officer's brief smile barely curved his mouth. "How about enemies? Perhaps a person holding a long-standing grudge."

"I—I can't remember anyone like that." She threw Jason a warning plea-filled glance. She didn't want to discuss her amnesia with the sergeant.

Jason understood and tried to change the direction

of Pete's thoughts. "Couldn't the brake tampering have been done by teenagers for kicks? Or by some drugged crazy just passing through?"

"Maybe," Pete replied, but obviously he didn't consider Jason's suggestions feasible. He didn't think Jason believed them either.

Sgt. Sandoval's interrogation had dead-ended, and Manda's strained, frightened look cautioned him that she'd had almost as much pressure as she could handle. Tucking the notebook and pen into his shirt pocket, he smiled. "Thank you, Miss Lethe, for the information. If you think of anything to help us identify the perpetrator, please call me."

He handed her a card bearing the patrol station phone number, then stood and turned to Jason. "Take care, my good friend." After giving Jason's shoulder a slap, he walked briskly out the front door.

Beneath a worried frown, Jason's black eyes studied Manda's face. "Are you all right?"

"No. I'm hungry."

They laughed, breaking the tension of the past half hour.

"While you're enjoying breakfast," he said, "I'll go back to what I was doing when Pete arrived. Cutting the eucalyptus shoots that sprouted along the entrance road from last fall's seed pods. They'd be trees by next summer, they grow so fast."

When Bess suggested Manda might like to eat on the sunny terrace, she accepted with delight.

"Fine," the housekeeper said. "You go sit, and I'll bring your food in a jiffy."

Tugging a white ornamental iron chair closer to a round table, Manda sat, propped her elbows on the glass top, rested her chin in her palms, and stared out across the golden-grassed meadow. In her mind she went over the session with Sgt. Sandoval. Stubbornly she agreed with Jason's suggestion. Some prankster, a total stranger, had messed up her car's brakes. The incident was over, and she intended to forget it.

But how *could* she forget it? What if somebody really had planned the accident, hoping to kill her? Who? And why? And how?

The how was fairly simple. Based on the highway patrolman's description of the process, no trained auto mechanic would have been required. Any how-to book on the maintenance and repair of automobiles would supply the information to damage her brake fluid line and turn her car into a coffin.

It might have worked, too, except for her lucky remembrance of a movie chase on a mountain road.

If Jason's theory of a stranger as the culprit was false, as Sgt. Sandoval obviously believed, then the possibilities of the "who" and the "why" were limitless and unbearable to contemplate. Somewhere out there, someone from her past, for some unimaginable reason, wished her dead!

Manda's fingers wrapped tightly around the edge of the white iron table.

For the first time in the two years, Manda's amnesia frightened her. She had been saddened, frustrated, angered, confused, and embarrassed by her memory loss, but never scared by it. Not until this moment.

Deliberately, as Dr. Nils had taught her to do when she was upset, Manda breathed deeply in, then out, again and again. She had learned to live bravely with unanswered questions, and she was determined that this morning would be no different. She willed her hurting hands to relax.

Gradually she became aware of the distant *put-put* of a gasoline engine. Was it a motorboat? No; the sound came not from the sea but from the woods beyond the inn.

The low, steady drone drew her to the north end of the terrace. Where the hill rose sharply to meet the shoulder of the highway, she spotted a large red tractor with a wide blade attached to its front. Fascinated, she watched the orange-shirted driver skillfully maneuver the cumbersome machine, its oddly graceful movements like a trained elephant's, dancing to the circus band's brassy rendition of "The Skater's Waltz."

"Here's your bacon and eggs," Bess called out, "and I brought an extra cup for myself. We can visit a while."

Smiling in reply, Manda hurried to the table. After Bess poured the steaming brown elixir and settled in the other chair, Manda asked, "Why is the man on the tractor scraping soil back and forth?"

"That's my husband, Clive."

"Oh?" Manda wondered why she hadn't seen him since her arrival at Tangletrees Inn.

"There used to be a deep ravine running from the highway down to the beach. When Jason decided to put the parking lot where it is—because that's the only flat place around here—he and Clive filled in the old ditch and dug a new one several yards to the northwest, so the water runoff wouldn't wash the foundation from under the concrete slab. But sometimes, after a torrential rainfall, a gully starts to form along the original drainage path and Clive has to bulldoze the ground level again. That's happened twice since Jason leased the property."

Manda stopped eating and looked at Bess in surprise. "Leased? Jason told me he's the proprietor. He doesn't own the inn?"

"No. He leased the house, which was converted from an old barn by the previous owner. Jason wanted a quiet place to live and write, and this is ideal. He knew money from the sale of his books wouldn't be enough income, not for a while at least, so he obtained permission from the estate lawyer to provide overnight lodging for tourists."

"Then it wasn't an inn before," Manda murmured offhandedly.

"Before the murder, you mean?"

"Murder?" Manda gasped. "Here? What murder?"

"Oh, my, I thought you knew." Bess's next words tumbled out in a rush of nervousness. "It happened a good distance from this house. In a shed. On the edge of a grove of ugly old dead trees. They were all torn down to make room for the parking lot." She turned her mug in uneven circles on the table. "I hope you won't feel uneasy about staying here."

Manda hadn't really listened to what Bess was saying. She only wanted to know about the murder.

"Who was killed?" she asked, her eyes silvery with excited curiosity. "How did it happen?"

"I don't know much about it." Bess sounded almost sullen. "I thought you knew," she repeated. "Jason doesn't like for anyone to bring up the subject."

"But I didn't bring it up!" Manda squeaked in frustration.

"That's right, you didn't."

Bess took a swallow of lukewarm coffee, made a wry face, and sighed noisily. At last she began to speak.

"Carlton Logan, the victim, was a rich jewelry designer who lived in San Francisco but spent most weekends here alone."

"No servants?"

"None. A local woman was hired to come in to clean every Tuesday after he'd gone. But on that Tuesday about two years ago, when she arrived, the man's car was still here. She finally located him in the workshop. He'd been beaten to death with a large wooden mallet that a homicide detective found up in the woods. Rain had washed away all the fingerprints. The blood, too. But a few shreds of the dead man's hair still stuck to the underneath side of the mallet."

"Yuk!" Manda groaned, repelled by the ugly picture Bess's words had evoked. "I hope they locked the killer away for life."

"They never caught him. Or her. They never figured out who did it or why or anything."

"How awful for the man's family! What did you say his name was?"

"Carlton Logan. He had no family. Parents deceased, no brother or sister, and he never married. According to his banker's testimony at the inquest, at one time Logan arranged for a monthly check to be sent automatically and confidentially to a Dallas lawyer. But that was stopped many years before the murder. When the California authorities checked, they learned that the lawyer in Dallas had died, so no one knows who or what the payments were for. Blackmail, probably. It came out after Logan's death that he'd led a very wild, free and easy existence as far as women were concerned."

"Didn't he leave a will?"

"Yes," said Bess, "and that was another strange thing. The twenty-year-old will specified that if no heir could be located within five years after his death, his estate was to be divided among a list of charities. The administrator of the estate assumed from the wording of the will that there might be an heir, but so far none has surfaced. During the murder investigation, the newspapers and television gave a lot of publicity to Logan's wealth, and a number of supposedly long-lost relatives appeared on the scene. But each claim proved false."

"What will happen to Tangletrees Inn after the five years?"

"Jason has the option to buy, if no heir turns up."

"And if one does turn up?"

"I just hope Jason can persuade the heir to sell to him. We understand someone else wants the property, and if the other party offers the heir more money . . ." Bess fidgeted with her mug on the metal tabletop. "Jason is so attached to this place, it worries me. If he lost it, I honestly don't know what he'd do."

From the intensity of Bess's last remark, Manda perceived the conversation to be skirting the edge of something personal and private to Jason. Having no wish to pry, she asked instead, "Why is it called Tangletrees Inn?"

Several times she had wondered. For some vague reason, she felt Bess's answer might be significant.

"Logan called it Tangletrees. I suppose because the woods grow thick and close around the house. Jason liked the name, so he used it when he opened the inn for business."

That made sense, Manda mused. What, then, disquieted her? Something Bess had said earlier. About trees.

Don't be ridiculous, she remonstrated herself. Since her hallucination at the parking lot the night she arrived, she seemed to have acquired a fixation regarding trees.

She shook off the uneasy feeling, smiled at the housekeeper, and asked, "Do you have many guests during the tourist season?"

"We could handle more." The older woman shrugged her shoulders. "Jason won't advertise the inn. He won't even let Clive put up a big fancy sign at the side of the highway."

"I noticed."

"Jason says he doesn't operate a hotel for noisy tourists. Instead, he provides a resting place where tired travelers can find quiet for their souls, as well as good food and refreshing sleep. That 'quiet for the souls' is his idea, not mine," Bess interjected with a chuckle. "I concentrate on the meals and the beds."

Manda laughed with her, then turned serious. "It would be a shame to have litter covering the beach, and boomboxes caterwauling around the clock. And people hauling away shells and driftwood, only to toss them into garbage cans a few weeks later."

"You sound just like Jason. I sometimes think he wishes he hadn't started the inn."

"He certainly was lucky to find you and your husband, both willing to live and work in this isolated area."

"Oh, no, Manda, we're the lucky ones. Clive had a

stroke three years ago, and I had to quit my job as nursing supervisor to take care of him. He's almost recovered now, praise be, except for some words he can't say sometimes, and when he chews his food, his mouth still pulls a little to one side. That's why he doesn't like to be around our guests. He feels embarrassed. Anyway, back then, I worried so much about Clive, and about our being forced to withdraw our savings to live on, I came close to a nervous breakdown.

"Jason knew about our misfortune. He'd been a reporter for the *Examiner*, where Clive worked for twenty years as maintenance engineer until his stroke. Because Jason was traveling so much of the time to research his books, he needed a couple to live here and look after the inn. He offered us the job. It was a godsend! There's absolutely nothing Clive or I wouldn't do for him." Her voice quavered on the last sentence. She busied herself with positioning her empty mug on the tray. "I've rambled on like a gossipy old woman."

"No, I'm glad we talked." Manda patted Bess's hand that clutched the mug handle. "We're friends."

The housekeeper blinked rapidly to dispel the sudden moisture in her eyes. "Humph!" Heaving her bulk out of her chair, she picked up Manda's breakfast tray. "I'd better go make the pineapple pie for tonight's dessert."

After Bess disappeared through the sliding glass door, Manda stood, stretched her arms above her head, and rocked her hips to ease her tight, sore muscles. She needed exercise; but she grimaced at the very thought of descending, then climbing, the hundred and more cliff steps. Yesterday she had noticed a dimly marked trail cutting off at a right angle from the path to the beach. Today she'd explore where it led.

The sandy path charted the rim of the bluff. Manda tried without success not to look out across the nothing. Her glances were intermittently drawn to the peril below. Jagged, ominous boulders crouched in the pounding waves, and for a moment, she could almost feel what it would be like to go over the edge and plunge screaming to the death-dealing rocks. A cold, clammy worm of premonition crawled along her spine. Her hands clenched into white-knuckled fists. Perspiration beaded her forehead. She couldn't breathe.

The cry of a seagull broke the spell, and Manda sucked air into her burning lungs. When she was able to think beyond inhaling and exhaling, she heard the footsteps. Once again fear grabbed her, and she started to run.

"Wait up, Manda, and I'll walk back to the house with you."

Her body almost wilted with relief at the sound of Jason's voice.

"I had no idea you were here," she said, as she turned to face him. Short, shallow breaths, leftovers from her fright, escaped between her smiling lips.

He stepped closer, and gently tugged her a foot or two back from the dangerous precipice.

"I'm sorry if I startled you," he said.

His thumb caressed the sensitive flesh of her upper arm. Her arm tingled. She tingled all over.

"That's all right," she mumbled.

How could she tell him she'd been picturing herself

thrown over the side of the cliff by some half-mad stranger? Jason would want to know why. Then she'd have to admit to being influenced by this morning's revelation of Logan's gruesome murder, and Bess would be in trouble for discussing the crime with her.

Looking up at Jason, Manda saw the puzzlement and concern in his asking ebony eyes. She had no answers for him. Shyly she pulled her arm from his grasp and moved down the trail ahead of him.

Sylvia, who had been looking out the front window, glanced over her shoulder to see who had entered the living room.

"Oh. Hello, Manda. I'm glad you weren't badly injured in your accident," she purred, somehow reminding Manda of a jungle cat not quite domesticated.

"Thank you, Sylvia. I hope you enjoyed your shopping in Carmel?"

Bess had explained why Sylvia left the inn early yesterday before Manda awoke. Sylvia must have stayed away overnight, because she hadn't shown up for breakfast or lunch today.

"It wasn't meant to be a pleasure trip," Sylvia explained with an air of patience. "I was checking out the competition."

"I'm sure you have competition everywhere. Even here."

The golden goddess could interpret that any way she chose, Manda thought with mischievous glee.

Sylvia whirled around, a hint of battle sparking her amber eyes for a brief moment, but Manda's genial smile placated her.

"Yes. Uh . . . I do." Sylvia fiddled with the drapery cord. "Some of the local shops carry fairly decent fashions." She turned back to the scene outside. "There's a car parked in the driveway. Two men are getting out. One in his mid-thirties and one . . . ah . . . not too old. Jason's greeting them."

Soon Manda heard voices through the open door. Jason's. Emory's. And Dr. Nils's! Why didn't he trust her to be on her own?

Jason came in first, carrying Manda's large Pullman case and a long garment bag. He introduced Sylvia to the newcomers, then took the luggage directly upstairs.

Emory, medium tall and slight of build, was dwarfed by the doctor, who had inherited his enormous shoulder span, barrel chest, and height of six feet six from Viking ancestors. Nevertheless, Emory nudged Dr. Nils aside and rushed to take Manda into his arms. Out of the corner of her eye, she watched Sylvia's grudging surprise, and she felt oddly triumphant.

"I'm so glad to see you," Emory exulted, his chin nuzzling her auburn curls. "This has been the longest two weeks." He held her slightly away as his steel blue eyes studied her serious face. "Is everything all right? Are you okay?"

The same instant Manda murmured, "I wish you'd come alone," Sylvia said in an upbeat manner, "She's very much okay, as you can see. Thankfully, the accident was a minor one."

"What accident?" Emory and Dr. Nils demanded in unison.

"There was some trouble with my brakes," Manda

said crossly, wishing Sylvia hadn't spoken out of turn. If Dr. Nils and Emory were told Sgt. Sandoval's theory about her minor accident, they would shove her into Emory's car and escort her home. "I run into an embankment and damaged the side of my car. But I wasn't hurt."

A frowning Dr. Nils planted himself between her and Emory.

"Surely you sustained *some* injuries," he stated categorically, without so much as a hello. "Show me your room, and I shall examine you."

"No." Manda detested his take-charge attitude. She glowered. "Mrs. Meecher, Jason's housekeeper, is a nurse, and she checked me over carefully. I have a few bruises, that's all."

"Why were you not taken to a hospital? I shall certainly see to it that someone is held accountable for dereliction of duty," he insisted in his most high-handed style.

Manda, recalling the sergeant's kindness and concern, straightened her shoulders and spoke, very decisively. "No. You won't take any action at all against anyone." Her storm gray eyes darkened with fury.

Dr. Nils gaped at her in amazement. One meaty hand combed through his thick shock of sandy blond hair.

Jason, descending the stairs, had overheard the exchange between Manda and her benefactor and felt like applauding her spunk. But he deemed it more expedient to calm Johannsen's troubled waters.

"The highway patrolman at the accident scene did urge Manda to see a doctor," he explained, "but she refused. I rather imagine, from what she's told me, she has had enough of hospitals."

The doctor seemed more agitated, not less. The reason became obvious when he scolded, "My dear Manda, you really should not confide in strangers."

"Jason's not a stranger." She staunchly held her ground; Dr. Nils just shrugged and turned away.

For an instant Emory's own annoyance uglified his classic features. Then, recovering his composure, he gave Manda an adoring look and asked her where they could talk.

"We can't stay long," he added, "and I need to speak with you privately."

"The terrace." Manda reached for his hand and led him away, making polite conversation through the hall and dining room. "Thanks for bringing my clothes. Before you leave, I'll see what Mrs. Hendricks packed. In case you'll need to tell her to send something else by bus. This is a lovely inn, don't you think? Did you have any difficulty finding it?"

"No. Dr. Nils has known all the time exactly where you were."

Outside, beyond the sight and hearing of the others, she wheeled to confront Emory. "Why did you bring him with you?" she yelped.

"To help me convince you to come home! He doesn't want you to stay here, and for once I agree with him." Roughly he jerked her against him and kissed her. Recognizing his kiss as emotional bribery, she offered no response other than to clench her jaws. Until he released her, she pushed on his chest with both hands.

"I *am* . . . going to stay here . . . *and* . . . work for Jason." Determination laced tight stubborn knots between each of her strung-out words.

Emory shifted to one side, but stood near enough to rake a finger down her forearm.

"Jason. You met the man less than three days ago," he grumbled. "You don't know anything about him, except that he owns this inn and he's a writer."

"I know he's a gentleman, and I like him," she said testily. Then her cheeks flushed crimson, and she quickly turned her head to avoid Emory's scrutiny, because he'd often told her that her feelings showed on her face.

"Should I be jealous?" he asked, keeping his tone light and teasing.

"You're making too much out of this. I like Jason—as a friend." That much, she rationalized, was true. As for what might develop later, who could foretell? At the moment she was only sure she didn't want to hurt Emory's feelings.

"I don't trust him," Emory declared, his mouth a grim line. "Tallfeather is hiding something."

Was Emory leading up to the fact that a ghastly murder had occurred here? Manda started to tell him she already knew about the unsolved crime, when he grabbed her shoulders, his fingers digging into her flesh. He forced her to face him.

Wild-eyed, he begged, "Please, Manda, come home with us! This place is unsafe for you. I can feel it! You're in *terrible* danger here. You *must* leave! Today!"

Chapter Seven

Manda stared openmouthed at Emory. He wasn't pretending. His raspy plea and flushed cheeks, his fists hitting the terrace wall, gave credence to his anxiety. He honestly believed she could be injured, or worse, if she remained at Tangletrees Inn.

Remembering her own broken hands, and worried that he might hurt his on the rough stones, she grabbed his fingers and held them briefly until they relaxed. Releasing him, she tried with a reassuring smile to allay his fear.

"Nothing bad is going to happen to me here." She shook her head at his beginning murmur of protest. "No, Emory. And please, let's not quarrel."

"I'd rather have you angry with me," he grumbled, "than have you hurt . . . or . . . dead."

"So would I." A small chuckle burbled in her throat. "But I'm not planning on being either one."

"This really isn't a safe place for you." Emory's mouth pouted. "Please, Manda."

"You just don't want me to stay here any longer, so you're trying to scare me into leaving." She patted his hand that spanned the brim of the stone wall. "But it's not going to work. My job with Jason probably won't last more than six weeks, if that. Then I'll come home. I promise."

"Okay, Baby, but I'll miss you like the very devil."

Manda sidestepped his embrace, a familiar irritation stiffening her posture. "I keep telling you. Don't call me Baby." Why did she hate so much his using that nickname? Had someone else, someone special, called her that?

"I'm sorry." Emory gave her one of his endearing lopsided smiles.

This time she permitted his hug, then pulled free.

"I'm going to see what clothes you brought," she said, and left him standing frustrated and alone on the terrace.

Twenty minutes later, a knock sounded on the open door of Manda's bedroom. Folding the last Downy-scented T-shirt into the dresser drawer, she spoke without looking up.

"Come in, Bess. You shouldn't have climbed the stairs just to help me unpack."

"Bess. Jason." Dr. Nils derisively enunciated the names as he entered the room. "You behave toward these people as if they were your friends."

"They *are* my friends." To vent her resentment of his intrusion into her private space and personal relationships, she slammed the drawer shut with a loud thump.

"I know nothing about the Meecher woman. She is, after all, merely a servant." He leaned against the dresser and dismissed Bess with a backward wave of his hand. Manda frowned and walked away from him. "However, I can assure you that I have obtained from a reliable source the information that Jason Tallfeather is a writer with, at best, a questionable reputation."

Manda whirled around, her anger no longer under control.

"You had someone check up on Jason?" The very words choked her. Fingernails dug crescents into her palms.

"There is really no need for hostility, my dear." Dr. Nils addressed Manda as if she were a recalcitrant patient, and she writhed inwardly at the insult. "Your welfare is my primary concern. When you telephoned from here that first evening, I recognized Tallfeather's name. I promptly contacted my editor, who asked around the publishing house and called me back."

"I don't want to hear this," Manda stated hoarsely.

The doctor, paying no heed, continued his singsong report.

"Tallfeather has been known to employ ruthless tactics when researching material for his so-called novels. He lives a completely antisocial existence—except for Miss Hathaway, with whom he has enjoyed a romantic liaison for quite some time."

Manda chewed on her lower lip and refrained from comment, as Dr. Nils absentmindedly toyed with the shells in the tray on the dresser.

"Tallfeather refuses to participate in autograph parties or to appear on talk shows to promote his work."

"Sylvia Hathaway told me he was on the Johnny Carson Show," Manda demurred.

Dr. Nils ignored the interruption, and with calculated determination finished his speech. "I surmise his royalty payments do not supply an adequate income; yet for some reason he does not advertise this inn or list it with travel agencies. And why do his book plots make the police appear oftentimes careless, even stupid? He seems to be mocking them. Can it be that he himself is guilty?"

"Guilty of what?" Bewildered and astounded, Manda paused. "Oh." Suddenly she understood. "Jason wasn't even living here when that man was killed."

For a few moments the doctor's expression went totally blank, then he asked sharply, "How did you find out about the murder?"

"Bess told me."

"Oh." A shell dropped into the tray with a tiny clink. Dr. Nils cleared his throat. "Not Tallfeather." He turned from the dresser and bestowed upon Manda his most eloquent I-told-you-so smirk.

"It's not the sort of thing an inn proprietor goes around broadcasting to his guests." Impatience sharpened her voice.

"No. Nor any of his other secrets, I should presume." His broad forehead wrinkled in a frown. "Manda, my dear, I will not allow you to work for this stranger in this isolated place with an unsavory past."

"Which has the unsavory past? Tangletrees Inn or Jason?" She grinned.

"Don't you dare make fun of me!" He spoke barely above a whisper, which only served to intensify his wrath.

The violence of his reaction bewildered her. She had expected the remark to tease him out of his tyrannical posturing. Instead, he was being utterly impossible.

"I don't like to go against your wishes," she said with calm firmness, "but I *am* going to work here. If later on, when my job is over, you don't want me to come back to your house . . ."

"Don't be ridiculous," he broke in. He paused to take a deep controlling breath. "I apologize for my display of temper. My sole excuse is that I'm fond of you, and I try to spare you from unhappy upsetting truths." He looked uncomfortable. Contriteness was for him an unfamiliar emotion. "I do make one request. If *anything* occurs to frighten you while you are here, you will please come directly home."

"I won't promise," she replied stubbornly, "but I'll consider it."

Why did he insinuate the very thing Emory had warned her about less than an hour ago? They both must be unnecessarily hung up on the fact of the unsolved murder.

"Let's join the others downstairs," she said, by way of ending a potentially stormy discussion.

"We might as well." A glower still shadowed his hazel eyes.

When they came within earshot of the trio sitting in front of the fireplace, they heard Emory say, "Manda, bless her, arranged that."

"No, don't get up," Manda admonished as Emory and Jason started to rise. After she and Dr. Nils took seats nearby, she turned toward Emory and asked, "What did I arrange?"

"My job with Dr. Nils."

"I did not," she disagreed with a fond smile. "You got the job on your own."

"But you did have a part in it," Sylvia prompted in a friendly tone.

"I suppose, yes, indirectly. I'd gone to the Cal Poly library to see an exhibit of paintings by college art students. Emory was the only other person there, so we introduced ourselves."

"For me it was love at first sight," Emory declared.

Manda blushed. He was half-jesting, but only half. She knew his announcement of a prior claim to her affection had been for Jason's benefit, and the subtle insinuation that Jason might care, one way or the other, mortified her.

"That's not how I remember it," she said testily. "When I walked into the display room, you headed for the door."

"I've told you before, I had just realized I was late for an appointment. But then I looked into those marvelous smoky gray eyes of yours, and I wasn't about to leave. Finding out who you were, so I could see you again, took priority over any job interview."

"How romantic!" Sylvia interposed. "Reminds me of our first meeting, Jason darling. Remember? You were waiting tables in the dining room of the UCLA dorm where I lived, and—"

"That's old history, Sylvia," Jason broke in impatiently. "Very old history." He missed seeing Sylvia's disappointed expression because he'd already shifted his attention to Manda. "Please," he urged with a teasing grin, "tell us more about the Manda Lethe Employment Agency."

"Oh, you!" she snorted, feigning annoyance.

Secretly, her heart danced a happy jig against her ribs. Could it be that the romantic liaison between him and Sylvia wasn't as firmly entrenched as Dr. Nils had inferred?

She caught the momentary flash of indignation on Emory's face, at the rapport between herself and Jason.

"Go ahead, sweetheart," Emory said, "tell them the rest of the story."

Manda resented the "sweetheart," but taking Emory to task in the company of others would merely reinforce his antagonism toward Jason. She wanted no more arguments. Whenever Emory drove up to visit her during the ensuing weeks, she hoped their few hours together would be peaceable.

"Well?" Sylvia's eager tone intruded into Manda's reverie. "How *did* you help Mr. Wade secure his job with Dr. Johannsen?"

"I didn't help—Well, maybe a little," she amended. "Emory asked if I was a student, and I said no, but I lived only a couple of blocks off campus. While we walked around, exchanging opinions of the paintings, Emory mentioned he was a newcomer to San Luis Obispo and needed a job. He told me he'd worked as a bank teller, a legal secretary, and a car salesman, among other things, and asked if I knew of any openings. As it happened, Dr. Nils's former secretary had recently moved to San Francisco. So I wrote down our address for Emory, and when I got home, I told Dr. Nils about the man I met at the library who might apply for the secretarial position."

"I did," Emory said, "the next day, and was hired. So you see? Manda did arrange it."

"I did not!" Manda denied once more. Then, with everyone else registering good-natured amusement at her vexation, she recanted with a reluctant grin of her own.

After the laughter died away, Dr. Nils rose from his chair. "Come, Emory," he said. "It's time we were taking our leave." To Sylvia he bowed. "Miss Hathaway." He shook hands with Jason, who stood beside him. "Good day, Tallfeather. No doubt we'll meet again soon, for I shall be keeping an eagle eye on my girl." His stern expression softened as he turned to Manda. "If you need me, my dear . . ."

"I know," Manda interrupted, her fingertips briefly touching his in a gesture of gratitude. "I'm glad you came, both of you." On impulse her lips brushed Emory's whiskery cheek.

Manda felt for a moment as if she were saying goodbye forever to one phase of her life, and the thought made her sad. There was such a tiny scrap of past for her to relinquish.

Still pensive a half hour later, Manda sauntered along the hard-packed beach. Not even the comical three-point landings of some of the gulls as they scrambled for the bread crumbs she tossed on the ground could lighten her mood.

She was sorry to have hurt Emory's feelings and disappointed Dr. Nils. What had motivated her to stay here in spite of their wishes? Stubbornness? Pride? Intuition? Perhaps a bit of all three. During the past couple of years, too many of her decisions and reactions had been engineered or influenced by Dr. Nils. Now . . . and here . . . otherwise she sensed it might never happen . . . she must find out who *she* was. Not her before-amnesia identity. She had little hope of ever learning that, after so much time had elapsed. But she did want to test her own strengths, come to terms with her weaknesses, discover the *real* Manda Lethe, whatever name appeared somewhere on her birth certificate. She was tired of feeling like an overprotected patient programmed by her physician, however well-meaning he might be.

Manda, glancing seaward, saw that an extremely low tide had made accessible the plateau of huge haphazardly joined rocks that before today had been far out beyond the water's edge. She kicked off her shoes and scampered across the sloping wet sand. Wading a short distance to the nearest boulder, she clambered up onto the mussel-covered surface. As she crouched over a tide pool, she became completely engrossed in the miniature world she found there—a puffy green sea urchin, tiny shreds of coral and kelp, a hermit crab inching along the bottom in its borrowed amethyst shell abode.

The scraping of footsteps on stone alerted her, but too late she remembered what Sgt. Sandoval had said about questionable strangers on the beach. A man's heavy work boots moved into her line of sight and stopped.

Manda's gasp seemed to steal all the air from her lungs. Her heartbeat faltered. Although her leg muscles suddenly ached unbearably, she remained rigid, too frightened to stand. Or even to look up at whoever he was.

Then he touched her shoulder. Manda sucked in a long breath and let out a squeak that she'd intended to be a resounding scream for help.

"It's all right, Miss Lethe." He spoke barely above the quiet slap of slack wavelets against the rocks. "I'm Clive Meecher."

"Oh." Her weak knees pushed her to an upright position.

The blue eyes of Bess's husband registered concern, and a bushy dark mustache, gray-flecked, partly obscured the sideways pull of his tentative smile. He was thin and bony; however, the biceps stretching his flannel shirt sleeves hinted at the man he must have been prior to his stroke.

"I didn't mean to scare you," he said.

"I know. You only startled me for a moment." He appeared skittish, and she longed to put him at ease. Noticing that he carried a child's tin pail whose contents rattled when he moved his arm, she asked, "Do you collect pebbles and shells, too?"

"Only the smallest ones. Bess wants them for her—ah—her gardens. Those little gardens she builds inside bottles and jars." He talked slowly, as if every word were considered in advance and then painstakingly uttered.

"Terrariums?"

"Yes, ma'am. I can't say that word." Embarrassed, he stared at his sand- and salt-encrusted shoes.

"Some words do get twisted on our tongues, don't they? I have trouble saying com . . . fort . . . a . . . ble." To prove it, she had enunciated each syllable very, very carefully. Then she smiled.

The man grinned back at her. A gold-filled tooth flashed in the sunlight.

"Thank you, Miss Lethe."

"For what?"

"You know." He turned to go.

"Wait," she said. He looked around. "My name is Manda."

"Yes, ma'am. Mine's Clive. You take care not to get . . . ah . . . stranded out here. Most flood tides, even the tall rocks are awash. And there's a real bad . . . ah . . . undertow here too."

A frisson of fear trickled down Manda's spine. As much as she liked being near the ocean, she was afraid of the water and had never learned to swim. If she believed in reincarnation, she'd have said in some earlier life she had died by drowning.

She shrugged off her disquiet and called after the departing man. "Thanks, Clive. I'll remember."

Chapter Eight

The next morning, when Manda took her charm bracelet from the hammered copper tray, she noticed that the fragment of green glass was missing. A search under the tray's fluted edge, on the floor at her feet, even in the wastebasket, proved futile.

Clasping the gold link chain around her wrist, she recalled seeing Dr. Nils fumble with the shells yesterday. Could he have picked up her "jade" and put it in his pocket, without realizing what he was doing? Oh, well. No matter. It was worthless, anyway.

Manda, eager to begin her first real job, fairly bounded down the stairs.

So she was disappointed at first, when during breakfast Jason informed her otherwise. "Before we start to work, I need to help Clive with some heavy chores around here."

"You're the boss," she said.

"Why don't you relax and enjoy our nature world," he grinned as if to hint that they shared a secret, "for a couple of days?"

Manda, forgetting her disappointment, nodded her head and flashed Jason a grateful smile. He was giving her the holiday she'd told him she needed the night she arrived.

"Too bad your car's still in the garage for repairs," Sylvia commented. "You could take a side trip into the hills. There are some lovely old ranch homes up there. And Lucia has a movie theater. Or you could drive down the coast to Hearst Castle."

"I had thought about stopping there on my way home." Then, the prospect would have afforded one more way to postpone confronting Dr. Nils's anger over her "escape" attempt.

"You can go today," Jason suggested. "Or tomorrow, if you'd rather. Take my car."

"I couldn't do that," Manda objected, although she was pleased by his offer.

"Of course, you could," Sylvia contradicted. "I think it's a fabulous idea."

Suddenly Manda understood. Sylvia had maneuvered Jason into the position of having to act as the unselfish host. Let the stranded guest use his car . . . and remove the guest from the premises in order that she, Sylvia, would have his wholehearted attention. Maybe the guest would even get bored with her solo company and decide to leave rather than to stay on and work as Jason's secretary.

The last contingency would never happen!

But the other . . . a day of unrestricted freedom to roam the treasure-covered grounds of Hearst Castle . . .

Jason, watching the expressive changes flicker across Manda's face, saw the beginning of her hesitancy.

"My car has an automatic shift like yours," he pressed. "It's small, easy to park. And the tank is full of gas."

Did Jason, like Sylvia, want her to go? Manda was unsure, and a little hurt.

Because she longed to be somewhere where no one tried to confuse or manipulate her, she made up her mind. "You've convinced me," she said.

Up in her room, Manda packed her purse, camera, tan windbreaker, and a Hershey candy bar in the large straw tote Mrs. Hendricks had sent her shoes in.

Jason awaited her at the parking lot. He handed her his keys and stood aside while she started the engine and put the bright red Geo in gear. Giving the door on Manda's side a noisy pat, and with a twinkle in his black eyes, he admonished, "Bring her back safely, Scarlett. Good secretaries are hard to find."

"Scarlett?" Manda laughed as the car started to move.

"With two *t's!"* Jason shouted after her.

Manda's good humor lingered as she negotiated the exit road and turned south on Highway 1. Traffic was light, and soon she was handling the strange car with ease. She drove leisurely, glancing frequently to her right to admire the broken rows of tumbling surf far below the roadway. Memories of the terror of two nights ago scattered through her mind, and she was never quite able to forget the precipice that lurked only yards away. Whenever she went around a blind curve that traced the cliff rim's outline, she hugged her lane tightly and kept a wary eye on the rearview mirror.

Perhaps no more than two or three miles from the inn, Manda noticed the low-slung black sports car behind her. A short, safe-to-pass stretch lay ahead, so she slowed to let the expensive, faster car go by. Instead, it dropped further back. Shrugging, she sped up again.

A half-dozen seconds later, the other car was crowding her rear bumper.

"Stupid idiot!" Manda accused. Tailgating infuriated her. Through the following car's darkly tinted windshield she could barely discern that the occupant was male. "And they call *us* lousy drivers!"

When she came to a semicircular turnoff, built for tourists to stop and look and snap pictures, she took the grass-centered lane that had been grooved into the sand by hundreds of tire treads. The sports car spurted by, and Manda let out a grateful sigh.

After waiting about five minutes, she pulled back onto the highway. Around the next bend she saw the black car parked on the narrow right shoulder, its flasher lights blinking. If that character thought she was going to stop and offer assistance, he was out of his gourd. Whatever was wrong with his car served him right for driving so recklessly.

Manda didn't even glance in his direction when she went by.

Singing along with the radio the somehow-remembered words of an old Jim Reeves ballad about four walls, she finally began to relax. The sun had moved high into a clear, Wedgwood blue sky and edged the curling waves with antique gold.

When out of habit Manda checked her rearview mirror, she gasped.

The black car was following her again!

As it swept around a hillside bend at near right angles to Manda's position, the sunlight glinted off the wide orange stripe along both shiny ebony doors. Black and orange. Halloween colors. The colors of witches and carved pumpkins with ghoulish faces.

Manda shuddered and reflexively pushed on the accelerator pedal. She rounded the next corner so fast, her momentum carried her across the yellow center line into the oncoming traffic lane.

She had to slow down!

And if she did, maybe, please God, the other driver would at last go around her.

She did.

He didn't.

Each time he gained on her and she responded by slackening her speed, he slowed also. Once, when he came up closer than usual, she stared so hard into her rearview mirror, trying to see the man's face, that the sharply sloped car hood blurred out of focus. That was when the grill, with all of its chrome strips missing, momentarily became the gaping, hungry mouth of some predatory monster.

Manda emitted a wail almost as inhuman as the bizarre creature she had envisioned chasing her.

She swallowed hard, then inhaled deeply, and, one at a time, removed her hands from the steering wheel and wiped her sweaty palms along her muscle-tense thighs.

That unknown maniac in the car behind her was driving *her* crazy!

She had to think. Calmly. Rationally.

He had done her no harm. He hadn't even been a threat . . . except to her screaming nerves, which understandably might be oversensitive regarding dangerous mountain roads. Most likely he was some kook who got his kicks out of frightening lone women drivers.

So far, she realized with chagrin, she'd been playing the game by his rules. From now on, she would not let his presence upset her. She'd spoil his fun by pretending he wasn't back there.

Her counteraction must have worked because, just before she reached Hearst Castle, her pursuer surprised her by dashing past and out of sight over the next rise.

Vastly relieved, Manda entered the grounds of the California historical monument and parked the Geo near a long row of sightseer buses.

Twice before, she had taken guided tours of the castle and a portion of the one-hundred-and-twenty-three acres on which it stood. She had no wish to see for a third time the lavish rooms filled with billions of dollars' worth of Renaissance art. Not even the private fifty-seat movie theater where it was said an unreleased print of *Gone With the Wind* was shown by William Randolph Hearst to a group of his cronies six weeks in advance of its legendary gala premiere in Atlanta.

Today Manda chose to remain outside, in the bracing salt-laden air and warm-for-November sunshine.

Since 1958, when the castle was opened to the public, hundreds of thousands of people had visited the gleaming white, twin-towered structure on the hilltop near San Simeon, and it seemed to Manda that a sizeable percentage of that number were on hand this morning. They certainly afforded her the anonymity she'd hoped for when she left the inn.

Or maybe not.

Once, as she moved along the walkway through a terraced garden filled with breathtaking topiary and statues, she felt a prickle on the back of her neck that warned someone was watching her. She wheeled, looked all around, and saw only strangers, not one of whom showed any interest in her.

Manda berated herself for allowing the incident with the black sports car to cast a pall of wariness over her outing. With a determined pleasure she continued her stroll. However, after an hour of being bumped and shoved by the crowds, Manda grew restive and sought a less congested spot.

She found it in a corner where a path ran along a high retaining wall. Low, thick evergreens had grown out over the walk, and visitors were avoiding the area lest the shrubbery, still damp with last night's fog, soil their clothing or shoes.

Manda stood there for several minutes, leaning against the smooth concrete upright, not minding that the moisture slowly dampened the legs of her pantsuit. The air smelled gloriously of late-blooming roses rather than cigar and cigarette smoke. Gradually the distant sounds of chatter, laughter, and crying infants gave way to the nearby twitter of a bird. Manda stooped to look into the fragrant juniper boughs that touched her knees.

All at once the bird's chirps coalesced into a single protesting shriek. Manda, expecting to see an approaching tourist, straightened up quickly and turned, her mouth in the shape of a greeting smile.

But she was alone. Everything was the same except for a subtle change, a palpable tension, in the surrounding atmosphere. Then the soft whisper of an artificial breeze stirred a ringlet on her forehead as a large whitish blur fell in front of her and crashed loudly at her feet.

For a moment Manda, disbelieving, stared at the heap of plasterlike rubble on the ground. Then she looked up . . . and saw movement as someone vanished into the gloom of the salon that opened onto the balcony above her. On the railing she spied the empty cylindrical base from which the enormous urn had tumbled. She could hardly breathe.

Suddenly the absolute silence that had followed the crash exploded into shouts of dismay. Folks were pointing excitedly at Manda, and some of them were running toward her.

Like magic, two uniformed guides appeared at her side. The younger one spread his arms wide and motioned for the onrushing group to halt. The other, a man with grizzled hair visible below his hat and with a worried frown, looked into Manda's pale face and asked, "Are you all right, Miss?"

"I—I think so." As all right as anyone could be after nearly getting killed. She was dazed with fright.

"My name is Colter. You had a close call. We have a nurse on duty at the security office. If you'll come with me—"

"Security office?" Manda repeated numbly. She clasped her hands against her waist to hide their trembling. "You'd never catch him now."

"Catch who, Miss?"

"The man—the person who tried to push the urn over on me." A growing anger was slowly taking precedence over her fear.

"Oh, no, Miss," the guide said, his tone that of a patient friend placating an overly imaginative child who had announced she'd seen a fire-spouting dragon. "The urn fell down entirely on its own."

"But I saw someone when I looked up! Someone running away."

"He was probably going for help. There! You see?" He gestured toward the parapet, over which a half-dozen curious faces peered down at them.

"Is anyone hurt?" a woman loudly inquired.

"No, Ma'am, but thank you for asking," Colter called

back, displaying a business-as-usual smile.

The well-trained second guide had already begun to lead the onlookers away.

Colter spoke *sotto voce* to Manda. "Mishaps do happen here, but not often. In spite of the careful and constant upkeep by our maintenance crew. No doubt the elements had loosened the adhesive holding that particular urn in place, and it became unbalanced and then fell of its own weight."

"No doubt." Skepticism crackled in her voice.

"If you would prefer to speak to someone in authority . . ." Colter offered. Obviously he was concerned about a law suit.

"Absolutely not!" Manda denied. "I'd like to forget the whole damn thing!"

"Of course, Miss. Perhaps that's best," he approved with a noticeable lessening of strain. "It gave you quite a scare. I could see that."

Manda coughed to squelch the near-hysterical laughter rising in her throat. She managed a tight polite smile, then picked up the straw tote she had earlier propped against the wall. After gingerly stepping around the pile of white alabaster chunks and shards, she said over her shoulder, "Good-bye, Mr. Colter."

Her neck stiff from holding her chin high and staring fixedly ahead, Manda strode at a brisk pace through the milling throng of castle visitors, some of whom she heard talking quietly behind her back about her lucky escape from injury. When she finally reached the parking area, she walked slower and allowed her whole body to slump. Her heartbeat still thumped loud and fast in her chest. She didn't know which she felt the most, fear or anger or confusion.

Had someone deliberately tried to harm her and fled into the building just as she looked up?

Or had the entire incident been a happenstance?

And if so, why on earth was she being plagued by weird coincidences? Like a huge statuary vase that leaped off a railing. Or a black car that chased a red Geo called Scarlett. Maybe the suave, darkly handsome sports car was named Rhett!

Manda, in spite of her frustration, grinned at her insouciant mind picture, then decided not to dither anymore about unsolvable puzzles.

Weaving among the lines of parked vehicles, she stopped so quickly she almost stumbled over her own feet.

There it was. A shiny black car with a downsloping hood profile and a wide orange stripe along its length. Could it be? Not possibly! It had to be another strange, unconnected happening in this nerve-testing morning.

But Manda couldn't ignore the knot of dread in the pit of her stomach as, with small hesitant steps, she moved around to the front of the car. Very slowly she lowered her gaze . . . and screeched. There were no chrome strips across the grill where they ought to be!

She ran the rest of the way to Jason's car. So fast that her sides burned with pain. Her fumbling fingers dropped the keys. When she bent over to pick them up, she had to fight off a wave of dizziness. After she scrambled into the driver's seat, she locked the door and threw her shoulders back to relieve the pressure on her thundering heart. Her hands shook. She licked her dry, dead-feeling lips.

Don't be afraid, she kept telling herself. *Don't be afraid. It's all over, and you're safe.*

But she could no longer trust coincidences. She was sure now.

From the very first, the driver of the black car had a nefarious purpose. The other traffic had probably prevented his harming her on the southward trip. To nullify her anxiety over having been followed, he'd passed her, then circled back and entered the castle grounds. It was he whom she had sensed watching her as she meandered through the garden. When he saw her stop to rest, he hurried inside the castle and out onto the terrace above her, where he waited until the balcony was deserted. Without a qualm he pushed the urn over the balustrade.

Only the suddenly changed cry of a bird had saved her!

Manda could not imagine how the man had known about the urn's being loose or off balance, but she *knew* he had trailed her from the inn with the evil aim of devising some means to hurt her. If it hadn't been the urn, it would have been something else.

For ten minutes . . . or an hour . . . or an eternity, Manda sat with her head on her crossed arms. Eventually the initial terror seeped out of her, leaving her weak and utterly spent.

But she couldn't turn off her brain.

Who was the driver of the black sports car? Someone from out of her unknown past? How had he happened to be on Highway 1 at the same time as she?

No. He had *expected* her to be driving alone to Hearst Castle. Who could have informed him of her spur-of-the-moment plans?

Suddenly the breakfast table conversation between her, Jason, and Sylvia played itself over in Manda's mind. She raised her head from her folded arms, stared into an unseen distance, and silently heard again those earlier words.

At the time, she had mentally accused Sylvia of manipulating her into an out-of-sight, out-of-mind situation for the one day. But suppose Sylvia had arranged for her to be permanently removed from Jason's life?

What about Bess? Or Clive? Manda remembered that the housekeeper had brought a pan of hot biscuits to the table while Hearst Castle was being discussed. Bess would have mentioned Manda's trip to her husband. Manda knew that, because Clive never ate with the guests, Bess relayed every news tidbit to him in the kitchen. So both of the Meechers had been aware of where she was going.

And Jason.

Manda wondered anew about the strange way he had looked at her, more than once, since the night of her arrival at Tangletrees.

She recalled his exact statement to Sgt. Sandoval the morning after her car accident: "None of us ever heard of *a Manda Lethe . . .*"

But what if one of the four at the inn had known all along that she was *Someone Else,* a person whose existence posed a terrible threat?

What if one of them had paid the man in the black car to wait on the highway for Jason's Geo and follow it until Manda Lethe, or whoever she really was, could be . . . eliminated?

Chapter Nine

Manda shuddered and sucked in a long breath that jerked like a dry sob. With clenched fists she banged on the steering wheel . . . twice . . . three times . . . until the pain in her hands became more urgent than her muddled, questioning thoughts.

She relaxed her fingers, massaging them until the hurt subsided. Then she scrounged around in the bottom of her straw tote until she found Jason's keys. After starting the engine, she emitted a sigh . . . and whispered, "Geronimo." She'd read somewhere that that was what World War II paratroopers shouted when they jumped out of the planes into uncharted danger. Manda didn't feel like shouting, but she certainly did need to bolster her courage.

Slowly, she steered the car out of its slot and commanded herself not to glance in the direction of the black sports car. But, in the manner of a person who pokes at a loose tooth with her tongue, she couldn't let well enough alone.

She looked.

The car was gone!

Manda delighted in that fact until she turned northward onto Highway 1, when it dawned on her that her adversary had probably departed the castle grounds first so that he could lie in wait for her.

Apprehensive and wary, over several tense miles Manda kept her eyes focused more often on the scene in the rearview mirror than on the scene through the windshield. Confident at last that she wasn't being followed, she berated herself aloud.

"Manda, you moron, you imagined ghosts where there were only harmless white sheets flapping in the breeze."

The man in the black car really was just a kooky driver. If he'd been hired to harm her, he would not have given up, but would have tried again on the return trip.

Manda still refused to agree with the castle guide's claim that the urn fell without provocation, but now that she had calmed down, there did seem to be a more plausible explanation than skulduggery. Children had been romping all over the place. Some youngster probably ventured alone out onto the balcony and accidentally bumped the already loosened vessel. When it toppled over the railing, the child had run back inside to avoid discovery and punishment.

"Yes," Manda said. "That must be how it happened."

She had not actually *seen* anyone, merely sensed a shadowy movement of hasty retreat.

Nor had she had any bona fide reasons to distrust the four waiting at the inn. She was ashamed of her misgivings.

There never were two nicer, friendlier people than Bess and Clive. As for Sylvia, why on earth should such a beautiful, sophisticated woman, who had remained an important part of Jason's life since their college days, be jealous of *her?*

And Jason had already told her why he sometimes gave her those puzzled looks. He was asking himself where or when—if ever—he'd seen her before. She trusted him to tell her the truth if he managed to solve the mystery.

She trusted him . . . period.

Missing him, yet knowing she had no right to feel so strongly about him, Manda made a wry face and pressed harder on the foot throttle to shorten the distance between them.

When she pulled into the inn's parking lot, she noticed two out-of-state vehicles, a shiny new van with an Oregon license and an old but well-preserved Buick from Arizona. In the kitchen she found a distracted Bess, who greeted her with, "Hello, Manda, I hope you had a nice day," then turned to stir something in a big aluminum pot on the range.

"I did, thanks."

Manda, relieved that Bess was too busy to press for details, hurried into the hall. She had already decided not to talk about her misadventures. Someone of her new friends might discern in her tale the mistrust, although unfounded, that had triggered her temporary paranoia.

As she walked past the telephone, Manda had an impulse to call Dr. Nils. He'd been so critical of Jason, and insistent that she get away from the inn. She'd tell him she'd spent the entire day at Hearst Castle, and that the trip had been made possible by Jason's unselfish loan of his car. Both pieces of information should please the doctor.

Mrs. Hendricks answered the phone. After a brief exchange of greetings, Manda asked to speak to Dr. Nils.

"He's not here. You know he usually sees the clinic patients on Monday." She sounded impatient, fretful. Manda realized she must be interrupting one of the older woman's favorite television programs. Mrs. Hendricks hated that.

"Yes, I do know, but I expected him to be home by now."

"Well, he isn't."

"Is Emory there?" Emory also left angry yesterday, and he'd be furious if she didn't talk to him today.

"No. They had car trouble on the way back from seeing you, so he took his car to the garage."

"Oh. Okay. Thanks. I just wanted to say hello. Nothing important. You don't even need to tell either of them I called."

"Good-bye, then!"

Manda heard the remote-controlled volume of the TV increase before the receiver thumped noisily into place. Laughing at Mrs. Hendricks's rather endearing idiosyncracy, Manda lifted her tote bag and headed for the staircase.

She met the other Tangletrees guests at dinner. David Hearne, who had shared a hitch in the Marines with Jason, had stopped off on the way to Disneyland to have his wife, Bernice, and seven-year-old twins, Steve and Sean, meet his old buddy. His parents, retired and living in Arizona, had been persuaded to join the family's trip in their own car.

After the meal, during which thankfully no one quizzed Manda about her holiday, she went with everyone into the living room. There she scanned the book shelves for something to read. Alongside Jason's hardcovers stood novels by Robert Ludlum, Sidney Sheldon, and Tom Clancy, and paperbacks—contemporary romances by Elizabeth Lowell and Sandra Canfield and historicals by Dorothy Garlock. Smiling, Manda approved of her host's taste . . . and of Bess's. She took the only paperback she hadn't read and, saying goodnight to Sylvia, Jason, and his visitors, climbed the stairs to her room.

The Hearnes departed shortly after breakfast the next day, with both generations promising to come back sometime.

While helping Bess return food to the refrigerator, Manda nibbled on the last flaky biscuit topped with orange marmalade.

Jason entered the kitchen and plopped down on the stepstool. Bess poured him a cup of steaming black coffee, which he accepted with a murmured, "Thanks."

Manda said to him, "I know you were pleased to see your friend again. He has a nice family."

"Yes. And yes. I remember, every night Dave used to take Bernice's picture out of his wallet and look at it. Sometimes with a silly grin, other times with a sad, lonely expression."

"I'm glad things have turned out happily for them. It's not always like that. Sometimes . . . someone dies . . ." Her voice trailed off into the past.

Jason saw the faraway memory in her eyes. He stood and spoke sharply. "Manda! What are you thinking about?" He'd forgotten Bess was there. He simply wanted to jolt into clarity the blurred picture he knew was forming in Manda's mind.

"She just told you!" Bess barked in defense of the young woman who stared silently into space. A space Bess had no inkling was populated with faceless, lost loved ones. But Bess did sense Manda's mood and tried to dispel it.

"Your little car will be fixed and painted like new by the end of the week. I forgot to tell you. The garage man phoned while you were away yesterday."

"Thank you, Bess." Manda smiled, a smile that somehow made her appear even sadder.

Jason watched her slow struggle to move back into the present. Fury burned in his heart. Fury at whatever—or whoever—had robbed her of most of her life. The desire to comfort her, to protect her from additional heartbreak, washed over him like a surfer's wipeout. For a few seconds he was not capable of thought. Only of feeling.

Then, recalling Manda's eagerness regarding her job, Jason knew how to cheer her. Helping Clive repair the tractor would have to wait.

"If you've finished disassembling that poor cold biscuit," Jason said with a chuckle and pointed to the crumbs she'd been pushing around on the counter, "how about helping Yours Truly write a book?"

"Oh, yes!"

Manda's new, brighter smile was his reward. Her big gray eyes gleamed like highly polished silver. Jason felt as pleased with himself as if he'd just been informed that he had won the Pulitzer Prize.

"Let's go," he said.

Manda followed him down the corridor, past the living room on their left, to a closed door on the right. Since her arrival at the inn, she'd seen no one go into that room. Now she knew why. It was Jason's office.

He twisted the knob, pulled on the door and motioned for Manda to precede him. She took a few quick steps, then stopped to survey her future workplace.

The pleasant no-frills room contained two gray steel desks with a covered typewriter on the smaller one, appropriate matching chairs, a four-drawer file cabinet and a long wooden table and straight back chair, both enameled white. On the table stood a card file, a stack of manila folders and a row of at least two dozen reference books propped between cubical white alabaster bookends. Directly opposite the hall door was a wide, sliding glass one, already opened to the terrace and flanked by eggshell-colored fishnet drapes. There were no windows, but the office was redolent with the crisp, tangy smells of the Pacific. The carpet was a monotone of smoky grays. Grooved panels of bleached driftwood covered the walls, their patina glowing softly under the fluorescent lighting recessed in the acoustical ceiling.

Manda's gaze was drawn to the only splashes of color in the room: a couple of paintings in narrow white frames, one on each of the side walls. Seashore scenes.

One showed a small yellow cottage partially concealed behind a pile of dunes. A diminutive figure, distinguishable as a female only by the cascade of straight, dark brown hair that fell to her hips, sat nearby, facing an easel whose legs dug deep into the sand. Masses of vivid blue-and-white-speckled flowers spilled over the dunes, covering the entire left half of the foreground.

The seascape depicted a narrow strip of tawny beach that fronted a wide, rolling expanse of sea colors. On the distant horizon hovered a squall line of ominous-looking charcoal and gunmetal gray storm clouds.

Both works of art had one thing in common, a huge black dog frolicking near the water's edge.

Even without the canine, Manda would have known they were created by the same person. The artist's style was truly unique.

Except for the flowers in the first and the ocean in the

second, all the features were vague, and the pale, lightly feathered watercolor strokes flowed together, subtly blending. But the royal blue blossoms with their viridian green foliage on the one canvas, and the cobalt, aqua, and indigo overlapping ribbons of waves on the other, stood out in brilliant, detailed three-dimensional contrast, the thick oils having been applied in several layers with a palette knife.

Manda, staring at the cottage scene, moved slowly across the floor. Strangely stirred, she stood on tiptoes, reached up and lifted it from its hanger.

She had forgotten Jason was in the room.

In the lower right-hand corner, almost hidden in the scantily etched salt grass, she spied a signature—a cursive "E" and what appeared to be "Jos" written over it, with the "O" nestling in the bottom curve of the "E."

"Elaine Joseph," Manda murmured.

"You know the artist?" Jason asked, astonished.

"No," she replied dully, replacing the painting. As she stepped back from the wall, she bumped into Jason. Glancing up to apologize, she met his intent, excited gaze.

"But you said her name," he argued. "Elaine Joseph. Don't you see? It fits. *J . . . O . . . S* is an abbreviation for the name Joseph, and the *E* could stand for Elaine!" His voice rose with impatience when she shook her head in denial. "If you don't think Elaine Joseph painted them, why did you stare at the signature like that and then say her name?"

"I don't know." Her dazed face turned ghostly white. "I don't know!"

Suddenly Jason understood. Over the span of a few heartbeats Manda had somehow penetrated the amnesia curtain that surrounded her, only to be quickly enfolded again within its terrible anonymity.

Manda felt like a statue. Lifeless and breakable. And colder than ice.

"It's all right, Manda, it's all right," Jason rasped, seizing her shoulders and shaking her ever so gently, hoping to return her to the bearable reality she had created for herself. He watched two big round tears leave her eyes and slide along the sides of her nose. Gathering her close, he bent his head and pressed his lips to hers. He had intended the kiss to be a calming, comforting gesture, but from the moment of sweet contact, he knew that for him it was everything but.

When Jason took her into his arms, heat surged through Manda's entire body and melted the numbness. His lips brushed softly across hers. Something moved deep within her, like the first fluttering of a butterfly's wings inside its imprisoning cocoon. The gentle kiss lasted only a few seconds before Jason's hungry mouth captured and held hers. She parted her lips to take a breath, and his tongue slipped inside, seeking the tender sensitive areas she'd never guessed were there. A flood of rapture washed over her. Behind her closed eyelids there flared a cascading fountain of red and gold and green stars—like a skyrocket exploding in a blue-black Fourth of July sky.

All of a sudden he released her. Manda wondered if her trembling rubbery legs would support her as she stood there, feeling deprived. And more than a little confused. His rugged features bore no trace of the magic that had enthralled her. Instead, he seemed quite distressed.

"I'm sorry, Manda. I had no right to do that." Jason averted his eyes from the questioning look on her upturned face. "I meant it to be a friendly kiss, to show you it's okay not to remember anything about the artist, and I—ah—let the situation get out of hand. I'm truly sorry."

Jason knew, inane as his explanation sounded, it was far better than the truth. *I want you, Manda, more than I've ever wanted any other woman.* Hearing that, Manda would have fled from his arms and probably out of his life. He had to give her time to know and to trust him. As for himself, he desperately needed to put some space between them, so he could secure a tight rein on his desire.

Too proud to let him see her hurt, Manda turned away. "Don't worry about it. I understand." She prayed her words were glib enough to convince him.

They were. But Jason recognized his relief as an empty triumph. Sighing inaudibly, he did what he'd come to the office to do.

Indicating the phone on the wall beside the hall door, he said, "It's an unlisted number, known only to my editor, the Meechers, and my family in Arizona. When I'm working, I can call out from here, but the ordinary business calls to the inn don't distract me."

Jason then showed Manda where to find the supplies she'd require for her tasks, and he pointed out the eccentricities of Amy Burke's filing system.

Mande listened carefully and asked about anything she didn't fully comprehend. All the while, in the back of her mind pulsated the memory of Jason's embrace, and the kiss that had awakened the very depths of her woman's soul. Falling in love proved every bit as surprising and awesome and giddy as she'd dreamed. And painful. No one had warned her about that side of it.

"Manda."

"Yes?" Had her woolgathering caused her to miss some

important instruction?

"I said . . . I don't expect this to be an eight-to-five job. Pace yourself, and take time off for your walks on the beach." He placed several cassette tapes beside the typewriter. "All I ask is that you transcribe these while I'm gone."

"You're going away?" She tried not to sound disappointed.

"For a few days. If I can get a reservation, I'll fly out of San Francisco tonight."

Searching for words to fill the strained silence, Manda touched the stack of tapes. "Where you're going, will you be doing more research for this book?"

"I'll be doing research, yes."

Without further explanation, Jason turned and walked out of the office.

At first Manda took offense that he hadn't told her where he was going, but then she reminded herself that she was a temporary employee, someone he barely knew. He would discuss his plans with the Meechers, not with her.

Just the same, his behavior puzzled her. The "friendly" gesture that went out of control, followed by his sudden coolness and the terse announcement of a trip to who-knows-what destination. Had her reaction to his kiss disgusted him, chased him away? No. Jason had thrilled to that special moment the same as she. Inexperienced though she was, Manda sensed that the spark of a young woman's primitive passion ignited only when the winds of a man's true yearning blew across the waiting fire.

Manda smiled a secret, pleased smile as she lifted the plastic cover off the typewriter.

Chapter Ten

When Manda came downstairs the following morning, Bess told her Jason had left to catch his plane. She suggested that Manda have breakfast in the kitchen with her and Clive.

"I'd like that," Manda responded, "but what about Sylvia?"

"She had coffee and toast and checked out a half hour ago. She'll be back as soon as Jason returns." Bess sniffed. "Sylvia doesn't stay here unless Jason's at home. She hates this—ah—godawful hellhole. Those are her words, not mine."

"I suspected as much." Manda barely succeeded in keeping a straight face.

She wanted to ask where Jason had gone, but it didn't seem fair to pump Bess for the information. He had said the trip involved research. She'd learn all about it later, when he was ready to tell her, or as she typed his notes.

The next four days turned out to be even longer and lonelier than Manda had expected. She missed Jason, his voice, his smile, his quick catlike footsteps in the corridors.

Drifting into a daily routine, she rose early and, before breakfasting with the Meechers, jogged along the tide-washed beach. Work sessions in the office consumed two or three hours of each morning and afternoon. Usually she prepared her own midday sandwich or salad and carried it outside to the sunny terrace, so she could look out over the Pacific while she ate. One day she persuaded the Meechers to join her there for lunch. They talked about their happy years in San Francisco, but clearly they had transferred their roots from The City to Tangletrees.

A few more guests stopped at the inn — a trio of young businesswomen from Kansas City on vacation, and later a Seattle couple in their sixties, who were touring the West Coast on what they charmingly referred to as their umpteenth honeymoon.

Manda did eat dinner with the guests, but afterward she hurried down to the shore line. The autumn evening tides ran high, so she trudged through piles of loose heavy sand that tugged not unpleasantly at her sedentarily lazy thigh and calf muscles. Tiring, she would sit at the base of the cliff and watch entranced while the sun, an enormous blinding orange ball, slid into a shimmering gilded sea. When the golden surface changed to purplish brown, signalling the finale of the daily spectacle, she returned to the inn by way of the kitchen door and climbed the stairs to her place of blue-decorated privacy.

On Friday it rained. The whole world changed to the color of lead: the sky, the sea, and all of the space in between. The surf's cadence no longer peaked and abated, but merged with the sound of the torrential downpour to create a steady, ceaseless thrumming. The dismal gray monotony outside made Manda restless. She ventured into Bess's culinary domain and found the normally sanguine lady to be as irritable as she herself felt.

Manda decided she'd use the rest of the drab afternoon to finish reading Jason's *Never Kill Again.* She went up to her room and, after switching on the portable electric heater to ward off the chill, settled in the high-back rocker. Already she had discovered that the axe Jason had to grind in his first book wasn't as sharp nor the style as erudite as in *A Rosary for Rosa.* But she liked this novel better. Maybe because its plot moved a sweet uncomplicated love story toward a happily-ever-after, and because Manda longed for her own old-fashioned romance.

Near twilight, Bess called up to Manda that the garage men had arrived with her repaired car. She hurried downstairs. At the front door she signed the necessary paper, accepted her keys and was informed that the Tempo had been left on the inn's parking lot. She watched the lights of the red pickup disappear into the gloom, and wished they belonged instead to Jason's returning red Geo.

Although Bess was hesitant at first, Manda coaxed her into serving dinner—a thick savory lamb stew—in the living room. Clive set up the card table and Manda covered it with a red-and-white-checkered cloth, then put out the silverware, napkins, soup bowls, and a basket of crispy breadsticks. For a festive touch she lit several pine-scented candles and turned off all but one of the lamps.

When the housekeeper entered with the steaming tureen, Manda grinned. "See? Isn't this cozy?"

"Humph," Bess grunted. But Manda understood her well enough by now to know that she was pleased.

After the dishes were cleared away and the dishwasher started to hum, Manda entreated, "Let's sit in the living room a while. The fire feels so good on a rainy night."

"And on a lonely one?" The older woman smiled knowingly. She had noticed the sometimes wistful looks on Manda's face. Manda probably missed the company of friends her own age, and, too, she'd been shut inside all of today. "All right. Clive is watching a football game, and I was going to read. But until the log burns low, I'll chat with you while I do my mending."

They talked about many subjects, exchanging the inconsequential tidbits of conversation that help two people get better acquainted.

"Other than being near the ocean, what do you like most?" Bess asked as she sewed a button on one of Clive's plaid flannel shirts.

Manda pondered briefly. "I guess I'd have to say visiting art galleries and museums. I'm crazy about paintings and sculpture."

"Have you seen Jason's bronze horse?" Bess pointed toward the Daniel Blue Eagle stallion.

"On my first day here. It's fantastic."

"You'll have to get Jason to show you his bedroom." Manda blushed and Bess, chuckling under her breath, hastened to explain. "He has a cabinet filled with pieces of carved ivory, and ancient Chinese vases and statues trimmed with real gold, and one-of-a-kind porcelain figurines so delicate you can see through them. Jason's favorites are a matched pair of jade dragons. He keeps them all upstairs, so our guests won't know they're on the premises."

"I think that's wise."

"Besides being irreplaceable and priceless, every item

has great sentimental value. Jason's Massachusetts ancestors owned and operated a shipping line, and generations of sea captains brought those lovely things back from foreign lands as gifts for their wives and daughters. Jason's mother, the last captain's only child, inherited them—along with the adventurous spirit of her seafaring kinfolk. Two months after she graduated from the fanciest girls' school in the East, Abigail Jason came out to Arizona to teach the Apache children on the San Carlos reservation."

"And that's where she met Jason's father?"

Bess nodded. "Running Buffalo, second son of Chief Three Tall Feathers and Canyon Flower, a Chiricahua princess. He anglicized his name to John Tallfeather when he enrolled at UCLA. About the time beautiful golden-haired Abigail Jason arrived from Boston, he had finished law school and returned to the reservation to help his tribesmen."

Manda silently watched the orange flames flicker and flare up again around the charring log. In her mind's eye, she could see the tall Indian man, copper-skinned and virile, perhaps a lot like Jason, excitingly different from any male the fair schoolmistress from New England had ever known. How naturally, how fatefully, Abigail must have been drawn to him.

As I am to Jason.

Enough daydreaming, Manda scolded herself as Bess stowed her mending in the wicker basket beside her chair.

Manda, with her random thoughts seeking a new direction, gave voice to the question that had nagged her for days. "Could you tell me where Jason got the paintings that are in his study?"

"From the attic. The cleaning woman who had worked for Mr. Logan stored them up there, along with a number of other things that were left here when the estate lawyers finished and went back to The City."

"Had they been hanging in the house for a long time before that, I wonder?"

"Oh, no, Manda, they weren't even framed. The cleaning woman worked for Jason before we came. She told Jason she first saw the paintings lying in a dresser drawer under some lady's clothes. She figured they'd been left in the bedroom that last weekend. Probably belonged to one of Mr. Logan's visiting . . . uh . . . ladyfriends. He had more than a few discreet affairs, if you can believe the newspaper stories that came out after his murder."

"But you told me he always came here alone."

"I said he had no servants here," she corrected Manda with a wry smile. "There were female . . . guests. The name Carlton Logan was widely recognized as that of a famous jewelry designer, but the man himself was not a public figure. Very little was known about his private life. The police and lawyers found that out when they tried to locate his heirs."

"I see."

Manda and Bess said good night and went to their separate rooms.

By morning the rain had ceased, but Manda decided to skip her run on the beach and to take her breakfast coffee and Danish to the office, and eat while she worked.

Later, when she rose from her chair to check the large dictionary for the spelling of a word, the cottage scene hanging over the long table drew her eyes like a magnet.

She sighed, lifted it from the wall as she had that other time. Now she propped it against a thesaurus. As she stared at the painting, the frame seemed to expand, and the features seemed to become larger and more clearly defined.

Manda opened and closed her right hand, as if she were clutching the bristly hair of the big black dog. It felt stiff and scratchy in her palm. She heard his gruff bark, endured the sting of his welcoming tail as it wagged against her bare legs.

"Brutus?" she whispered. "Good dog, Brutus."

Her wide-awake dreaming continued, but her concentration shifted to the woman who sat on a stool in front of an easel and gazed across the water. Manda knew the artist was young, petite, and darkly tanned, gray-eyed, with straight brown hip-length hair. As Manda watched, the woman would intermittently lift her brush from the canvas, turn, and speak lovingly to a small red-haired girl building sand castles nearby.

"Mums?" The word stretched out, Manda's voice thin and reedy like that of a pleading child.

Manda blinked, and suddenly the dreamlike visions were gone.

But the memories, the realities, remained. Brutus had been her beloved childhood pet, and the pretty creator of those two masterful paintings was—her *mother!*

"Mums!" Manda exulted. "Oh, my God! Mums."

Her heart thundered in her ears, and above the pounding she heard herself gasping for breath. Tears slid down her pale cheeks as she realized . . .

She had actually *remembered* something of her past!

At first she was so stunned, all she could do was repeat over and over in her head: *I have remembered! I have remem-*

bered!

She had always hoped it might happen. But after months went by, with only brief infrequent sensations that hinted at more but triggered nothing, her belief in the restoration of her memory had dwindled to a trifle. If Dr. Nils still thought her total recovery was possible, he hadn't said so in a long time.

He'd be so happy for her!

With trembling fingers, Manda lifted the telephone off the wall and punched the San Luis Obispo number.

Emory answered on the second ring. "Good morning. This is Dr. Johannsen's residence."

"I have to speak to Dr. Nils!" Manda insisted. "If he's with a patient, interrupt him, because—"

She heard the intercom buzzer, a click as a second phone was picked up, and then the other familiar voice on the office extension: "Dr. Johannsen speaking."

"Dr. Nils! I can remember! You said I would someday," her words ran on in a frenzied quavering, "and I have. Oh, Dr. Nils, it's incredible! And scary, too. I know who—"

"Say no more!" the doctor broke in. "Not over the phone." He paused, then spoke harshly. "Emory, are you still on this line?" There was no response. "Manda, my dear," his tone softened, "I'm delighted. But I must warn you. This breakthrough may only be partial. In any case, you will require my counseling. I have a patient scheduled for today who cannot be postponed. I shall arrange for her to come in at once, and then I'll drive up there."

"You don't have to—"

"Yes, I *do*. And, Manda, in the meantime, say nothing about this to anyone. Do you understand me? Not one word!" he ordered, and he hung up before she could argue.

His wanting to be with her made sense. He was her guardian, after all, and although he was not a demonstrative person, Manda had frequently sensed his deep affection for her. Also, as her analyst, he'd long been thwarted by her stubborn case of amnesia.

Now maybe that was over.

Her remembering, she realized, had really not begun this morning, but rather last week, when in Jason's company she had first seen her mother's paintings hanging in this room. The once well-known signature had sparked an awakening, however fleeting. From that moment, her subconscious mind had continued to prod and search through her beclouded storehouse of memories, until finally, a few minutes ago (was it only a few minutes?) she had perceived within the narrow framed picture a scene that, when remembered as life-size and real, she had recognized as a piece of her childhood. Preserved forever on canvas by her mother. By Elaine Joseph.

Her mother's name was Elaine Joseph. *Her* name . . .

"Manda Joseph. My name is Manda Joseph." She said it aloud a half-dozen times, listened hungrily to the strange sound of it.

Her pulse throbbed in her temples. She felt dizzy. *Steady, Manda Lethe. No—Manda Joseph. Take a deep breath,* she told herself, applying the panic-fighting rule Dr. Nils had taught her. *Don't give in to weakness.* She had used the surname Lethe for . . . for as long as she could remember. It was perfectly natural that another name would seem odd, even upsetting.

Something else puzzled her, too. The notes the doctor

had showed her after the truth drug session indicated that when she stumbled out of the desert, she'd cried out to someone in Sandy Springs, "I want Mommy! Take me to my Mommy!" Yet just now, when she envisioned her mother sitting before her easel, that remembered Manda-child had called her mother "Mums."

She understood how Dr. Nils could have made the mistake. Anxious about his hysterical patient, and in his haste to record her reactions while she was still under the drug's influence, he had jotted in his notebook the word most young children would have shouted: Mommy.

The plausible discrepancy didn't change the fact that she had truly recalled a portion of her past. Full remembrance might take weeks or even longer, but now Manda believed it would happen.

Her whole being was electric, humming with the joy and triumph of the morning's revelations. Ignoring the unfinished page in the typewriter and the half-eaten roll and mug of cold coffee atop her desk, Manda paced the gray carpet, never taking her eyes from the painting that leaned against the reference book. Where was her mother? How had they become separated? Intuitively Manda knew they'd been exceptionally close. Where was the yellow seaside cottage in which she'd lived as a little girl? No wonder she felt drawn to the ocean. In the purest, soul-embracing sense, the seashore had always been her home.

No, not always.

Suddenly Manda remembered in her late teens having stood in the cottage, empty except for a couple of cheap tan suitcases stuffed to the point of obesity and four cardboard boxes tied with rope. Winter rain trickled like tears down the outside of the curtainless windowpanes, and, inside, real tears slid down her mother's pale drawn face. Mums's words echoed hollowly in the cold bleak room as she held out the paintings, one in each hand.

"Manda, my sweet, we may never live near the water again, so I want you to have these to remember the happy years we've spent here together. I had to sell the others . . . the furniture, too . . . everything but our clothes and a few keepsakes . . . to pay the hospital bills. But these two paintings are yours. To keep forever."

As her mother's voice faded, so did the memory.

Utterly frustrated, Manda hammered a fist on the edge of the enameled office table. A gut instinct told her she was standing on the fringes of the past. Why in heaven's name couldn't she step over onto whole cloth? Massaging her smarting hand with her other palm, she considered her mother's words as they had lingered side by side in the small vacant house, words that intoned a somber farewell to a way of life. Where were they moving to? Whose hospital bills had Mums referred to? Manda wondered. Her father's? Did he die after a long and costly illness? None of her memory flashes had touched even vaguely upon a father. Why was that? Why were there so many blank, black spaces in her life? It was as though she stood before a row of dark windows, unable to see the light of truth beyond.

An inexplicable chill pervaded Manda's entire body. She hurried out to the terrace, where sunshine quickly warmed her shoulders and consumed the eerie cold, one more product of her strange morning.

I ought to go check on my car's new paint job, came the non sequitur thought. She looked toward the parking lot.

What was it Bess had said about the laying of the concrete slab? To make a place for it, Jason and Clive had demolished the building in which Logan had been found beaten to death, and they had uprooted "a grove of ugly, old trees—dead trees." At the time Manda had been so shocked and curious about the murder that the housekeeper's comment regarding the trees hadn't registered. But now it did.

The few gnarled, weather-beaten Monterey cypress *had* been there! And the ravine, too! The one Jason had rerouted, the one she'd seen Clive bulldozing smooth after the runoff from heavy rains just prior to her arrival at the inn had washed it out again. Those feelings of *déjà vu* hadn't been based on craziness, after all.

"The blue room!" Manda exclaimed. "That first night, Jason said the room I started to go into used to be blue, and I didn't understand. But now I do. I slept in that other room! When it *was* blue."

Without a doubt she had visited Tangletrees during the period of Carlton Logan's ownership, before Jason leased the property and made certain changes. Totally unthinkable was the idea that she had come here to be alone with a womanizer. Then why had she come? And when? Who else had been here? Could the answers lie with her mother's paintings?

Mums gave them to her to keep, and somehow Manda was absolutely certain that she would have starved, literally, rather than part with them. Yet they had been found here in a guest bedroom, hidden under some female articles of clothing, *immediately after the murder.*

Only she herself could have brought those paintings here.

God in heaven, was she the murderer? Was that what

she had blocked out of her mind, together with everything else that had occurred before?

Her anguished shriek of denial tore mercilessly at her throat, and rose on the breeze to mingle with the mournful cries of the seagulls soaring overhead.

Chapter Eleven

Bess's grip on Manda's sleeve tugged the younger woman loose from the paralyzing shock and horror over the possibility that she had committed murder.

"What happened?" Bess demanded, a worried look beclouding her brown eyes. "Are you all right?"

"What? I . . . ah . . . Of course, I'm all right." The travesty of a smile curved her lips.

"But I heard you scream."

"Oh, that. I walked into a spiderweb." Her shudder, if not her explanation, was genuine. "They give me the creeps."

"All that fuss over a little spider," Bess grumbled, then walked back inside the house.

Manda regretted having lied to Bess, but before she told anyone about her fear that she could have killed Carlton Logan, she must try to understand the significance of the fragments of her past that she had recalled thus far. Dr. Nils, if he knew where her thoughts were heading, would take her back home for intensive therapy. Emory's solution to her problem would be to ignore it, get married immediately and go far away, but pushing the awful deed she may have done still deeper into her subconscious wasn't the answer she sought. Jason, if she told him, would use his reporter's expertise to ferret out all the facts regarding the crime, but first he'd contact the police, in which case she'd be taken away for questioning.

Although Manda at that moment felt more insecure and confused than at any time since she'd arrived at the inn, she was positive of one thing: The best way for her to remember everything was to stay here. And she wanted—needed—to remember everything. If the remembering process meant reliving unhappy, frightening, or even shameful experiences, so be it. She would handle them like any normal young woman—with poise and courage and a sense of perspective.

For now, of uppermost urgency loomed Dr. Nils's arrival. Because of their earlier, brief telephone exchange, he'd be expecting her to announce some new memory. She'd comply but without divulging her prior visit to Tangletrees.

Late in the afternoon, Manda greeted Dr. Nils at the front door.

"Tell me, my dear," he blurted. "I barely managed to stay under the speed limit driving up here."

"In Jason's office," she suggested. "No one will disturb us there."

Entering her workplace ahead of her companion, she noted at once that Bess had removed the remnants of her breakfast and rehung the cottage scene. Without preamble Manda motioned toward it, then toward the seascape.

"What do you think of those?" she asked.

The doctor, a connoisseur of art, examined each painting carefully.

"The artist's technique is amazing," Dr. Nils said at last, obviously impressed. "Different from anything I've seen anywhere, anytime. He must have used countless extra tubes of oil to achieve that three-dimensional effect."

"She." A soft smile flickered across Manda's mouth.

"I'm sorry, Manda, what did you say? The man is truly a genius!"

"The woman," she corrected Dr. Nils again, louder this time.

"The woman? The artist is female?" He paused as comprehension dawned. "You know who she is? Fabulous! I'll contact her. I definitely intend to purchase some of her work."

At that precise moment, with Dr. Nils's back to the door, Jason stepped noiselessly into the office. Manda's heart leaped in her throat. Excitement and delight flushed her cheeks, and she started to speak to him, but in a silencing gesture he placed his index finger against his lips.

She made a valiant effort to ignore his presence as she responded to Dr. Nils's last remark. "Her name is Elaine Joseph. I don't know where she is, or even if she's still painting. I do know . . . she's my . . . mother." Her voice broke on the final word.

"Ah! It was the recognition of your mother's uniquely splendid work that triggered your memory."

"Yes!" The grin belonged to a proud and happy daughter.

"Manda, my dear, I am so very pleased. Is it not what we have both wished for?" He paused, took a deep breath. "What else have you remembered?"

Glad she'd prepared herself in advance for his query, but not quite able to meet his gimlet gaze, she replied, "Nothing. I'm still hoping, but—"

"Nothing about Sandy Springs, Arizona?" That was Jason's strained voice from just inside the doorway. Dr. Nils's face reddened as he whirled around. "Tallfeather, you are intruding!"

"In my own office?" Jason's peal of laughter held no mirth.

"It was my idea, Jason," Manda said, puzzled by his hostility. "I wanted to show Dr. Nils my mother's paintings."

"Of course, you did," he agreed. But his mouth stayed a tense angry line.

"Then what's wrong?"

"Johannsen knows." Jason glowered.

The doctor moved toward the door, but Jason blocked his exit.

"What is this about?" Manda insisted. "You're being rude to Dr. Nils."

"Rude?" Jason fairly shouted. "I'd like to throw him out of my house! But first, Manda, my dear," he sarcastically mimicked the doctor's often used endearment, "I'm going to tell you about Sandy Springs."

"Tallfeather, don't!" the doctor pleaded shrilly.

"You shut up!" Although Jason didn't so much as glance in the other man's direction, there was no doubt as to whom the command was addressed.

Walking around the doctor, who moaned but made no further attempt to leave, Jason came close to Manda.

His black eyes were no longer angry. Instead, she thought she detected a deep sadness in them.

"Manda, for two years, or for whatever length of time it has been," Jason's hushed velvet voice told her, "Dr. Johannsen has let you believe a terrible lie."

"He wouldn't do that," she declared.

Of all Jason's unexplainable actions and words since he'd entered the room, his accusation of Dr. Nils was the ultimate absurdity. Anticipating an irate denial, Manda looked at Dr. Nils. His shoulders drooped, and in utter silence he hung his head.

Wary but with a need to know, Manda turned back to Jason. "What lie?" she asked.

"As a small child you did not stagger alone into Sandy Springs from out of the desert." Disgust sharpened the rugged planes of his face.

Bewildered and tense, Manda waited for Dr. Nils to say something. Why should she listen to Jason who, after all, was practically a stranger?

"I don't believe you!" she spat at Jason.

"Yes, you do. That's why you're so angry."

Damn him! she thought.

"Dr. Nils has been like a father to me." She realized she was arguing with herself. "But you—I hardly know you. You expect me to accept every word you speak as gospel."

"I'm a reporter, Manda. The first stop on my trip was Sandy Springs, and I found a solitary way station. One tumbledown adobe building that's a service station and sandwich shop for travelers who put up with the dust, cobwebs, and roaches just to get out of the blinding scorching sun. The Navaho owner has lived in the rear of the store for thirty-six years, and he certainly would have remembered an event as unusual as finding a lost half-starved child."

"Then how did I know the name of the place?" she wondered aloud as she dried sweaty palms on her thighs.

"You didn't. I did," Dr. Nils finally spoke, his voice bleak. "I made up the part about your being lost."

"But the therapy session notes." She still didn't understand any of this.

"I made those up, too. I substituted the lie for—for the truth that was on the tape."

"What was the truth?" Jason demanded in an accusatory tone.

"Nothing."

"Nothing?" cried Manda and Jason together.

"Nothing," the doctor repeated. His raspy breathing sighed through the room. "Do you remember, Manda? After each unfruitful counseling session, you talked about running away and hunting a new identity of your own. You were desperately melancholy."

"It was pretty awful." Her face reflected the anguish of that earlier time.

"So you begged me—only one more session, no matter what the outcome." She nodded her confirmation, and he continued. "You did agree to try the truth serum. By the end of a half hour, you had recalled nothing that we did not already know. I had to make a quick decision. I could let you go on becoming more despondent every day, until you did possibly run away, or worse. Or—or I could give you a small portion of your past to hang onto, something to kindle your hope for the future.

"So while you were still drugged, I removed the tape from the recorder, locked it in a safe place, and hastily scribbled some notes as a basis for the fabrication about your desert experience. The name Sandy Springs popped into my head from a newspaper article I'd read that morning about a remote Indian trading post well off the main roads. A place no one would bother to visit to check out my story. Or so I believed." He glanced at Jason, then turned back to Manda, his face contorted, his eyes stricken. "Yes, it was underhanded. But I don't think it was wrong. Given the circumstances and your state of mind, I considered it the right thing to do. And—" Grimly defensive, he drew his shoulders up straight. "And I would do it again."

"Well, I'll be damned," Jason murmured. Fading anger erased the tightness of his mouth.

Manda stood speechless, her tired brain trying to assimilate what the doctor had done for her in violation of his code of ethics. It confounded her that she felt no gratitude.

"I'll leave you to finish your private conversation," Jason told them. "In *my* office." He chuckled at his feeble joke as he strode out into the hall.

An uncomfortable silence filled the room. Manda, completely overwhelmed by Dr. Nils's dishonesty, wondered what the man expected her to say.

Finally he spoke, his voice at a lower pitch than normal. "I hope you will forgive me. As your doctor, I acted in the manner I deemed best for you at the time. But I should have told you differently long ago. I had no inkling that Tallfeather —"

"Leave Jason out of this," Manda interrupted. "The lie was yours, and so is the blame."

"But if I had had the chance to tell you myself—"

"You've had more than a year of chances," she broke in again, hurt and bitterness filtering through her ire. Dr. Nils started to reply, but she warned, "No more. Not now." She paused to reach for control. "You'll be spending the night here?"

"Yes. I'm much too upset to drive home."

He closed his eyes for a second. When he opened them, he was alone.

Manda would never have believed that she'd be glad to see Sylvia again, but Sylvia's presence at the dinner table that evening saved the dining room from being a disaster area. By pretending an interest in the lovely returnee's glib chatter about places and people she and Jason had known, Manda succeeded in ignoring Dr. Nils. Until she got used to the cataclysmic realization that the one person she'd trusted above everyone else had deceived her—however justified he claimed his reasons to be—she had no inclination to speak to him again.

She did, however, plan to speak to Jason, alone, at the earliest opportunity. So when he declined dessert, rose and started down the hall in the direction of his office, Manda excused herself and called after him, "Jason! Can you give me a few minutes of your time?"

He stopped, glancing over his shoulder. "Sure. We really should go over the work you've done for me this week." Shortening his stride to match hers, he completed the walk in silence. Once inside the office, he flicked the light switch, waited for her to enter, then closed the door.

The room had shrunk or . . . Jason stood too close. Manda smelled the musk of his cologne, heard his soft, easy breathing. She moved one step to the side as she tried to recall what he'd said. Oh, yes.

"I didn't quite finish typing the fifth chapter," she murmured, avoiding eye contact.

"I don't want to talk about the job."

"But you said—"

"I know what I said. That was to throw Sylvia and the Meechers off the track." He smiled. "You want to ask about my trip."

"How did you know?" The words squeaked with amazement.

"It's what I'd do, if I were in your place." He motioned for her to sit in the more comfortable padded armchair. Then, pulling the white enameled chair away from the table, he turned it around and straddled the seat, resting his clasped hands along the back with his chin propped on his thumbs. "You've figured out that the trip to Sandy Springs took only one day, and you're wondering why I didn't return immediately to tell you what I found out."

Manda rolled her eyes toward the ceiling. "Jason Tallfeather is a mind reader."

"No. Just the great-grandson of an Apache shaman." Laughter rumbled low in his throat.

Manda joined in for a moment, until she did a bit of mind reading of her own. Jason was trying much too hard to get her to relax. Her slate gray eyes widened with apprehension as she asked, "What else did you find out?"

He was sitting close enough to reach out and grasp her clenched fist. Slowly, one by one, he loosened her fingers, stroked their tension away, then wrapped his bronzed hand gently around them.

"We can do this later," he offered.

"Not later. Now. whatever it is, no matter what, I need to know now." Fear and bravery, wariness and determination flip-flopped in her eyes like an on-off neon sign.

Once again he was struck with the urge to protect her, but this time he assigned his emotion a new name: caring. Caring deeply. Love? He shook his head. This was not the right time for self-analysis.

Manda misunderstood the shake of his head.

"Please, Jason, you have to tell me."

He sighed and released her hand, sensing in her an inner strength that at the moment surpassed his.

"After the Sandy Springs fiasco, I drove back to Phoenix. Surely I could learn *something,* a crumb of truth to substitute for Johannsen's lie." He swallowed to cut off further condemnation of the doctor. Manda didn't need to hear that.

He really does care, Manda thought. Her shy radiant smile bridged the awkward silence.

"I planned to check with the several Catholic schools and convents in Phoenix," he told her, "but then it occurred to me that that part of Johannsen's story would probably also prove false."

"Oh," came the breath of sad acceptance.

"There was an ocean picture in my hotel room. A ghastly amateurish one. But it made me think of my paintings and the moment when you recognized—or seemed to recognize—the signature on them. If you *had* by some chance known the artist, and her name *was* Elaine Joseph, then maybe I had a new lead."

"I don't understand. Bess told me you knew nothing about Mums's paintings."

"Mums's?"

"I called her that." Manda's eyes shone.

"Well, it's different anyway." Jason grinned. "I'm glad you've remembered."

"What new lead?" She wasn't about to let him distract

her from the purpose of this dialogue.

"Something Amy Burke said."

"Your secretary?"

"That's right. On the first or second day she worked here, she informed me that one of my paintings is dumb. Her word, not mine," he added, as Manda bristled. "Amy, who lived in Texas until she married, explained that bluebonnets, which she assured me those flowers definitely are in the painting with the little house, abound in her native state but not on its beaches. I reminded her that the artist could use poetic license the same as a poet, but she'd have none of my rationale. 'The picture's still dumb,' she said."

"So?" All of Jason's talk about Mrs. Amy Burke's criticism of her mother's masterpiece was beginning to annoy Manda.

"So, there in my Phoenix hotel room, it suddenly occurred to me that Elaine Joseph, who knew exactly how bluebonnets looked, at some time or another probably lived in Texas. Early the next morning, on Thursday, I took a flight to Austin, where a friend who helped with the research of my third book is a librarian at the University of Texas. For hours we hunted through art texts and catalogs. Finally, in a pamphlet listing more or less obscure Texas artists, we found brief mention of an Elaine Joseph."

"Mums." Manda whispered because the lump in her throat almost prevented any speech at all.

"According to the one paragraph, although Elaine Joseph was not yet well known throughout the state, her work, which featured an unusual treatment of a three-dimensional effect, was growing in popularity. Her hometown was listed as Port Aransas, a fishing resort on

Mustang Island in the Gulf of Mexico."

"Oh, Jason! We both lived there. In the yellow seaside cottage."

"Right." The knowledge that his efforts had brought about the rapt expression on her face made Jason almost as happy as she looked. "Yesterday I rented a car and drove from Austin to Aransas Pass, the city on the mainland directly across the Intracoastal Waterway from Port Aransas. From there I took the island ferry, and that's when I lucked out. While we crossed the channel, I left my car to chat with the ferryboat captain. I'd overheard him gossiping with the locals about their families and jobs. He'd apparently been piloting the ferry for a long time, so I asked him if he knew an artist by the name of Elaine Joseph who lived somewhere on the island. He told me she'd moved away five or six years ago, but he remembered her as having been petite and pretty with big gray eyes and long dark brown hair. Friendly enough, he said, but always closemouthed about her personal business. She had owned an ancient Volkswagen whose motor, after being shut off during the crossing, sometimes refused to fire up again, creating a traffic problem on the ferry till the captain or his assistant could help her restart the engine." Jason paused purposely for effect. "The artist with the ailing jalopy was usually accompanied by a redhaired girl and, for many years, by a black Labrador."

"That was me and Brutus, the dog in the paintings." Manda's proud joyful smile very nearly took Jason's breath away.

"Right," he agreed huskily.

"What about my father? Did the ferryboat captain remember him, too?"

"I asked, but he knew nothing about your father. He did suggest I go talk to the retired postmistress, who lives at the hotel and who was Elaine Joseph's closest friend."

Chapter Twelve

The Sandpiper Hotel, built in the twenties, had survived hurricanes, depressions, and, more recently, a conglomerate's attempt to replace it with a row of ultra-expensive condominiums. The two-storied clapboard structure was a city-block long, freshly painted white, with multiarched verandas running its entire length on both levels.

Under the lower shaded porch roof sat two white-haired women, chatting. When Jason inquired for Miss Prudence Rutherford, the older lady peered at him over wire-rimmed glasses that had slipped to the tip of her nose. Although her near-transparent skin was wrinkled from seventy-odd years, her brown eyes were sparklingly alert and evinced a curiosity about the stranger who stood on the broad hotel steps.

"I am Prudence Rutherford," she announced rather grandly. "May I be of assistance to you, young man?"

"My name is Jason Tallfeather," he told her. "I live near San Francisco, and I'm a writer."

"My goodness! You're *that* Jason Tallfeather?" Her formal pose transformed immediately into a wriggle of excitement. "I loved your books!"

"Thank you, ma'am." He smiled in acknowledgement of her praise.

"Anything I can do for you, Mr. Tallfeather, you just name it."

"Thank you, ma'am," he repeated. "And yes, perhaps you can help me. I'm trying to locate Elaine Joseph, an artist who used to live here."

After he spoke, Miss Rutherford rose stiffly from her rocker. Tall and spare, she carried herself ramrod straight to the far end of the veranda. Jason followed to a slatted wooden porch swing that hung by two galvanized chains from the ceiling. Holding the swing steady for both of them to sit down, he said, "The ferryboat captain thought you might know how I could contact Mrs. Joseph. Or her husband," he added deliberately, making the last phrase sound as though it were an afterthought.

"Husband? I always figured he was dead. Elaine never mentioned him, and there was never any correspondence between her and a Mr. Joseph. I would have remembered handling any mail like that. I remember everything. Even if they do say I'm too old to work."

"Of course," Jason said. "Probably Mr. Joseph was dead, then. The captain said she moved away. Would the post office still have a record of her forwarding address? Or do you remember it?"

The swing squeaked as they moved slightly back and forth.

"She didn't leave a forwarding address," the former postmistress said. "It seemed a careless thing for her to do, and Elaine wasn't a careless person. She'd been quite ill—still was, from the looks of her—and we all knew that she was selling everything she owned to pay her current and upcoming medical bills. And when Elaine failed to tell anyone where they were moving to, I worried for months about Samantha."

"Samantha?" Jason gulped, but he already knew the answer.

"Her daughter. Everybody else called her Manda. But me—I don't hold with nicknames. Lazy nonsense, nicknames." She uttered a disgusted, huffing sound. "Samantha was a dreamy elfin child, always small for her age, with big gray eyes like her mother's and curly auburn hair. They were very close, those two, and like I said, it really bothered me to think of that shy sensitive little girl—sixteen, seventeen, up till then sheltered from any contact with the big bad world—having to fend for herself. Because, let me tell you, Mr. Tallfeather, Elaine was slowly but surely dying, and she had to know it. That's why I couldn't understand her not leaving a forwarding address. Cutting Samantha off completely, she was, from any help that someone here might have wanted to give the child later on."

"Too proud?" Jason suggested, his expression grim and his black eyes sorrowing at the obligation to pass along to Manda what he'd just heard.

"I think not," Miss Rutherford demurred. "Under those circumstances, pride would have been foolish. Elaine loved Samantha—worshipped her, you might say. No, she had a more important reason to keep her daughter's whereabouts a secret."

"Why do I have the feeling you know more than you're

telling me?"

She gave Jason a keen measuring look. "Young man, are you here to cause trouble for Samantha?"

"No, Miss Rutherford, I am not."

He met her gaze unflinchingly, but if she asked, he would never tell this kindly gentle lady where Manda was. Not after hearing that Elaine Joseph had deprived her apparently soon-to-be-orphaned daughter of the aid and comfort of friends rather than reveal where her daughter would be. Until he discovered the woman's reasons, he owed her, and Manda, that much. He felt guilty enough, poking around in Manda's past without her permission.

Miss Rutherford, who had been eyeing him intently, briskly nodded her head, as though satisfied with his answer to her question.

"Right after Elaine and little Samantha moved here—she was a tiny mite of four or five—Elaine got a letter from one of those uptown law firms. You know the kind, with four last names in the envelope's return address. Forwarded from her former address in Dallas, the letter was.

"She asked me to send it back, unopened and marked 'Addressee deceased.' I told her that would be illegal, but I did offer to return it with 'Unclaimed' stamped on the outside, and I told her that would be the same thing. If she really didn't want to know what was inside, I said. She looked me straight in the eye, and I could tell she was mad—and maybe scared, too—and she said, 'I *know* what's inside, and I never want to see one of those letters again. Please, for as long as they keep coming, send them back.' So that's what I did."

"Do you recall the name of the law firm?" Jason asked.

"I told you, young man, there's nothing wrong with my memory!" she snapped. "But the law firm disbanded years ago. The senior partner died, and the others scattered to the four winds. They wouldn't tell you anything anyway."

"I expect you're right." He liked this sharp, straightforward woman.

"After four months the letters stopped coming," she volunteered. "Then the man came."

"What man?" His nose for news twitched like that of a nervous rabbit.

"Well, he *said* he was her second cousin from Amarillo, and to prove it he was all duded up in brand-new jeans, cowboy boots, and a white Stetson. But he looked too fancy, and he wore those western duds like he felt unnatural and conspicuous. He was shifty-eyed, too, and surly, and he fairly demanded the address of Elaine Joseph and her female child. Those were his exact words: her female child. Now, I ask you, would a cousin, even a cousin twice removed who didn't know Elaine very well, refer to her daughter as 'a female child'?"

"It doesn't seem likely," Jason concurred, his heart racing with the old thrill of chasing down obscure facts.

"He was some kind of citified detective, sure as anything. And with him showing up right after those lawyers' letters stopped coming, I figured he was involved with them, some way. And when I remembered how set Elaine was on not seeing those letters, I knew she wouldn't want to see the man either. So I got rid of him."

"You drowned him in the Gulf," Jason whispered, melodramatic and solemn.

She let forth a hearty chuckle and Jason smiled. Then she said, "I told him Elaine and her *daughter* had moved to Galveston."

"Didn't he ask for a forwarding address?"

"Sure he did, rude as you please, and I gave it to him. The Galveston street and house number of the highest-priced brothel on the whole Gulf Coast!"

"Why, Miss Rutherford, however did you know that address?" He pretended to be shocked, when in truth he was delightfully amused.

"Not first-hand, Mr. Tallfeather." She laughed.

"Call me Jason," he urged, grinning his admiration.

"Thank you, Jason." She'd put her serious face back on. "Every man in the state has heard of that address. A Texan would have hee-hawed and accused me of pulling his leg. But that man just growled 'Thanks' and slammed out of the post office."

"He didn't come back? After he checked in Galveston?"

"No. I guess he got my message the first time."

"Did you tell Elaine Joseph about him?"

"Sure I did. She turned white as a ghost and thanked me over and over for sending him away, and afterward she and Samantha kept strictly to themselves for a couple of weeks. I remember, Samantha missed out on her Sunday school swimming party. I doubt if she minded, though, because a month or two before that, she had fallen off a jetty and nearly drowned. Come to think of it, I don't recall ever seeing that child play in deep water again.

"Well, Jason, like I started to say, I got worried about neither of them coming in to town, so I finally walked to her cottage with her mail and a sack of fresh fruits and vegetables and milk. Nearly pooped me, too, traipsing all that way."

"Wouldn't the neighbors have let somebody know if Mrs. Joseph or Ma—Samantha were ill?"

"No neighbors. No public road. Just a trail across the dunes. But Elaine didn't mind being isolated. Good for her painting, she told me once."

"If there's no road to her house, where did she keep her car?" He read the puzzlement on Miss Rutherford's face. "The ferryboat captain said she had one."

"Oh. Jasper Mapes. That old gossip. *He* told you about me. Sure, you said that before. I remember."

Nodding, Jason prompted, "Mrs. Joseph's car?"

"She parked it at my place, of course."

Of course. Jason's grin flashed briefly, then he said, "I'd like to see the cottage." Manda would be pleased to hear about her Texas home.

"You can't. The fellow who bought it from Elaine tore it down and built a hamburger place. There's a two-lane asphalt road out there now."

"All in the name of progress," Jason muttered.

His own unspoiled Tangletrees came immediately to mind, and he sighed, wondering how long he could keep it that way. He sat silent for several seconds, listening to the lazy swish of the surf behind the hotel.

Miss Rutherford shifted her position so that she gazed directly into Jason's black eyes. Her words came out hesitant, even a bit wistful. "Jason, when you see Samantha . . . please . . . would you give her my love?"

"I will, Miss Rutherford, ma'am," he promised gravely as he covered her brown-splotched hands, clasped in her lap, with one of his. He stood up, gave her a small respectful bow, and added raspily, "And we both thank you."

Chapter Thirteen

". . . And the last thing she said to me was, 'Please, when you see Samantha, give her my love.' "

While he had narrated the Port Aransas interview, he watched the moisture overflow Manda's eyes and track down her face, which registered a heart-squeezing mixture of sorrow and relief.

"Samantha. My name is Samantha," she said in a tremulous voice. "Somehow it doesn't feel right."

She rose from the swivel chair and walked over to stare at the cottage scene. Jason followed, leaned his hip against the table as he gave her a smile that was forced and, he hoped, cheering.

"Maybe because Miss Rutherford was the only person who called you that?"

"You liked her, I can tell." She managed a feeble smile of her own. "I wish I could remember her."

"I wish you could, too." His obsidian eyes glinted with a compelling warmth, and he raked the knuckle of one finger across her cheek to remove the final tear.

For an instant or two, she permitted herself the extravagance of the sublime torment his touch set in motion. Until another truth overrode the thrill.

"My mother is dead." The pronouncement sounded absurdly calm.

As for Jason, he felt excitement, then shame because he was excited. But, he rationalized, if Manda actually did recall Elaine Joseph's demise, however heartbreaking . . .

"You remember?" he prodded.

"No, not in the way you mean. I just *know.*"

Helpless to erase the defeat he witnessed in her grief-clouded eyes, he glanced away and murmured, "I'm so very sorry."

"Why can't I sense something about my father? It's as if he never existed." She pulled in a ragged breath. "Oh, Jason, maybe he didn't. I mean . . . What if I—I'm illegitimate?"

Roughly he jerked her close, one of his hands cradling her auburn head to his chest. Twenty-four hours ago he'd considered that possibility and prayed she wouldn't.

"What if you are?" he asked now, softly. "Whoever your father was, whatever your name is, you're still the same pretty, bright, spunky Manda I lo—know you to be."

"There are so many questions." Her words were muffled against the fabric of his shirt. She could feel the heat of him sifting through. "Where did Mums and I go after we left the Gulf Coast? What has happened to both of us in the five, six years since then? Why was she hiding or running away from something . . . or somebody?" His arms felt so strong, so warm, so . . . strangely tugging at a hidden string tied deep and low inside her.

"I don't have the answers," he told her, twining a satiny russet curl around his finger. "But I won't quit till I find them. The puzzle pieces . . . your mother's paintings, your charm bracelet, Miss Rutherford's information about the law firm letters and the citified detective . . . None of the pieces fit yet, but they will before I'm through. I was a darn good investigative reporter, remember, and I welcome the challenge. The mysteries in *your* story are more intriguing, more complicated than those in any of my published books."

Manda's body stiffened for a moment, before she pushed herself out of his embrace. She took an unsteady step backward, then another, then another.

"Oh, dear God." Her voice was quietly desperate. "You've been checking into my past so you can write a new book."

"No! That's not true!" With both hands outstretched in supplication, he moved toward her, but she retreated again.

If he touches me, she thought, *I'll scream. Quite literally scream.* Misery contorted her features.

She had reached the office's outside wall.

"I believed you were my—my friend," she accused hoarsely, "but all this time you—you've been *using* me!"

Her hands jerked and groped behind her until they found the door latch. In a near panic she shoved the heavy glass aside and stumbled over the threshold and out onto the terrace. Immediately a thick fog encompassed her, making her invisible to Jason, but she hadn't escaped his voice. "No, Manda, no! Dammit, Manda, you've got it all wrong. I can explain. Manda, please." Her deep-seated fear of the impenetrable mist was as nothing compared to her frantic need to get away from the man inside that office. As if pursued by some demon, she ran the length of the terrace. By the purest instinct she managed to race down the steps without falling.

Once on the ground, she was compelled to slacken her headlong flight. The fog, a giant cauldron of bubbling wet smoke, swirled and shifted around her in curlicued layers. Through the misty darkness she gingerly groped her way along the familiar path. Blinded by the mist, heavy as raindrops, and by the tears that drenched her face, she couldn't see a thing.

Jason's betrayal had been the final torment, the cruelest blow of the whole incredible shock-filled day. To have him snoop into the uttermost secret places of her life, then arrogantly insinuate that the details surrounding her amnesia would serve as fuel to feed the plot of another book—! She'd trusted him. Like a mighty underground atomic explosion, his callousness had rocked the very foundations of her world.

She didn't know Jason Tallfeather at all. Because she was falling in love, and because she wanted to love a certain kind of man, she had artlessly endowed him with attributes he didn't possess. Like decency . . . and fairness . . . and compassion. She was a naive fool, a fool in love with an impossible dream.

At last she came to the steps leading down to the beach. The chill clammy salt air smote her face. She could still see nothing but fog. She was frightened of the fog, but even more upset by the idea of going back inside to face Jason. One hand clutching the wooden banister, she felt with a cautious foot for each slick plank. During a pause to change her grip on the railing, Manda thought she heard footsteps on the stairs above her. Her breathing, and her heart, too, it seemed, stopped momentarily.

"Jason?"

She stared straight ahead. No way could she talk to him again, until she'd pulled herself together.

Waiting and listening, Manda heard only the fog-muted roar of the breakers and her own pulse thudding in her ears. Jason wasn't there; he would have answered by now. Exhaling slowly, she relaxed her tense muscles and stepped down onto the cool sand.

That noise sounded again. Closer. Like a shoe sliding softly, stealthily, on wood.

"Jas—?"

Before Manda could turn, something struck the side of her head. After one brief second of searing pain, she crumpled to the ground in an unconscious heap.

At first she was aware of being very cold. Had she left her window open wide by mistake, and in her sleep thrown off her bedcover? With her eyes still closed—she had a dreadful headache—she thrust one hand out to pull up the blanket. Her fingers came away wet. She patted the surface on which she lay.

This wasn't her bed. She was lying on her back on something hard and rough—in water! Because of the numbing cold, she hadn't initially felt the wetness, but now . . . Where was she?

She sat up gradually and opened her eyes. Dark, looming shapes and pockets of pearly light spun together, blurred, separated, and joined again in a different pattern, an out-of-focus black-and-silver kaleidoscope. And her head hurt terribly.

She remembered. She'd been standing at the base of the cliffside steps in the fog, when someone hit her on the head!

Manda blinked a few more times until her vision cleared. The fog was gone, probably blown away by the same strong easterly gusts of wind that were rapidly drying her hands. The moon, a brilliant globe high in a cloudless, star-speckled sky, afforded ample light for her to determine that she was sitting on the rocky area where she'd first met Clive.

"Don't get stranded out here," he had warned. "At floodtide it's all under water, and there's a bad undertow, too."

How had she got this far from the cliff steps?

Suddenly she figured it out. Someone had brought her here unconscious at slack tide and left her to . . . to drown!

Already the stone floor on which she crouched, shivering in the gusty offshore wind, was awash with three or four inches of frigid frothy water. Soon it would be covered so deep that the treacherous riptide would drag her out to sea.

Manda's whole body shuddered, more from the fear that assaulted her than from the cold. Terrified, she leaped to her feet.

"Jason!" she shouted, not knowing what else to do. "Help me, Jason!"

Then she hushed. Even if Jason were out there and could hear her above the noise of the surf, he wouldn't come to her aid. He had *put* her here! To perish on this godforsaken outcropping. Or in the ocean, already roiling above her ankles and, with each receding wave, tugging harder at her slippery, tenuous footholds.

She had no inkling of why he had done this to her, but he was the one person who knew where she'd gone. It must have been Jason's footsteps she'd heard on the stairs, seconds before he knocked her unconscious.

The tide was rising at a merciless rate. Did she dare try to swim for shore? She could barely manage to keep afloat in a pool. Once she left the rocks, the undertow would surely seize and destroy her. She'd rather wait here and skip the useless struggle.

If only there were someone walking on the beach or along the rim of the cliff, to see her silhouetted against the moon-silvered water. But everyone at the inn would have been asleep long ago.

She yelled anyway. "Help me! Somebody, help me!" In desperation she closed her eyes, her heart clamoring a wordless prayer.

Had that been a flash of light across her eyelids? Her eyes popped open, and through her tears she scanned the beach. No. The light had merely been a product of her frenzied imagination.

Manda slumped to her knees, sat back on her heels, and let her head droop forward in hopeless surrender. The briny water, almost on a level with her chin, sloshed into her mouth as she sobbed, making her choke and sputter.

Because in those last panicked moments her brain had mercifully switched off her acute, tormented senses, Manda recalled few details of her rescue.

Dimly she remembered Jason's arrival at the sea-washed boulders with a life preserver, then his strong arms supporting her weight as he guided her along a taut rope to safety. And she remembered his words, urgent, shouted into her ear, but barely audible above the tumult of the breakers:

"I'm here, Manda. Don't give up! Hang onto the rope. That's right. Please, darling, please don't give up!"

Darling . . . ? Yes, that was the word. But she'd been too exhausted to think about it. Or even to care. What mattered was that she wasn't going to drown.

When she reached the shore, Clive had wrapped a scratchy woolen blanket around her, and the two men led her, shivering uncontrollably, along the beach through shin-deep water. She staggered once, reached for their hands or arms, anything secure to hold onto.

Jason grabbed her by the wrist to steady her, then exclaimed, "Your charm bracelet! It's gone!"

"I—I wasn't wearing it," she told him between gasps. That afternoon, in her haste to be downstairs before Dr. Nils's arrival, she hadn't taken the time after her shower to put the bracelet on.

"Thank heaven," Jason said, for it surely would have been lost forever if it had come off in the ocean. He'd begun to think it was not only a talisman, but also a possible clue to what had happened to her after she and Elaine Joseph left Port Aransas.

Jason and Clive helped Manda up the cliffside steps, along the path, and into the house. Jason insisted upon carrying her, still shaking and weak, up the stairs. As soon as he laid her ever so gently on her bed, Jason turned to confront the doctor, who waited nearby.

"Why in the hell weren't you in your room when I went to tell you Manda hadn't returned from the beach and could be in bad trouble?" Jason's accusing eyes flashed black fire.

"I *was* in my room," Dr. Nils answered calmly, as he moved toward the bed.

"No way! I banged on the door and called—!"

"Not now, Jason," Bess chided. "We have to take care of Manda."

"Oh. All right, Bess." He stomped out of the room.

With sympathetic mutterings Bess exchanged Manda's dripping clothes for a silky nightgown and settled her beneath an electric blanket. Already her trembling had begun to lessen.

While Dr. Nils examined her, he gradually coaxed from her a halting story of what had happened. He checked the painful spot behind her ear and tested her eyes and her reflexes. He diagnosed a slight concussion and assured her that the sensitive swelling on her head would disappear in a few days.

"You were extremely fortunate, Manda." He displayed one of those professionally condescending smiles that she despised. "And quite foolish to have lingered so long out on those rocks when you had been forewarned about the undertow."

"But I didn't!" she protested. "I told you! Someone knocked me out on the steps—I mean, at the bottom of the steps—and took me out there to—to *die!*"

"Shush, my dear. You know how high-strung you can be. In your weakened physical state, you should not upset yourself further. Perhaps you took a nap while on the rocks and had a dream, a nightmare. In your haste to reach the shore, once you saw the danger from the tide, you tripped and fell and hit your head—"

"No! No, Dr. Nils!" She raised herself and slapped at his hands as he tried to push her back down on the bed. "You *have* to believe me!" she begged. "Oh, please, somebody has to believe me!"

"I believe you, Manda." Bess's voice rang out loud and firm, and her stern look challenged the doctor's vexed glance. "I'm sorry, Doctor. I would never presume to question your medical judgment, but I cannot agree with you about this. Manda has spent countless hours on our beach. She knows its every hazard, and she would never have taken the risk you suggested. She—"

"Very well, Mrs. Meecher, very well," he placated. "We must not aggravate the patient's distress by arguing in her presence. She is in need of restorative rest."

"Yes, sir," the former nurse agreed, but with a lingering annoyance in her tone.

"Someone should sit with her tonight and awaken her every two hours, as a precaution against torpidity."

"I'll do that, Doctor."

"Excellent. Then I shall retire once more to my room. Wake me if necessary, but I feel certain she'll be all right by morning except for a—" He made a poor attempt at humor as he patted Manda's arm, "—sore head."

"What is torpidity?" Manda wanted to know as soon as he left the room.

"If you're alert enough to ask," Bess evaded with a pleased grin, "you don't have to worry about it. Dr. Johannsen's right. Tomorrow you'll be fine."

No, I won't, Manda silently disputed, *because I'll still know somebody wants me dead.*

But surely not Jason! Otherwise, why would he have rescued her?

Manda had intended to lie quietly and try to figure out the who and why of her dilemma. What she did was fall at once into a deep sleep of total mental and physical exhaustion.

A little after 3:00 A.M., Jason tapped lightly on Manda's bedroom door, then opened it a crack. In the dim glow of the shell nightlight at the bed's baseboard, he saw Bess motion him inside.

"She okay?" he whispered, when he'd tiptoed close to the chair where Bess sat.

"Perfectly okay. I woke her an hour ago. And we don't have to whisper." By way of sharing his concern, she reached up and gave his hand a squeeze. "Couldn't you sleep?"

"A couple of hours, maybe. How about you?"

"Just a catnap. She needs watching."

"That's why I'm here. For the changing of the guard." He ignored her murmur of protest. "Your work day begins in a few hours, and you can use some real rest in your own bed. I promise to keep a close eye on her."

Bess rose stiffly from the rocker.

"Thank you, Jason."

When the door shut behind Bess, Jason walked over to Manda's bed. She lay on her back. In the dark he couldn't discern her features, just the pale circle of her face below the arch of curls against the pillow. An errant ringlet broke the straight white line of her forehead, and before he realized what he was doing, he reached down and touched it with his fingertip. As though alive, it clung and wrapped ever so silkily around his finger. In much the same manner, he mused, that Manda had wrapped herself around his heart.

Jason relived seeing the disbelief, then the anger and the hurt in her eyes when she thought he'd betrayed her trust. A breath caught in his throat, exited as a flowing sigh. Manda stirred. Quickly he freed his hand and retreated three quiet steps to the only chair in the room.

No sooner had he settled himself than he heard Manda's whimper, like the mewing of a kitten. Tense, he stood up, unsure whether to rouse her. Suddenly Manda began to thrash about, and her wailing "I can't swim, I can't swim!" tore at his insides. He rushed across the narrow space and dropped onto the side of the bed. After a couple of tries, he stopped her flailing arms by seizing her hands. He transferred them both to one of his, and with his free hand lit the low wattage lamp on the nightstand.

Sheer terror ravaged her face, twisted her mouth, hazed her staring, unseeing eyes. She was wholly enmeshed in memories of her brush with death. A sound he could only define as a whispered scream escaped through her gaping lips.

Jason held her close to his chest, rocking her gently back and forth as he repeated over and over again, "It's all right, Manda. You're safe now. It's all right. You're safe."

Bit by bit she relaxed against him. Her eyes were

closed. A few inches at a time, he eased her back onto the bed. The instant her head met the pillow, she lunged up again, and her eyelids raised to reveal the same panic as before.

"I'm scared!" she cried. "Oh, please, I'm so scared."

Before Jason could react, Manda's beseeching hands grabbed his shoulders, then clasped together behind his neck. She drew his surprised face down to hers.

He understood her dazed condition, half-in, half-out of the nightmare. He also understood she needed him. And yes, he needed her.

Gently he put his mouth to hers, traced the shape of her trembling lips with the tip of his tongue. She opened for him, and her moan was swallowed up in his "Manda . . . So sweet . . ."

Ashamed of having taken advantage, he reluctantly broke off the kiss. What she needed now was a caring friend, not a lover.

"Hold . . . me."

Hearing her soft, breathy plea, Jason reached out and switched off the lamp, as his hips nudged her to the far side of the bed. One brown suede slipper, then the second, hit the floor. Jason loosened the front of his robe. When the cool air touched his bare skin, he realized he couldn't crawl naked into bed with a woman he guessed to be as pure as a newborn babe. Snugging the tan velour robe about his frame, he re-knotted the belt. He slid under the blue blanket and lay on his right side, facing Manda.

Instantaneously she turned, placed her back toward him, and wriggled until her body fit his spoon fashion. She felt so warm, so wondrously . . . female. Jason hissed his frustration through clenched teeth. He knew she was more asleep than awake, and that she was seeking the comfort of a human body, *any* human body, to blot out the horrors of last night.

Jason couldn't find a place for his left arm. Finally he draped it across Manda's waist. As he bent his elbow, his hand unintentionally brushed the underside of her breast. He gasped when Manda took his hand and pushed it upward, until it rested fully on the small firm mound.

"Ummm," she murmured.

Almost of their own volition, Jason's thumb and forefinger coaxed the satin-covered tip into a swollen bud.

"Ooooooh," Manda responded, squirming her backside even tighter against him.

Jason's body surged hot and hard with desire.

Jesus, what am I doing? he admonished himself, summoning all his willpower in order to take his hand away from the enticing globe of flesh. *She's been through hell and she's completely zonked out. I'm acting like a real jerk.*

A jerk maybe, he admitted guiltily, but an aroused one who loved—yes, dammit, loved!—the woman cuddled so sensuously near his passion.

In her sleep Manda had reflexively captured his hand and returned it to cup her breast.

She uttered a long blissful sigh and went limp, dissolved into peaceful slumber.

Jason wondered when he'd revert to a relaxed state. Then, from out of nowhere a silly grin spread across his face. It was still there when, some twenty minutes later, he dozed off.

Chapter Fourteen

"Manda! Wake up!"

"Jason?" Manda whispered sleepily, then opened her eyes. "Oh. Dr. Nils."

"You thought I was Tallfeather?" He sounded surprised . . . and angry.

"I—I must have been dreaming."

Had it all been a dream? she wondered. *No. I'm wide-awake now. No fatigue or fuzzy thoughts . . . but I can still feel Jason's warm body curled so right . . . so real around mine, and his hand caressing my—*

"Your face is suddenly quite flushed, my dear." The doctor held his palm against her forehead. "However, you don't appear to have a fever."

"I don't," she said testily. "When can I get up?"

"Don't be in such a hurry."

Hurry? She wasn't eager to go downstairs where Jason was, but sooner or later she had to. A moaning sigh rumbled in her throat.

"Are you experiencing any pain?" Dr. Nils frowned and reached down to open the black alligator medicine bag at his feet.

"No."

Her heart hurt, all right, but the ache couldn't be detected by the cold stethoscope the doctor placed here and there on her chest while she went through the inhale-exhale routine.

"Good," he announced.

It wasn't good at all. She had the kind of heartache no physician could cure. Jason had planned to exploit her memory loss in his next book, for the whole world to read about! When she protested and ran away, he'd followed, struck her down, and carried her out to the rocks to drown.

Then why had he rescued her?

Suddenly, with the clear reasoning possible in terror-free daylight, Manda thought of an answer to that question. Maybe Jason didn't want her to *die.* What if the entire incident had been a ruse, a scheme quickly devised after she fled from the office? Put her in danger, save her, then play upon her gratitude to obtain her consent, although reluctant, for the writing of his "real life" novel about the experiences and emotions of a lonely amnesiac. Could he really be that manipulating, that cruel?

Manda sucked in her breath. Had last night's . . . tenderness . . . in her bed . . . also been a pretense, a deliberate phase of Jason's plan?

Her eyes teared a bit, only partly because of the intense penlight Dr. Nils was using to test them.

"Ah. Both pupils are reactive."

"I'm fine. I told you that," she snapped.

"Any double vision? Dizziness? Or nausea?"

After each query Manda shook her head no. She

lightly rubbed the lump behind her right ear.

"You do have a headache," Dr. Nils said.

"Not much of one. Honest." She smiled, realizing her gruffness toward him was unfair. He was her doctor, after all.

He smiled, too; for the first time since waking, she'd looked up into his face. "I expect you're hungry."

"Ravenous."

"I'll have Mrs. Meecher bring you a light breakfast."

"Can't I get out of bed? I feel okay. Except for the tiny headache." Again she grinned at him.

"You want to go downstairs?"

"Yes, I do. I need to walk around, get my brain in gear. I have to figure out—"

"Manda, my dear, I must ask your forgiveness for ly—for telling you that stupid story about Sandy Springs." His hazel eyes begged for tolerance as a shaky smile curved his mouth. "If that therapy session hadn't upset me so dreadfully, I could have come up with something more believable."

In her misery over Jason's betrayal, Manda had completely forgotten about the doctor's little white lie.

"That's all right, Dr. Nils. I understand that you were trying to help. And you did admit your mistake as soon as I remembered something that really is true."

"Your mother's name. Her paintings are exceptional."

"I knew you'd appreciate them." She uttered a soft, sad sigh.

"Yes, I do value beautiful works of art. Which reminds me. Now that I am reassured of your recovery from the unfortunate . . . accident, I will be able to keep my appointment with Mr. Wong, if I hurry. Following that, I shall return home."

The Carmel merchant, Wong Yi, frequently notified his friend of the purchase of an unusual jade piece before making it available for public sale.

"Be sure to tell Mr. Wong hello for me."

"I shall. Good-bye, my dear, and take care." He seemed nervous. Anxious, probably, to add to his collection of jade.

Watching Dr. Nils quickly pick up his medicine bag and leave the room, Manda almost wished she were going to Carmel with him. The Wong Teahouse boasted such delightful sights, smells, and sounds: Chinese bronzes and jade and iridescent silk cheongsams; burning incense and aromatic tea blends; wind chimes of brass, rattan, or shell that swung into a discordant but pleasurable symphony each time the opening of the shop's front door changed the air currents.

But her place was here. Her memory return had begun here.

So had the danger.

Manda at last was forced to admit to herself that someone wanted her dead. She faced the daunting truth that, over a period of only eight days, three attempts had been made to end her life. After last night she could no longer blame the earlier events on a prankster, metal fatigue, or a mischievous child. Someone *had* tampered with her car brakes, and she had escaped injury by a hair's breadth. Then a second effort to kill her occurred at Hearst Castle, and again her enemy's scheme had been unsuccessful . . . although Manda could not even guess why the culprit had disappeared without trying once more that day.

Last night's episode had been more carefully planned . . . and cleverly, stealthily, carried out. In spite of what Dr. Nils called it, her near-drowning on the rocks could never be construed as an accident. Someone had deliberately, cold-bloodedly, placed her out there to perish and, by so doing, had removed all doubt from her mind that the other incidents were unrelated or coincidental.

Until the foggy night when she stopped here in need of lodging, she'd been perfectly safe. So *where* she was, Manda deduced, was one clue to her imminent danger. The unknown factors were the *who* and the *why*. And although Manda was scared half out of her wits by the eventuality of a fourth attempt to destroy her, she was determined to look for the answers.

Somewhere among those tangled threads of mystery, she knew as surely as she now knew her name was Samantha Joseph, lay the pull cord that would raise the curtain that had hung between today and her forgotten past. She intended to find the string that tied her now to her yesterday or . . . quite possibly, die trying.

Manda gave herself a mental shake and stowed away her fearful thoughts for the time being. Still, an insistent chill clung to her, emotionally and physically. To ward off the physical part, she dressed in a loden green sweatsuit. Getting rid of the emotional uneasiness would not be so simple.

Later, as Manda descended the stairs, she heard Jason speaking. "You can check, but you won't locate any footprints. The tide came all the way up to the base of the cliff."

"I waylaid the doctor before he left," another male voice said. "We talked about last night's events. He told me Miss Lethe has been—ah—ill."

"She's a victim of amnesia, Officer Watson. She's not ill . . . or abnormal, as your tone suggests. Her current memory functions perfectly. If *she* says—Oh, good morning, Manda."

Both men rose politely to their feet.

"I assume you suffered no serious aftereffects from last night," Jason commented, "or Dr. Johannsen would have stayed."

"That's right." She avoided eye contact with him.

"I phoned the sheriff's office last night, right after we took you up to your room, but I told them they couldn't interview you until this morning."

Jason introduced the deputy, a bald-headed giant of a man whose thin-lipped smile failed to reach the gimlet eyes below thick reddish brows.

"Officer Watson," Manda acknowledged.

"How do you do, Miss Lethe." His gaze was barely short of accusing. He didn't really care how she did.

"I'm normal," she replied. Then she did look directly into Jason's eyes, and discovered them laughing at her. He winked, and for a moment she forgot anyone else was in the room.

The deputy's face reddened beneath his tan, but he staunchly carried out his assignment.

"Miss Lethe, I'd like to hear your account of what happened here last night. From the beginning, please."

She proceeded to tell him in chronological order, everything she remembered about the incident.

Well, not quite everything. Manda didn't explain how she had dashed out of the study because Jason had betrayed her trust. Instead, she indicated she'd gone for a stroll. And when she reached the place in her story where she had heard footsteps behind her on the steps, she stammered a little, omitting her belief that it was Jason.

The deputy squinted his eyes and pursed his lips. Did he suspect that she was telling him half-truths? Haltingly she described having been struck on the head, and she hoped he was fooled into thinking that her stammering had been caused by remembered fright.

"Please continue, Miss Lethe."

"Yes, sir. I—I don't know how to swim, so when I realized where I was, I just crouched there, expecting to drown. But then, like a miracle, Jason came, and he swam beside me to the shore. Through that awful undertow." She could almost feel it yanking at her failing strength. "We held onto a rope that Jason had anchored to a boulder on the beach. Clive—Mr. Meecher was waiting for us. He put a blanket around me. They halfway carried me back here to the inn. Jason did carry me up to my room. Mrs. Meecher helped me into some warm dry clothes. Dr. Ni—Dr. Johannsen said I had a mild concussion and asked Bess—Mrs. Meecher—to stay with me." She made no mention of Jason's part in the vigil, but she blushed. "I woke up this morning feeling fine, and here I am." She smiled, glad to have completed her story.

"Yes, and you're lucky." The man frowned, then added in an undertone. "That's the same story Dr. Johannsen said you told *him*." He gave the last pronoun an insinuating emphasis.

Manda's smile abruptly faded. "Because that *is* what

happened."

"The doctor doubts—he thinks you imagined—" The deputy stopped as her dark gray eyes blazed with fury. "Are you absolutely certain that someone hit you on the head as you stood near the steps?"

"I'm certain. And I do not intend to discuss with you what Dr. Nils chooses to believe. If you have no further questions about what *did* happen, I'm going to eat my breakfast." Whereupon she rose and marched, her backbone stiff with indignant pride, toward the kitchen.

Jason's chuckling dismissal of the deputy followed her down the hall. "And that, Deputy Watson, is how it was."

Chapter Fifteen

A short while afterward, Manda sat on the sunlit terrace. Between bites of toast and poached egg, she had concentrated on watching the easy rollers fold over into low, lazy waves. The surf whispered. Every motion of the water seemed lethargic, as if the ocean, too, were taking a rest following last night's powerful churning about.

Jason's quiet words startled her.

"Here you are. We need to talk."

Manda clenched one fist in her lap and kept her gaze seaward. It was too soon. She hadn't yet decided what she wanted to say to him. About anything.

Deliberately blocking her view of the Pacific, Jason lowered himself into a chair between her and the stone wall.

"Manda, look at *me*."

She did.

He cringed at the hurt and confusion he saw on the beloved expressive face. How could he hope to break down the emotional barriers between them? An old Apache proverb came to mind, one his grandfather, Chief Three Tall Feathers, had been fond of quoting to his people when confronted with a stressful situation: *In the forest, even the strongest brave can cut down only one tree at a time.* Now Jason translated his own version: *I have to start somewhere.* He inhaled a deep breath and released it as a ragged sigh.

"I did not check into your past to get facts for a new book!" He paused. Shouting wouldn't help. He licked his dry lips and began again. "But I can see why you might have suspected that. You knew I'd been dissatisfied with the novel in progress, and I've talked about scrapping it and hunting for a brand-new set of clues. And last night I did infer that what I learned in Texas has challenged me to find out more. But I want to do that for *you,* Manda, not for me. Never for me," he added, his black eyes begging her to accept the truth.

For a few moments Manda remained still and silent. She thought if she spoke or moved, she would surely float up and away. Gone was the burden that had weighed down her spirit, her very soul, since the heart-wrenching scene in Jason's office. She took a sip from her coffee cup to swallow the constricted tears of relief lumping in her throat.

"I—I guess I misunderstood," she whispered.

The brightening spark in her eyes struck Jason like a laser beam of hope. Maybe she would hear him out. Ever so tenderly he dared to remove her hand from the mug handle and hold it between his.

"At first I was furious with you for questioning my motives and for running out on me. To get my mind off the whole mess, I started to read the pages of the revised manuscript you typed while I was away, and I lost track of the time. I decided my editor might approve after all of what I've done thus far. When I remembered the misgivings about the plot that I'd expressed earlier to you, I suddenly realized there was some basis for your doubting me."

"I put two and two together and got five." Manda's smile was as soft as her voice. She tugged her hand from his grasp, because she still had some questions to ask, and she couldn't think straight while he uncurled her fingers and gently stroked each one from palm to tip.

"That's understandable. I'm just sorry I didn't chase after you."

"I thought you had," she blurted, looking away from the compassionate downturn of his mouth.

"You thought—?" He stopped, sucked in a short breath of amazement. "You thought the person behind you on the cliff steps was me?" Manda nodded. "Why didn't you tell the deputy?"

Defensive gray eyes met dumbfounded black ones.

"Because you saved my life." Her no-nonsense look called to Jason's mind her parting verbal jab at Officer Watson. She was saying, *That's the only reason I'm going to give you.*

"Well, . . . thanks."

Had Manda had another reason for keeping quiet about her suspicions? Could it be that her response to him in bed had been more than the pure reflex of a woman with exhaustion-dulled senses? Jason squelched the urge to grin.

"You're welcome," Manda said, then blurted, "How

did you know where I was?"

"I figured it out as soon as I saw you weren't in your room."

Manda said nothing. She found herself re-living another occasion when Jason had been in her room . . . and in her bed. The recalled sensations of the gentle touch of his rough palm on her tingling, taut breast, of his musky male scent as he held her against his lean, hard body, brought vivid color to her cheeks. She refused to meet his gaze.

Jason noted her reaction and hoped the flush on her face was engendered by a natural embarrassment rather than by shame or, worse, her utter disgust at the memory of his recent physical closeness.

Raspily he cleared his throat before he spoke again. "When I passed your room on the way to mine, there was a light under your door. I decided not to wait until morning to clear up the misunderstanding between us. You didn't answer when I knocked, so I knocked a second time and called your name. Still no answer. Then I got worried and opened the door. Of course the room was empty and your bed undisturbed. I realized it was Bess who had turned back the blanket for you and left the table lamp on. I knew immediately you hadn't returned to the house after you ran out of my office. That could only mean trouble. I rushed to the doctor's room for help." Frowning, Jason paused.

"But he wasn't there, was he? I remember you yelling something at him about that, right after you carried me upstairs. I wonder where he—"

"He claims he was in his room," Jason growled.

"He told Bess he'd been so unnerved about your learning that he'd lied to you—or about my finding out and telling you—whichever—that he took a sleeping pill. Supposedly he was so drugged, he couldn't respond immediately to my banging on his door and shouting that you might be hurt down on the beach. He says he came out into the upstairs hall a few minutes later, after I'd dashed downstairs to wake Clive and Bess."

"I've never known him to take a sedative, not even when he was too tired to sleep and had an early appointment the next day. He must have been more upset than I thought."

Manda wished *some* man she liked would also like Dr. Nils. First Emory, and now Jason, oozed animosity toward the man who had willingly and expertly assumed the role of her surrogate father. Her exasperation with Jason prompted her to offer an excuse for the doctor's behavior that she would ordinarily have rejected.

"Dr. Nils must still have been upset this morning, too," she said. "That's why he told the deputy I only imagined being hit on the head, and that I really fell and hurt myself."

"Maybe. Incidentally, Officer Watson came up with a different theory after you walked out on him." Jason smiled as he recalled the proud, sassy picture she'd made. "A couple of ranch houses in the hills northeast of here have been robbed recently, and Watson believes one of the burglars was scouting out the inn when you surprised him in the fog, and he hit you."

"But wouldn't he just have left me there at the bottom of the steps?"

"That's what I asked the deputy."

"And his reply?"

" 'Guilty people do weird things sometimes when they're scared.' "

So perfectly had he mimicked the bald-headed giant's bored uncaring tone that Manda giggled.

"I'm glad you can laugh about it." Jason's own velvet voice was back. He reached out to touch her hand again, then glanced at his watch. "My editor should be in his office by now, even if he took a long lunch hour. I'm going to call and ask if he'd like to have my first four chapters and synopsis next week."

In one continuous flow of motion, he gave her fingers a squeeze, rose from his chair, and leaned over to kiss the top of her head. The warm spot on her scalp vied with the cold shiver dribbling down her spine. Before she could summon enough breath to wish him luck with the editor, Jason had crossed the terrace and entered the dining room.

Manda had much to think about.

At times she sensed that Jason cared for her. He teased, he smiled his special smile, he touched, he kissed—her body pulsed at the memory—but he *said* nothing about loving her.

A wrenching truth pierced her heart. She was in love with Jason, but she didn't trust him.

Maybe he hadn't searched out her Texas childhood in order to write a book. He could, however, still have placed her on the rocks at low tide and then gone to her room, knowing he'd find it empty, and acted according to the remainder of his story. But what had motivated him?

Someone had threatened her life—three times—and circumstances finally compelled her to admit to herself that Jason had had ample opportunity to tamper with her car brakes. And had it been a cunning ploy, offering his car for her castle trip so he'd not be suspect? As she had conjectured that day, he certainly could have arranged for an accomplice to imperil her.

Her skittery uneasy mind kept going back to her initial response to Tangletrees. Why hadn't Jason publicized the inn? His present life-style suggested he could use the cash. He fretted about not having sold a book in a year. Although the furnishings of the inn were comfortable, they were plain, and most of them needed to be refinished or replaced. The building's cedar-shake exterior could stand a fresh coat of paint. And that was another thing. Why was the inn a dull green, practically invisible to people on fishing or pleasure boats motoring close to the shoreline?

Bess once told Manda that she didn't know what Jason would do if he lost the property. What was so important, so special, about this leased undeveloped land that would make Jason do something awful if he couldn't own it outright? Had she, Manda, known the answer to that question before her amnesia? Was that possibility the basis for what had happened here since her arrival?

Why did Jason insinuate, by his attitude if not in words, that Dr. Nils had been somehow involved in last night's danger to her? Just because the doctor had lied about the taped therapy session was no reason to think he lied about the sleeping pill. Why shouldn't a father figure want to give a totally depressed "daughter" something to hold onto? Like the rope to which she'd clung as she inched shoreward from the sea-washed boulders, the doctor's small falsehood had served as a lifeline. Jason shouldn't fault Dr. Nils for that.

Besides, if for any reason Dr. Nils wished her harm, he could have acted upon the desire many times during the past two years. Physicians have access to lethal drugs, and an intelligent, analytical mind like Dr. Nils's could easily have circumvented discovery and punishment.

Manda jerked her ruminations to a guilt-ridden standstill. *What am I thinking of? Dr. Nils is the last person on earth who would hurt me.* She couldn't believe that for a few crazy moments she had permitted Jason's intolerance of Dr. Nils to send her ponderings off on such an absurd, regrettable tangent.

The white metal chair almost toppled over as Manda leaped to her feet.

"I'll call Emory," she decided aloud, hurrying inside. "He'll help me get my head on straight."

What she saw as she glanced toward the foot of the staircase halted her reach for the phone.

Jason and Sylvia stood body to body, and Sylvia's hands, tousling the sides of his thick crow's-wing hair, pulled Jason's face down to hers as their mouths collided. Manda felt like a Peeping Tom, but was unable to tear her misting gaze away. When the kiss ended, Jason's devastating, dark velvet words wafted down the hall: "You're one terrific lady, Sylvia Hathaway. I'm happy you can share with me."

So much for special smiles and tender touches, Manda thought, as she blinked away the moisture pooling in her eyes.

With shaking fingers she lifted the phone. Because of her insecure grip, the receiver slipped out of her hand and thumped on the desk. The noise, embarrassingly loud to Manda's ears, announced her presence, and the embracing couple abruptly stepped apart.

Manda, not wanting to see the amusement she knew would be registered on their faces, refused to look their way. Nervously she gathered up the phone, making it clatter all over again, and jabbed the right numbers.

Emory answered on the fourteenth ring. Manda had been counting to keep her mind off Jason and Sylvia, as they walked past her into the living room.

"Dr. Johannsen's residence." Emory's voice was gruff.

"I'm so glad you're home."

"Manda? Is that you, Manda?" He cleared his throat. "Are—are you all right, Baby?"

"Don't call me—!" She broke off. He'd probably always use that name sometimes, and today she didn't want to fight with him. She inhaled slowly and started over. "I'm all right. You shouldn't worry so much about me."

"Since that car accident a week ago, I worry. And—why are you calling so early?"

"Early? It's almost noon." Suddenly she understood why his voice sounded so husky. "I woke you, didn't

I?"

"I—I guess I am a bit addle-headed," he admitted with a nervous laugh. "Don't tell Dr. Nils I slept this late. He left a hundred pages of notes for me to type. To say nothing of a half-dozen other tedious jobs." He chuckled again. "I confess all, Manda, my sweet. I watched the late-late movie on cable, and it turned out to be so erotic that I lay awake till dawn, wishing you were here so I could hold you."

"You know I don't like it when you talk like that."

"Sorry. But I miss you."

He really did care for her. And now that she knew what it was like not to have her own feelings for Jason returned in kind, she could sympathize with Emory. And, despite a few minor faults, Emory was a fine man, a trustable friend. Would she ever be able to forget Jason and give her heart into Emory's keeping, where it would be appreciated and cherished? She didn't relish the bleak prospect of being alone and lonely for the rest of her life.

"Could you drive up here today or tomorrow?" she asked Emory, more wistfully than she intended.

"I'd love to, Ba—Manda. But I told you. The doctor expects me to—"

She interrupted with her best argument. "Emory, last night somebody knocked me unconscious and left me on some offshore rocks when the tide was rising, and if Jason hadn't rescued me, I'd be dead."

"So now he's your knight on a white horse," Emory grumbled.

Not mine, Manda demurred. *Sylvia's.* A sudden anger bubbled through her bloodstream. Jason had no right to beleaguer her, however subtly, with his empathy and charm . . . and sexiness . . . when he was committed to Sylvia.

"Like him or not," Emory was saying, "I owe him thanks for saving my girl."

"I'm not your—" Manda stopped.

Being Emory's girl during the last few months hadn't been so bad. At least he'd never pretended to be something he wasn't. He loved her; he said so; she could believe him.

"Manda! Have we been cut off?"

"I'm still here."

"That's the problem!" Emory stormed. "You're still there! I don't trust that place! I don't trust Tallfeather, either!" His tone softened. "If anything happened to you, I couldn't bear it. Please, Manda, come home."

The pleading expression of Emory's love touched Manda deeply, and she wished she could do as he requested, but . . .

"I can't leave now. I've been here before—at the inn—" she told him breathily, "and I'm starting to remember things. I have to stay."

She suddenly hung up the phone and leaned against the wall, overcome with the agonizing and bitter knowledge that she must continue to work and spend time with Jason, whom she loved with all of her battered heart.

With luck Manda managed to keep to herself the rest of the day. She explained to Bess that she had a headache—she did, but actually not enough of one to matter—and felt tired. No one came to her room to disturb her while she played solitaire . . . and sadly wished she'd never met an unforgettable man named Jason Tallfeather.

When Bess brought her dinner tray upstairs, Manda suffered a brief pang of guilt, until the housekeeper assured her she had to climb the steps anyway to put out fresh towels for a late-arriving overnight guest.

"Jason wanted to come up earlier and invite you to go with him and Sylvia to see a Patrick Swayze movie in Lucia," Bess said.

"I wouldn't have gone," Manda stated grumpily.

"I know. That's what I told him."

Manda raised a worried gaze to hers. Had Bess guessed why she was hiding out, and had she imparted that information to Jason?

Bess's countenance was deadpan as she added, "Because you're still recovering from last night's shock, of course."

"Oh . . . ah . . . yes . . . ah . . . Thank you, Bess."

"Enjoy your dinner," Bess advised, the instant before she clicked the door latch shut behind her.

Manda awoke with a new resolve.

In the lonely nighttime darkness, she'd lain wide-eyed for hours making plans. No longer would she wait and hope for her memory to return. The answer to her shut-away past was here—she knew it!—and she intended to extend every one of her senses to its furthest outreach, search every crack and corner of the inn, walk every inch of the grounds, until she discovered the secret.

And last night she'd figured out exactly where to start.

According to Bess, some items belonging to Carlton Logan had been taken to the attic after his death. But Elaine Joseph's paintings, which also had been stored up there, hadn't belonged to the murdered man. They were—always had been—Manda's. Could something else of hers have been put in the attic along with the paintings? She proposed to find out.

For a change Sylvia appeared for breakfast at the designated hour, and her sentences overran with sexy comments about the movie and its star. "Yes" and "Ummm" and "I suppose" constituted Jason's unimpressed responses, but at least they prevented Manda's having to make polite conversation.

When Bess came in from the kitchen to refill their coffee cups, Manda inquired, "Would you mind if I went exploring in the attic?"

"Certainly not, but there's nothing up there. Just the usual discarded things that every household accumulates and folks never get around to throwing away."

"I thought I might find a small table to serve as a kind of desk in my bedroom."

"I can buy whatever you need in Carmel," Jason offered. "The attic is terribly dirty."

Did he have a reason to keep her out of the attic? Manda wondered. Or was he simply being a thoughtful host? She wished she could trust him.

More than that, she wished she didn't love him.

"It wouldn't be practical to spend money for something I'll be using only a few weeks." *Or less,* Manda tacked on mentally, *if I can solve my mystery, and not have to be around here one day more than necessary to watch you hold Sylvia in your arms.*

Forty-five minutes later, the key Bess had given her grated rustily in the lock, and the door hinges squeaked. Obviously no one had gone up to the attic for quite a while. The staircase was steep, the treads narrow and uncomfortably far apart for Manda's short stride. A small wooden ball dangling on a heavy cord thumped her on the forehead. She tugged it.

The light of the naked bulb created grotesque shadows around the murky space, weird immobile monsters that were in reality a cracked cheval mirror, a drawerless bureau with rounded, bulging sides, and a listing three-legged armchair whose cotton padding swelled from a slit cushion.

Manda sniffed at the noxious odors left behind by vermin and dusty years.

She stood stock-still in the middle of the large gloomy room, her gaze slowly roving over every visible object. She had no inkling of what she was looking for, but she knew she would recognize it when she saw it.

First she inspected the contents of three lidless cardboard boxes left near the stairwell. *Lapidary Journals* and hardcover volumes concerning mineral deposits and gem cutting. Some of the color photos in the magazines intrigued her, and she thought she might enjoy the articles, but not this morning.

What she sought was something that was her own, not old periodicals that had belonged to the inn's murdered owner.

She dusted her palms against each other and walked away from the cartons. Out of the corner of her eye, she caught the dull gleam of something metallic. There, in the dark tight V where the sloped roof met the floor, sat a small brownish rusting tin trunk.

After several tugs, Manda pulled it out into the light. Scratched on the brass keyplate she could make out the initials, *C. L.*

"Carlton Logan's," she whispered.

This possession of the dead man psychically begged to be opened and examined . . . *now.*

Manda stooped over and reached out with a tremulous hand. Slowly, almost prayerfully, her heart jackhammering, she raised the lid.

On top were strewn three glossy photos of seductively posed, scantily clothed young women. The suggestive autographs made Manda blush. Evidently Logan's posthumous fame as a ladies' man had been earned. Manda found herself intensely disliking the man.

Did I kill him? she asked herself, as she had so many times during the last couple of days. She shivered in spite of the stuffy warmth of the attic.

Anxious, her mouth as dry as the Mojave, Manda laid aside the photographs, which had partially hidden a wool Army uniform with a corporal's chevron on the shirt sleeve and the crossed-rifles Infantry insignia pinned to the collar. Manda wrinkled her nose at the faint but unmistakable smell of mothballs. When she picked up one side of the neatly folded trousers, she cried out in sudden, happy surprise. She dropped to the splintery floor beside the open chest, leaned forward, and lifted the khaki-colored pants to peer at the object beneath.

The black lacquer box that had belonged to her mother!

She remembered how as a small child she had been allowed on special occasions to run her freshly-washed hands over the shiny smooth lid and trace the outline of the mother-of-pearl lotus blossoms. Later, when she reached the age of understanding, her mother had explained that the glistening black box contained very private papers, and was *never* to be unlocked without her permission. After that, if Manda saw her mother sitting sad-faced, holding the box, she always refrained from asking questions. Somehow she had known that the never applied to discussion of the box, as well as to any unauthorized peek at its contents.

But Elaine Joseph was dead. Manda was sure of that now. And who besides Elaine's daughter had the right—the obligation, perhaps—to examine what was in this keepsake? Tenderly Manda set the box in her lap. Shaking fingers slid across the surface, slick and cool to the touch, just as she remembered it.

Without any conscious forethought, she used the tiny, ornate gold key on her charm bracelet to release the locked clasp.

Inside lay two envelopes, a manila one that fit

tightly into the box's bottom and, atop it, a slightly smaller white one of the size used for business correspondence. The latter, raggedly torn as though it had been opened in a frenzy, was stuffed to near bursting and its front bore a handwritten message:

"For Manda—To be opened after I am gone.
Elaine J."

Sitting on the rough grimy floor and gasping with urgency and suspense, Manda pulled the pages out of the white envelope, unfolded them, and moved her eyes over the beginning sentences.

"Manda, my dearest one . . . So often I've tried to tell you. But I was a coward . . ."

Suddenly Manda recalled, as though it were yesterday, the first time she had read the words . . .

Chapter Sixteen

The dreaded graveside service was over at last. Reverend Caruth, who officiated, had hurried away to catch his plane back to Dallas. Off-duty medical and office staff from the Houston hospital murmured their condolences and departed. The cold morning-long December drizzle had changed to sleet.

Dr. and Mrs. Grandy drove Manda home to the three-room efficiency apartment above their garage, where she and Mums had lived since they left Port Aransas.

Three years ago, Keith Grandy, the cancer hospital's chief radiologist, had found it impossible to remain objective toward the plight of the pretty young woman who so courageously endured the ravages of her disease, but who burst into sobs at the thought of her sheltered seventeen-year-old daughter having no one to look after her. Dr. Grandy and his wife Lorene, in their early fifties and childless, moved Manda from the seedy rooming house into the quarters which they had previously rented to medical students.

During the outpatient periods of Elaine's illness, she had been too frail to hold any kind of job. To pay the token rent, Manda, until she finished high school, helped Mrs. Grandy with the household chores and worked Saturdays in a nearby dime store. After graduation she continued to cook and clean for the Grandys, and she obtained a clerical position in Medical Records at the hospital that allowed her—when Elaine was confined there—to drop by her mother's room for frequent visits.

Now Mums was gone. It hit Manda like a bomb burst, not only the loss and the grief, but also the realization that she was completely, forever alone. She had been set adrift in a rudderless ship.

While Manda wept, Lorene Grandy held her and made crooning, comforting sounds. At last Manda's racking sobs quieted to snuffles and hiccups, and she raised her tear-streaked face.

"You've been so good to us," she said. "To—to Mums." A sorrowing grimace twisted her features. "I—I hope you'll let me stay here a few weeks. Until I can decide where to go, what—what to do."

"Oh, Manda, dear, certainly you may stay," Mrs. Grandy told her. "For as long as you like."

Dr. Grandy pulled from his inside pocket a long, fat, white envelope, and said, "Perhaps this will help you plan for the future. Elaine gave me this letter to hold for you. When she was sure—" He stopped, took a ragged breath, then went on. "Several nights during the past month, when I would stop off in her room after visiting hours, I found her writing. I didn't ask any questions and I didn't order her not to write and save her strength. Her big gray eyes thanked me, and then the last day before she slipped into the coma, she took this from under her pillow and whispered, 'For my sweet girl.' " Manda's choked outcry stabbed his heart as he held the envelope toward her. "Maybe she has told you where to go from here, what you should do."

With a trembling hand, Manda accepted her mother's last communication.

"Shall we stay while you read it?" Mrs. Grandy offered.

"No. But thank you."

As they moved rapidly out of the apartment, Dr. Grandy's parting words were, "I'll be back—afterwards—to see if you need me."

Manda stared at the words scrawled on the outside of the envelope: "For Manda—To be opened after I am gone. Elaine J."

When the seal resisted her nervous fingers, she ripped the paper. A great number of pages fell out, some written in pencil, some in different colors of ink. She visualized Mums's ordeal, physical and emotional, as she surmounted the pain to add a few paragraphs at a time to this final message.

Manda moaned deep in her throat. Dropping limply onto the recliner, she read the letter. Frequently she had to stop and wipe away the tears that washed out her vision.

"Manda, my dearest one. So often I've tried to tell you. But I was a coward. Your father is alive. I let you think otherwise, because I could not bear to talk about him. But now I must. Because you should have the choice to contact your father, or to get by on your own. Right now there are a thousand questions running around in your curly red head. Let me tell you what happened, in the order it happened, and I pray for your understanding.

"You already know that when I wasn't quite four, my parents were drowned in a boating accident, and my grandmother, old and crippled with arthritis and so very poor, had to put me in the Waco orphanage. It wasn't so bad, maybe because I never knew anything else.

"But when I turned sixteen, I became restless. I hated the orphanage's strict rules, and my high school classmates made fun of my hand-me-down clothes. All I could think about, dream about, was having my own money to buy a white pleated skirt and a red sweater.

"There was a convention in town, and an ad on the school bulletin board for usherettes. Girls sixteen and over, it said, with nice figures and pretty faces; uniforms and on-the-job meals furnished. I applied and was hired. By the time the school got around to notifying the orphanage of my absences, I hoped the convention would be over and I'd have my wages.

"Your father had an exhibit at the convention. He was exactly twice my age, handsome, and oh! so exciting to be with. His attentions flattered me beyond belief. Made me feel like a grown-up Somebody, you know?

"On the last day of the convention, I played hooky from my job to spend a few bittersweet hours with him, knowing I'd never see him again. We went to a movie, to a carnival, took a long walk in a little park.

It was late fall and chilly, but we sat on a grassy knoll covered with autumn leaves, and I didn't even feel the cold. He held me in his arms and kissed me again and again, and he wanted to make love. I loved him, I said, truly I did, but I'd never give myself to a man, unless we were married.

" 'Then we'll get married,' he told me. 'But it will have to be tomorrow, because I'm leaving town.'

"Looking back on it, I realize I was a gullible, lovesick adolescent. Then, it seemed like a storybook romance happening to an orphanage Cinderella.

"We were married the next afternoon in his hotel room, by a tall gray-haired judge, impressive in his black robe. The hotel manager and a maid witnessed the ceremony. I'd already decided to advise the orphanage superintendent of my plans after the fact, by telegraph from my new hometown.

"Your father was a wonderful passionate lover, sometimes nearly insatiable. I was blissfully happy, and his—our—apartment reminded me of a fairy castle. Fancy, gilt-trimmed furniture, rugs I could bury my bare feet in, and a fantastic view of the bay.

"During those first two and a half months, I met none of his friends. He worked late a lot, and a couple of weekends he had to go out of town. The rest of the time he said he wanted me all to himself. When he was away, I was content to keep house and study cookbooks from the lending library, so I could prepare the dishes he liked.

"Then, alerted by certain telltale symptoms, I made an appointment to see a doctor, who confirmed my pregnancy. I could hardly wait to get home to tell my new husband!

"My bus wasn't due for a half hour, so I went into the coffee shop on the ground floor of the doctor's office building. I sat in one of those high-backed booths, and while I waited for the waitress to bring my tea and toast, I overheard a man talking in the next booth. In vulgularly explicit language, he said he wanted to have sex with this young girl, who stubbornly refused because he wouldn't marry her. Then, loud and clear, I heard another man say, 'That's easy. Pay some distinguished-looking old actor who's down on his luck to dress up in a rented black robe and say the right words. If your girl's as dumb as mine, you can have a lot of fun, and quit whenever you're bored. No divorce, no alimony.'

"You've probably already guessed. That second voice belonged to your father. My fairyland world had collapsed. Crying all the time, I ran from the coffee shop, spent the last money in my purse for a taxi to the apartment, where I packed a few plain, sturdy clothes, took five hundred dollars from his jewelry case (I figured I'd *earned* that much, for being a satisfactory bedfellow!) and caught a city bus to the Greyhound station.

"I bought a ticket to Dallas, a place close to my beginnings, and large enough for a pregnant unmarried girl to get lost in. I slept some, but mostly I stared out the bus window and thought about how I had been shamed, betrayed, violated.

"But then I began to think about the tiny spark of life growing inside me. The baby was mine, completely and solely mine, forever separate from the man who had sired it. And Manda, my sweet, in all the years to follow, that never changed. For you, a father simply didn't exist.

"Near the Dallas bus terminal, I walked past a storefront church, went inside, and sat down on one of the benches, where I asked for a blessing upon my unborn child and for the spiritual cleansing of my sinfully used body.

"The pastor came over to ask if he could help. Sobbing, I told him everything, adding that I knew no one in the city, had no place to go and very little money. God must have led me to that church. Rev. Caruth's wife was confined to a wheelchair, and the girl who had been living with the Caruths and helping with the housework and the care of the two Caruth boys had recently married and moved away. He offered me the job.

"Three months went by. I had settled comfortably into the Caruth household and was seeing a neighborhood OB. I felt a lot better about myself. I was absolutely unprepared for what happened next.

"A detective, a cold, almost rude man, came to see me. He had been hired by your father to find me. The doctor who had confirmed my pregnancy had phoned the apartment to ask my 'husband' why I hadn't returned for my monthly check-up. The detective assured me that your father would agree to a real marriage, because he wanted a son. What if it was a daughter? I asked. The detective shrugged and reminded me that my child would have a name, whether or not his employer decided to acknowledge a girl baby. I screamed curses and futile threats at the detective, till Rev. Caruth came out of his study and ordered the man to leave.

"That evening the detective phoned Rev. Caruth.

Your father insisted upon giving me a monthly check to cover my medical bills, and hoped I'd come to my senses about marriage. Angry and bitter, I wanted to refuse the financial assistance, but the Reverend counseled me to reconsider. Your father could well afford it. The next day a lawyer told us that my taking the money would obligate me in no way, as long as I signed no contract and never put into writing the identity of my baby's father. That's why your birth certificate, which you'll find in my black lacquer box, specifies 'Father unknown.' I hope you can forgive that lie. That box, Manda, is a rare antique, the only one of the gifts from your father that I took with me when I ran away. He'd given it to me *before* that awful fake wedding ceremony, so that to my girlish mind it wasn't tainted.

"Anyway, within a few days a verbal agreement with your father was worked out by the lawyer, who was a sponsor of Rev. Caruth's church and the senior partner of a big downtown law firm. A monthly check would be made out to the law firm and mailed to the attention of the Reverend's lawyer friend. He would deposit that check and issue another one in the same amount from his own personal account, made payable to me. There would be no legal, traceable link between me and your father.

"I hated the idea of taking the money, but pride was a poor substitute for survival. I put some of it into a savings account every month, too.

"After you were born, we stayed on with the Caruths for two years. I paid a girl to come in and sit with you, so I could attend night school and get my high school diploma. I'd always fooled around with drawing and painting, and the art teacher said I had talent and encouraged me to study further. I found a position as sales assistant at an art gallery-studio and painted there on weekends. We moved into an apartment on the same block as the studio, and close to a nice day nursery for you. We lived very frugally. My only extravagance was a weekly private lesson with one of the finest art instructors in the Southwest. During my first year of study with him, he was instrumental in my securing my first commission: ten cheap landscapes for the units of a small Fort Worth motel. You'd have thought I'd been assigned to redo the Sistine Chapel, I was so proud!

"Later I sold several of my paintings through the gallery where I worked, and soon after your fifth birthday I signed a lucrative contract with a seafood restaurant chain to furnish a dozen seascapes for three new locations to be opened for business within a year.

"It was a glorious day, I can tell you, when I became self-supporting, and could return that first uncashed check to the lawyer, with a note saying I wouldn't need your father's money anymore.

"I decided we'd spend the summer on the Gulf Coast, so I could study the sea and shore. But before I finalized our plans, I happened to spot an ad in the *Dallas Morning News* regarding a 'well-constructed, in need of repairs' Gulf frontage cottage, for sale at an astonishingly low price. I left you with the Caruths and took a bus to Port Aransas.

"For the second time in my life, I fell in love at first sight. This time with a house. The shutters hung askew; one of the porch steps had rotted out;

circles on the kitchen ceiling told me the roof leaked. But pink hollyhocks grew shoulder-high around the back stoop, and at the side of the cottage was a big sandbox under a faded red vinyl canopy. An ideal place for you to play while I sat on the porch and painted the Gulf of Mexico less than a hyndred feet from our front door. We spent twelve wonderful years there.

"Island visitors bought my paintings, and a Corpus Christi gallery sold some on consignment. Our expenses were meager. We were comfortable and very happy.

"It nearly broke my heart (and yours, too) to leave Port Aransas. But when I was told that I had an inoperable cancer, I realized you were far too dependent upon me. You reminded me of myself at your age, utterly naive and ill-trained to cope with the practical everyday world. I needed to be close to the hospital, and I'd spend what time I had left teaching you some of those grown-up, big-city lessons.

"You know the rest. How the Grandys befriended us. How they took you under their wing when I had to spend weeks at a time in the hospital for tests and chemotherapy.

"I expect you wondered why none of our Port Aransas friends contacted us. I told *no one* where we would be. You see, a short while after we arrived in Port Aransas, a detective came there looking for us. He inquired at the post office, because General Delivery was the address he'd probably gotten from the Caruths. Earlier, I had asked Prudence Rutherford, the postmistress, to return a check—and any others like it from the law firm—marked 'Unclaimed.' She'd guessed that I wanted anonymity. She convinced the detective we didn't live there anymore. I never doubted for a moment that he was sent either by your father or by the Dallas law firm at your father's behest.

"When I learned I was dying, I couldn't bear the possibility that after I was gone your father might somehow track you down and force his way into your life. That's why I decided when we left Port Aransas to cut *every* tie with our past. Even with the Caruths. That way, any more nosey detectives would run smack into blank stone walls. It was hard on me, too, losing touch with good friends we'd made over the years, and I was so glad that you didn't pressure me to know why.

"This letter has become much too long, but I think just putting the details down on paper has turned out to be an emotional catharsis."

Here her mother's handwriting deteriorated to the point of being almost illegible. Mums must have used her last bit of strength to finish. Manda uttered a faint, whimpering sound and continued to read.

"Upon the advice of Reverend Caruth, who came to see me after I wrote him, and of Dr. Grandy, who has watched you mature into a strong, sensible twenty-year-old, I have sent a telegram to your father. It's as much of a surprise to me as it is to you—after all the trouble I've gone to, to prevent your knowing each other. But those two wise friends persuaded me that you have a right to meet your father if you choose, and then to determine for yourself what course your future will take. I wired him that soon he will be your only living relative. What he will do, I have no idea. If he doesn't get in touch with you, you can decide whether to contact him.

"Throughout this whole confession, I've referred to him as your father, because writing his name over and over again would have been too painful. In spite of the way he treated me, and after all these years, I still love him. Below are his name and business address . . ."

An urgent knock sounded on Manda's front door, and she raised bleary, tear-swollen eyes from the page. She was strangely willing to postpone the moment of revelation. Once she knew who her father was, she could never go back to being the exact same person ever again.

"Come in, Dr. Grandy," she called out to her friend who'd returned to check on her.

But the man entering her apartment was a tall, well-built, middle-aged stranger with wavy red hair graying at the temples.

Manda leaped to her feet, spilling her mother's letter across the carpet.

"Don't be afraid," the solemn-faced man reassured her. "Dr. Grandy knows I'm here. He told me where to find you."

Benumbed by the past few hours' sorrowing events, Manda felt no alarm, only disgust and dismay at this man's untimely call—because obviously he was Mums's insurance agent, whom Dr. Grandy had mentioned yesterday.

"You are Samantha Joseph?" her visitor inquired.

"Yes, I am." Manda's tear-reddened eyes flashed a warning. "But I don't want to talk about insurance *today!"*

The stranger nervously cleared his throat. "Samantha," he said, "I'm Carlton Logan. I'm . . . I'm . . . your father."

Chapter Seventeen

Sitting on the dirty attic floor, Manda gathered the pages she had let fall one by one as she read them. Dazedly she recalled what had happened after Carlton Logan's unexpected appearance at her Houston apartment.

At first she'd felt a burning outrage at the man's bad taste, bursting into her life on the same day as her mother's funeral. Her eyes steely with antagonism, she told him so.

Paling, he had tried to slow the onrush of Manda's hostility by explaining that he'd been in Amsterdam when Elaine's telegram reached his San Francisco office, and that he'd caught the first available flight from the Netherlands to Houston after his secretary relayed the message. At the hospital he'd been informed that the patient had expired, nothing else. He'd obtained Elaine's address from a phone directory in the waiting room, and hailed a cab parked outside the hospital.

By the time he finished speaking, Manda had begun to recover from the initial shock of confronting a father she hadn't known existed until a few minutes ago. At her invitation, Carlton Logan sat down and sipped the hot coffee she'd poured with a shaky hand.

Manda had tried hard to be open-minded about the other things her father told her on that dreary unhappy afternoon.

When Logan had found out about Elaine's pregnancy, he sincerely regretted his callous treatment of her and attempted to make amends. She made it clear she wanted nothing from him except the financial help that circumstances forced her to accept. When she stopped cashing his monthly checks, he hired another detective to find her and her child, but every lead proved to be a dead end.

Learning after so many years about Elaine's terminal illness had swept him up afresh into a maelstrom of guilt-ridden memories. He had never forgotten the young orphan girl with the incredible gray eyes, the teenager who had loved him completely, holding back none of herself. Together they had created a daughter, a love-child he wanted to know, and now had the chance to claim as his own.

Listening to his intimate expressive voice, and watching the emotional nuances play across his handsome features, Manda understood how her mother could have been enchanted by his sophisticated charm. Although Manda was determined not to succumb to that magnetism, she did agree to see her father again during the two weeks he planned to be in town.

Logan escorted her to a dinner theater and to the Summit to see a Rockets' basketball game, and they spent one entire day at the Lyndon B. Johnson Space Center. He visited her often in the apartment. They talked a lot, on her part self-consciously at first and very politely. Little by little she grudgingly began to like the man. She doubted if she'd ever feel a deep love for him, but Carlton was fun to be with and he lightened her somber moods. Gradually they became friends, good enough friends that Manda frankly admitted that she'd miss him when he returned to California.

"Then why not come with me?" he suggested.

She shook her head. "I wouldn't enjoy a ride on your social merry-go-round."

"I realize that. I'm not a complete ogre, Samantha."

He still called her that sometimes, usually when his emotions were nearest the surface, and she had stopped correcting him. After all, he hadn't been around when she was learning to talk and, unable to pronounce Samantha, had shortened it to Manda. Or when as a toddler she had willfully refused to answer to Samantha. Mums had capitulated, allowing even her school and employment records to bear the name Manda Joseph.

"What if I can offer an alternative?" Carlton asked. "A place where you can stay at least through Christmas and the New Year, and where we can get better acquainted without becoming involved with other people."

"I don't understand."

He described his secluded converted-barn home perched on a cliff overlooking the Pacific Ocean. It sounded wonderful.

"We could fly to Santa Barbara," he told her. "Hardly anyone knows me there, and it's a small airport, so there'd be no publicity hounds lurking around. I'd rent a car and drive us up the coast to my house. You'd be completely alone. No servants. Just a cleaning woman once a week, and if you like, I'll tell her to take three weeks' vacation. And I'd join you at Tangletrees on weekends."

"Tangletrees?"

"A bit of whimsy on my part," he grinned. "Near the house there's a small grove of Monterey cypress, seven or eight old trees, twisted by decades of ocean storm winds, with an ugly system of arching air roots. They're practically the last of their kind, except for those on the Point Lobos preserve a few miles south of Monterey. I'm afraid they'll all be gone someday," he finished a bit sadly.

Manda, delighted at the prospect of living near the sea again, even for a short time, had accepted Carlton's invitation. She told the Grandys she'd be with her father, but not one word about his oceanside house or its location. When her grief had lessened a bit, she'd have to look for a permanent home and a job, but she had no qualms about letting her father support her for a few months. Mums wouldn't object; she had bequeathed to Manda a free choice.

Descending from the attic with the lacquer box cradled in the crook of her arm, Manda thought back to that first time at Tangletrees. Many details were still hazy. She remembered the incessant winter rain that had imprisoned her inside for two days, then her walks on the beach after the sun finally came out. Once she'd removed her shoes and socks and splashed around briefly in the icy cold bubbles of the shallow, spending waves.

Carlton, as promised, had driven down from his

San Francisco penthouse both weekends. They engaged in long quiet talks and strolls along the shore. One particular stroll nudged at Manda's memory. She vividly recalled the dazzling burnt orange spread across the water by the sunset, and the sanderlings, gulls, and sandpipers vying noisily for food before darkness fell. With a stafflike piece of driftwood, Carlton had drawn a picture in the firm sand . . . and there the memory blurred.

A multitude of other mysteries still remained, but Manda was absolutely sure of one thing. She had *not* killed Carlton Logan! Now it was all right to tell Jason she'd visited Tangletrees before; she no longer felt tongue-tied by the shame and dread that she might have been a murderess.

She hadn't solved the puzzle of who wished her harm, or why, but she did know who both her parents were, and what had happened to them and to her during the past twenty-two years. The rest would come later. It had to!

Manda left the shiny ebony box on her bed while she washed the attic's dust from her face and hands, then she sat in the rocker and eagerly opened the large manila envelope stuffed in the box's bottom. It contained her birth certificate, her mother's night school diploma, and a child's crude crayon drawing of a pink dog standing in front of a row of crooked purple waves. Manda's eyes brimmed with tears. Elaine Joseph, estimable artist, had cherished her baby daughter's handiwork as though it were a Winslow Homer. Manda aloo found a small faded blue stationery envelope, out of which she slid three photos—five-year-old wallet size color photos of herself and of Mums, and one black and white snapshot of Manda at age nine or ten, sitting on the steps of the Port Aransas cottage and hugging an enormous black Labrador.

"That's all?" Her plaintive question applied to more than the contents of the manila envelope. She was railing against her mother for having saved so little of her early years. Manda understood her mother's reasons, but she didn't have to like them.

Numbly she looked around the bedroom, and her vision focused on the clock on the dresser. Two-thirty. Where had the hours gone? Quickly she changed into clean jeans and a long-sleeved denim blouse with calico flowers appliqued on the back. After tucking the two color photos from her mother's lacquer box into her shirt pocket, she hurried downstairs.

Emory stood in the living room talking to Jason and Sylvia. Manda, pleased to see him and overstimulated by her new discoveries, raced across the floor and into Emory's quickly outstretched arms.

Sylvia watched the surprise and jealousy flare in Jason's eyes. Anger tightened her mouth. She looked thoughtful, then resumed her customary self-assured smile.

"I'm so glad you came," Manda told Emory. "When did you get here?"

"About five minutes ago. I was about to ask Mrs. Meecher where you were. Tallfeather didn't know, he said."

"I was in my room. Before that, up in the attic."

"Since mid-morning?" Jason asked, as Manda stepped out of Emory's embrace. "You skipped lunch to hunt for a table amid all that filthy cast-off junk? I could have driven to Carmel in less time and bought—"

"No table," she interrupted breathlessly, her gray eyes wide and sparkling with excitement. "I found something far more wonderful. I found my father!"

"Your father?" Jason gasped.

"What?" Emory fairly shouted.

"There's a man in the attic?" Sylvia shrilled.

All three had spoken at once, and Manda laughed, not sure whose reaction delighted her the most.

Jason recovered first, his expression grim. "I think you'd better explain."

"Carlton Logan was my father! I can prove it!"

"That's where I'd seen you before!" Jason exclaimed, slapping his forehead with his palm.

Before Manda could open her mouth, Emory demanded, "What do you mean, that's where you'd seen her? Where?"

"I saw her picture. In a dark room in Santa Barbara. I was there on a holiday, spending a few days with a newspaper photographer friend of mine. He'd been out to the airport to cover the arrival of some extradited embezzler and, as Sam was wont to do, he'd snapped a close-up of a pretty young woman with enormous sad eyes. I saw it in his darkroom, hanging to dry. I remember, I asked him who she was and he shrugged and said, 'Some babe travelling with Carlton Logan, the Frisco skirt-chaser.' I'm sorry, Manda," he finished lamely.

"That's okay," she responded with a wry smile. "I know from my mother's letter what kind of a man he was."

"What letter?" Jason sounded stunned.

Emory's mouth fell open in shock.

"That's what I found in the attic. Her last letter to me. You see, I figured out that I had to have been the one who brought Mums's paintings here. I'd remembered earlier that she gave them to me, the only two she didn't sell, and I knew *I* would never have sold them. Bess said they'd been stored in the attic together with some other things, so—"

"What paintings?" Emory broke in impatiently. "Your mother was an artist?"

"I'll explain later," she promised him in an aside. "So I decided to look in the attic. Not really for a table," she confessed to Jason. "And I found the letter she wrote to me just before she died of . . . of cancer. She said Carlton Logan was my father. Then I actually *remembered* having come here . . . just before he . . . died."

"What about his murder?" Emory almost whispered. Manda knew the worry in his pale blue eyes resulted from the same assumption she'd made days earlier: that she had somehow been involved in Carlton Logan's death.

"Whose murder?" Sylvia gasped.

Jason ignored Sylvia's question and hastened to refute the inference in Emory's. "Don't be an idiot, Wade. Manda had absolutely nothing to do with Logan's murder."

"Thank you, Mr. Tallfeather, sir," she smiled, curtseying playfully. She felt absolutely giddy with happiness because Jason believed in her.

"I didn't mean—I know Manda wouldn't—" Emory stopped, looking embarrassed.

Manda's short stubby fingers worked the photos out of her pocket and handed them to Jason.

Elaine's was on top.

"A beautiful lady," Jason commented. Then he studied Manda's likeness. "Now I see why I didn't recognize you right away. In the picture Sam took, you were wearing your hair like it is here, almost to your waist. And, of course, his was a news photo, black and white. No short auburn curls," he ended with a half-bewildered smile, as he passed the photos to Emory.

"The weight of Manda's long hair would have straightened out most of the natural curl," Sylvia offered, apparently pleased at being a part of the conversation at last.

Manda's face lit up anew, and her laugh tinkled bell-like through the room. "I remember now! I'd never in all my life worn my hair short, but I decided to have it cut at the hotel salon while I waited for Carlton to keep an appointment, before we drove up the coast. I wanted a new-me image, to go with my brand-new life," she added shyly.

"It was the expression in your eyes that was so familiar to me that first night you walked in here." Jason spoke as if there were no one in the room but him and Manda. "That sad, lost look, the same as in the picture Sam had taken."

Emory frowned at Jason's intimate observations and returned the pictures to Manda.

"Did you find those in the attic, too?" he asked, his words raspy with held-back emotion.

"Yes. With my mother's letter. In a rare old Chinese lacquer box that I remember from my earliest childhood." Manda turned to Jason. "You told me once that you thought the key on my bracelet was old and Oriental. You were right. I used it to open Mums's box, which she wrote was an expensive gift from my father."

"And you were correct in feeling that your bracelet was a link with your past." Jason's smile was soft and thoughtful.

"Whatever are you two talking about?" Sylvia asked, confused by what was going on and irritated that she was excluded again.

They ignored her still further.

Manda's gaze remained fixed on Jason's.

"Since I came down from the attic, I've remembered about the medallion with my name on it," she told him. "Mums gave it to me on my sixteenth birthday. Until she died, I wore it on a chain around my neck."

"So now you understand how you got all three of the charms. I'm glad."

"No, not the green pebble."

"But I assumed—" Jason stopped abruptly, and the dark honey color of his face paled.

"Do you know something about my pebble charm that you haven't told me?" Manda demanded.

Jason wished he could say *abracadabra* and vanish in a puff of smoke. Manda's expression registered an increasing fury. As long as he'd been able to cover up . . . but he couldn't tell her an outright lie. When she discovered the facts for herself—and she would eventually—she might never trust him again unless he was completely honest with her now.

"Logan designed it," he finally admitted as he met Manda's reproachful eyes. "The caging of an uncut polished stone with gold wire as thin as a human hair was Logan's trademark. Especially when he worked with jade."

"Jade?" cried Manda and Emory together.

And Manda added, her voice sharp with denial, "This is *not* jade!" Grabbing the green charm between thumb and forefinger, she thrust her wrist toward Jason. "Dr. Nils would have told me."

"Maybe the doc had his reasons for keeping quiet," Emory suggested *sotto voce*.

Manda gave Emory a quelling look before turning back to Jason.

"Why didn't *you* tell me?" she demanded.

Her anger was draining away, leaving a residue of sorrow and unhappiness. Jason had deceived her from the first. All along, he could have identified the jade charm as Logan's workmanship.

"You told me how important the bracelet was to you," he said, his eyes begging her to listen with her heart as well as with her ears. "I was afraid if you knew your green pebble was an expensive piece of jade jewelry designed by Carlton Logan, you'd get the absurd idea that you might have been one of his—ah—girlfriends and had come here to kill him after he had broken off the affair. Bess told me that you and she had talked about the murder, and the newspaper stories that disclosed what a womanizer he had been. And there were the times when Tangletrees seemed familiar to you, as if you had been here before." Manda gasped in astonishment. "Oh, yes, I've been aware of that. Your pretty face is no great shakes as a secret-keeper, you know." He dared a brief, faint smile.

"Hah!" Emory grunted, in agreement with Jason for once.

"When you first came here, you felt insecure and confused," Jason continued, solemn again. "It was the amnesia, of course, but I didn't want what I knew about your jade charm to compound your self-doubt."

"Amnesia?" Sylvia uttered a totally unsophisticated squeal. "Manda has amnesia?" She fluttered a hand toward Manda, then quickly pulled it back, and stepped aside. "Oh, my dear, how simply ghastly for you!"

"It's not contagious," Manda blurted.

Before the words were out of her mouth, she was sorry. But Sylvia's supercilious attitude sometimes stretched Manda's patience beyond the bounds of amiability. And right now Manda was in no mood to be patronized. Not by a pretending Sylvia, and *definitely* not by a pitying Jason.

"I appreciate your concern, Jason. I guess." Indignation negated her statement of thanks. "But I still don't think my charm is real jade. Dr. Nils would have told me."

Jason now realized that she'd said the same thing earlier, but he'd been so caught up in devising a way to soften his covering up the truth that her exact words hadn't penetrated.

"How would Dr. Johannsen have known?" he asked.

"He owns a huge collection of jade artifacts, that's how."

Emory enlarged upon Manda's reply. "Spends every spare dollar he can get his hands on to buy the stuff. I've known him to cancel patient appointments on an hour's notice, to fly cross-country to the auction of some dead or bankrupt jade fancier's estate."

As Emory spoke, Manda witnessed puzzling changes in Jason. First he looked surprised, then disbelieving, then distracted. No . . . more alert than pensive. Suddenly his expression became totally unfathomable. She would have termed it blank, except for the cold steel-hard glitter of his eyes.

He wheeled around and strode briskly to the fireplace. Manda saw his hand *tremble* when he reached for the poker. Hot red embers sprayed out onto the hearth as he struck the charred log a vicious blow.

"Damn!" he muttered, his toe kicking the biggest chunk of smoldering charcoal back underneath the grate.

Manda watched the long deep intake of breath lift his shoulders. Slowly he replaced the poker in its stand and turned. His gaze, now as gentle as the remembered feel of his hand on her skin, met hers squarely.

"I'd like to talk to Dr. Johannsen. If you'll okay it," he added with a wry grin, which she accepted as his unstated apology for having held back information about the Logan-designed charm.

"I don't mind. But why?"

While Jason had busied himself stirring up the fire, Emory and Sylvia had drifted off to another part of the room and were engrossed in their own scenario, probably discussing Manda's amnesia. Jason threw a cautioning look in their direction, then spoke quietly.

"We know the doctor lied about what was said on your sodium pentothal session tape. Maybe he didn't realize the importance of something you *did* say." He paused. "Did you tell him about my trip to Texas?"

"No. I didn't really have a chance. I was so angry at first, when I learned he'd lied, and then he left yesterday morning as soon as he examined me and said I could get out of bed."

"Right." Jason paused again, closed his mouth, and

swallowed. "If the doctor knew what I found out in Port Aransas, and about your mother's letter, and what you've remembered so far, he might be able to make a vital connection between those facts and some thus far obscure detail he recorded during your early counseling sessions. Maybe he'll let me see your case file. My reporter's instinct could help. If I could, I'd like to prevent your having to read through the doctor's old notes and relive those bad times in the hospital and right afterward."

"You'd do that for me?" His willingness . . . no, his eagerness . . . to save her further hurt made her proud.

"Manda . . . darling . . . I'd do anything for you."

The caress in his dulcet voice reawakened her hopes and dreams, and they broke free of her wounded heart and fluttered warmly through her veins. Jason touched her lips with a fingertip. She imagined his mouth there instead, and he smiled sweetly as he divined her thoughts, her wish. His desire-clouded eyes promised her everything. Her breathing quickened.

Out of the corner of one eye, she noticed Emory walking toward them. Jason saw him, too.

"Then it's settled." Jason spoke matter-of-factly, not at all as if he'd just been making silent, motionless love to her.

"What's settled? If it involves Manda, count me in." From the controlled iciness of Emory's voice, Manda knew he had observed the emotional undercurrents between her and Jason.

Shifting nervously from one foot to the other, she avoided Emory's piercing stare. She couldn't alter her demeanor as rapidly as Jason had. Thwarted passion still hammered at her inner being. Uncertain whether her voice would sound natural, she was relieved to hear Jason respond to Emory's remarks.

"I'm going to San Luis Obispo to discuss Manda's recent remembrances with Dr. Johannsen."

"When?"

"Tomorrow morning."

"I'll go, too. Follow you in my car. Maybe I can help. I was planning to spend two or three days here with Manda, but—"

"That's the best way for you to help," Jason interrupted. "You can stay and protect her. In case the person who's been making attempts on her life should try something else, while I'm away."

"All right," Emory said. "If that's okay with you, Manda."

"Fine." She did feel vulnerable, exposed, as though she were the dot in the center of an enormous target, and her waiting unknown assailant were a champion marksman. "Fine," she repeated, as she threw Jason a grateful look and a wobbly smile.

And so it was agreed.

Chapter Eighteen

"Come in, Bess," Manda called out in response to the knock on her door.

Still in her robe, she had been gathering her soiled clothes for the housekeeper to launder, hurrying because she hoped to dress and be downstairs to see Jason, and to wish him good luck before he left for San Luis Obispo.

"It isn't Bess," Sylvia informed her. "May I still come in?"

"Of course."

Sylvia stepped . . . no, floated as always . . . through the doorway, leaving the door ajar.

"I'm sorry if I upset you yesterday," she purred as she took a seat on the side of the freshly made bed. "The amnesia thing threw me."

The ensuing lengthy silence unnerved Manda. She was uncomfortable, playing hostess to the woman Jason had loved for so many years. He was compassionate and caring and—yes, flirtatious—toward her, and for a little while she had let herself forget the passionate embrace she had witnessed at the foot of the staircase. How could she have forgotten Jason's words to Sylvia about sharing? Manda knew he liked her and worried about her mental and physical welfare, but Sylvia was his lover, and the one with whom Jason would spend the rest of his life. Manda ached with the knowledge.

"I don't quite know how to put this." Sylvia's gold-tipped fingers toyed with the bedspread fringe.

"Just say it." Manda wondered what could be bothering the golden goddess.

"All right, I will." No longer jittery after Manda's permission to speak, Sylvia looked completely in control again.

"Emory has told me how much he cares for you, and I could see that for myself. He's a nice man. Handsome. Earthy. A promoter, too. It takes one to know one, I suppose." Brittle laughter escaped from her long lovely throat. "He'll be a good provider, Manda, and with your amnesia you'll need that. You'll need a dominant husband, too, like Emory."

"I don't *need* a husband, dominant or otherwise." Manda spoke with a composure that astonished herself. Holding back the tirade of harsh words that burned deep in her very soul, she quietly added only four. "I . . . don't . . . love . . . Emory."

"But you do love Jason," Sylvia smirked.

Momentarily overcome with a devastating humiliation, Manda stared at the woman sitting regally on her bed.

Sylvia had fired her best salvo . . . and won. Manda couldn't even retreat because this room, until now her place of refuge, had become her battleground.

Two and a half weeks ago, she might have succumbed to the fleeting urge that assaulted her, the urge to cower in the bedroom closet.

But not today.

Manda lifted her chin and glared at her arrogant accuser. True, she loved Jason, but she refused to apologize for that, and somehow she would cope with the heartbreak of losing him. She did not need or want—nor would she accept—Sylvia Hathaway's pitying scorn.

During the past few minutes that had severely tested her, Manda at last gained a total, proud sense of who she was. She felt the inherited inner strength and fighting spirit of Elaine Joseph flowing like adrenalin through her veins. She would find out who killed her father and see that the culprit was punished. Then she would thank Dr. Nils for all his aid and support, get herself a job, and march fearlessly out into her shiny new world.

She would *never* marry Emory—or any other man—to gain a provider. Samantha Joseph Logan could and would provide for herself . . . and never, never settle for second best!

"Jason belongs to me," Sylvia declared with haughty triumph, "and someday soon he'll ask me to marry him. If he doesn't," she smiled smugly, "that's all right, too. We've been lovers ever since college, and—"

"Good morning, ladies."

Jason's brusque voice and blazing eyes contradicted the relaxed image of the man leaning indolently against the doorjamb.

"Jason, darling!" Sylvia leaped from the bed and

rushed—neglecting to float—to his side. "Good morning! I was just telling Manda—"

"I *heard,"* he snapped.

She stroked his arm and pointed adoringly. "Darling, you probably misunderstood—"

"I heard it all, Sylvia." He seized her placating hand and literally threw it down to her side. "I've been standing out in the hall the whole time." His mouth clamped tight.

"But, darling—"

"Stop calling me that!" he raged, unable to check his fury. "I am not your darling. I haven't been for years. If I ever was. The only *darling* of a selfish arrogant woman is herself." Jamming clenched fists into his pants pockets, his tone changed to shards of ice. "Sylvia, I've never before asked a guest to leave this inn, but I'd be most grateful if you'd pack your belongings at your earliest possible convenience and drive away from here and out of my life."

Her honey-sweet aura melted, exposing a core of naked wrath. "You are cruel!" Sylvia practically stumbled out of the room.

Manda, who had been listening and watching with dismay, felt sad for Sylvia. And for Jason.

"I'm sorry," she mumbled and slumped weak-kneed into the rocker, covering her face with both hands.

She smelled Jason's maleness and cologne, felt the brush of his suit trousers against her bare leg, heard the whoosh of his sigh as he knelt in front of her. Gently he clasped her hands and lowered them from her emotion-flushed cheeks.

"Why should you be sorry, little one?" His smile was tender, his eyes no longer frosty.

"Because I let Sylvia make me mad and we both said some unkind things to each other and you overheard us and you're sending her away and you love her and that will break your heart and—"

Jason ended her breathy nervous chatter by placing his mouth roughly over hers. He watched her eyes widen in surprise, and then close the second after ecstasy turned them a heart-stopping hazy gray. Her lips opened for him, and he hungrily sipped the sweetness inside, until he remembered why he'd kissed her. There were some matters that required straightening out. Reluctantly he lifted his mouth from hers.

"Manda, I don't love Sylvia, and my heart certainly won't break when she's gone."

Manda could hardly believe it. Jason was *smiling!*

"But you're—" She barely managed to pronounce the word, "lovers."

"We *were* lovers. Past tense." He stood up, assisted her to her feet and guided her to the bed, where they sat side by side. With the fingers of one hand interlaced with hers, he elucidated.

"I met Sylvia when we were freshmen in college, over thirteen years ago. I was a green, impressionable kid, fresh from the Indian reservation school. She was sophisticated, magnificently beautiful, and the most sought-after date on campus. I admit it, I was smitten. And I couldn't believe my luck when in our English Lit class she made me aware that she was interested in me. After we went out a few times, we did become . . . lovers." He squeezed Manda's hand, as though saying he hadn't forgotten she was there or who she was. "I naturally assumed Sylvia and I would be married. To get money for our life together, I took a proofreading job at the city newspaper. I worked there four nights a week and waited tables in the dorm dining room twice a day, and I sat up all night two nights studying. My one free night in each week, I spent with Sylvia. I was constantly sleepy, hungry, and exhausted, but for her I thought all my sacrifices were worth it.

"God, was I stupid! Just when I decided my bank account could handle a cheap apartment for us, I happened to discover that on those nights when I worked or studied, Sylvia had been dating the sons, younger brothers, and nephews of rich influential men who could further her modeling career. In order to save a few more pennies for us, I'd been depriving myself of adequate food—while she had been enticing the Big Men on Campus to wine and dine her—and possibly more!"

"How terrible for you." Manda sorrowed over the heartache of the young disillusioned Jason.

"It was at the time." Now he could chuckle at the memory. "I broke off with her, of course. And I learned a valuable lesson."

Not much of a lesson, Manda said to herself. Aloud she put it differently. "But you took her back."

"No! No, I didn't. That's what you've been thinking all this time? Manda, my sweet one, you couldn't be more wrong. Our paths crossed about a year ago, when I'd gone to New York to see my editor, and Sylvia was there on a fabric-buying trip. We just happened to stay at the same hotel. I saw her in the lobby, went over to say hello, and she invited me to have a drink with her for old times' sake. I saw no reason to decline. The next evening I took her to dinner and the theater . . . as a friend. Since then she's come here four . . . no, five . . . times." Jason shifted uncomfortably. "I suppose I knew she wanted . . . expected to renew our . . . relationship, and maybe I'm at fault for not being up front with her from the very first. But I didn't want to hurt her feelings. Or damage her ego. She was, after all, a paying guest of the inn. What I hoped was that she'd eventually give up and go chase another man."

"That's why you kissed her," Manda stated sarcastically, as she loosened her fingers from his.

"Ah! You did see us. And you dropped the phone." Jason caught her chin with one hand and forced her to look straight into his twinkling eyes. He wore that mischievous little boy smile again. "Usually a gentleman doesn't kiss and tell. But in this case—Manda, *she* kissed *me*. Sylvia had just been informed that she won a national award for her wedding gown designs. I gave her a hug and told her I was glad she'd shared the news with me. She . . . took advantage of the situation to—. I didn't hear you come into the corridor, but I'm sure now that Sylvia heard you. She staged that whole scene for your benefit."

"She must be a lonely, unhappy woman," Manda deduced, pity saddening her features.

"And you . . . are an unbelievably wonderful one," Jason murmured in her ear. Lightly he kissed the tip of her nose, both of her blushing cheeks, and then her beckoning, waiting mouth. He stood up, groaning at the necessity to leave her.

"More of this later," he promised solemnly as he tapped her chin with his forefinger. "For now, I'm going to San Luis Obispo."

He had traversed half the length of the upstairs hall before Manda remembered.

"Good luck," she whispered, staring across the room that felt suddenly very bleak and empty.

Chapter Nineteen

An hour after Jason's departure, Manda and Emory sat on a warm dry boulder, high up on the beach. He'd listened intently while she told him the gist of her mother's letter, and about the "awareness" episodes at the inn that started her to remembering: how she'd known the hazards of the entrance road before traveling it; how she almost went into the wrong blue room: how she'd envisioned the Monterey cypress trees that once had grown where the parking lot now stood. Lastly, she recounted her first actual remembering, the recognition of her mother's paintings in Jason's office.

"I wish I hadn't lost them," she ended wistfully.

"But you haven't."

"They belong to Jason now." After a deep breath, she licked her lips and tasted salt from the spindrift.

"No. They don't. The paintings, the inn, this beach—it all belongs to you. To Carlton Logan's daughter."

As the waves slapped and swished, Emory watched

the changing emotions on her face: shock, comprehension, joy. His jubilant whoop reverberated across the water and against the cliff behind them.

"You own it all!" he rejoiced.

"Yes, I do. I remember now. Carlton told me, that last weekend," she said in a soft, faraway voice. "He was going to change his will, identifying me and declaring me his legal heir."

Suddenly she experienced another one of those two-of-Manda sensations. On the normal level, she shared with Emory his pleasure over her good fortune. On the dreamlike plane, she stood to one side, observing that other, happy girl with a strange regret, hearing the troubled voice of her father.

I trust you to take care of it, Samantha. Always. If people knew our secret, they would forever destroy the natural beauty of Tangletrees.

What was Carlton talking about? What secret? Take care of what?

"I don't understand," Manda said aloud to the ghostly presence in her head. "Please. Make me understand."

"Make you understand what?" Emory came up behind her. "You look positively spooky. Are you okay?"

She shuddered violently. The ethereal Manda—and the beseeching Carlton—had vanished.

"I . . . I'm not sure. I thought I remembered . . ."

Emory stared at her, a baffling expression in his blue eyes.

"You're cold," he said finally. "Let's walk back up to the house, find you a sweater, and go for a ride, get you away from this depressing place."

"We can't. Remember what Bess told us? Jason left

instructions that under no circumstances am I to leave the premises before he returns."

"I don't take orders from Tallfeather," Emory growled.

"No, but yesterday you told him you'd stay here while he was gone."

"I said I'd protect you. I can do that in my car."

"No. If we left, it could cause trouble for Bess and Clive, and I don't want to do that."

In exasperation Emory rolled his eyes entreatingly up toward the sky. A four-letter expletive hissed from his mouth, followed by, "Damn nosey old watchdog!"

Manda looked where he pointed.

Clive, his feet planted widely apart, his arms akimbo, peered down at them from the rim of the towering embankment. Apparently the inn's caretaker believed in the literal interpretation of his employer's admonition to watch over Manda. His behavior might have been amusing, were it not so dear.

"Clive!" Manda shouted. "Stand back from the edge!" Softer, she worried to Emory. "It could crumble and send him to his death."

Clive retreated a couple of steps, but reassumed his on-guard stance.

"You care more for a servant than you do for me," Emory complained.

"That's not true, Emory." Manda sighed. His unreasonable jealousy, no longer annoying, simply bored her.

"Well, you can be a prisoner here all afternoon if you want to let Tallfeather boss you around," Emory said. "Me, I'm on vacation, and I'm going to drive up the coast, maybe as far as Point Lobos."

"All right. Have a nice day," she urged with genuine sincerity.

Emory snorted and trounced off toward the cliffside steps.

Jason stopped for lunch at a McDonald's on the outskirts of the college town. Thanks to the directions Wade had given him, he had no difficulty finding Dr. Johannsen's pretentious, pale pink stucco house with the traditional Spanish red-tiled roof. He parked his car at the curb, stepped out, and traversed the pink flagstone walk that bisected a lawn of vivid green winter grass, symmetrically landscaped with hibiscus, oleanders, and dwarf palm trees. Like the doctor, the landscaping of his front yard was regimented and off-putting.

Under the shaded arched passageway, Jason rang the doorbell and waited.

In a few seconds, the deeply carved door swung outward to reveal a short, graying blonde in her sixties, slightly overweight and amply endowed.

"Yes?" she asked curtly. Her brows almost met above her nose in a frown.

"Good afternoon. My name is Jason Tallfeather. I don't have an appointment with the doctor, but it's important that I speak with him."

"Come in."

As he followed her into a sunless room furnished with massive antiques, his heels thumped on the bare wax-darkened floor.

"You're the owner of the inn where Manda's staying," the woman said.

"Right. And you must be Mrs. Hendricks."

"She told you about me?" she asked as a pleased smile suddenly brightened her stern visage.

"Yes. She's quite fond of you. She talked about you a lot." Jason hesitated, then restated his purpose. "If I could see Dr. Johannsen?"

"I'm sorry. He's not here. He's been away all weekend." She noted the flicker of dismay on the visitor's face. "Is Manda ill? Or . . . or very upset? Is that why you came?"

"Oh, no," he hastened to reassure her. "Manda is fine. In fact, she's remembering new things every day."

"I'm so glad." Now she understood. "That's what you want to discuss with Dr. Nils, Manda's remembering her past."

Jason turned to go. "If you would please tell him I was here—"

"He'll be back this afternoon. Maybe soon." The doctor might not approve of her volunteering the information, but Mrs. Hendricks wanted to do her bit to help that sweet girl.

"Oh?" Jason faced the housekeeper again, his eyes alight with renewed expectation.

"Last night he phoned from Santa Maria, told me he had a very early appointment this morning and would come straight home as soon as he finished."

"I see. He's on the hospital staff there, too."

"Oh, no. This was personal business, he said."

"If you really think he'll be home before too long, I'd like to wait."

"I think that's a fine idea," Mrs. Hendricks decided. "I'll show you to his study."

She quickly led the way along the dim corridor to a

room on the opposite end of the house. Jason noticed that the lavishly furnished study opened onto the arcade and fronted a wing that jutted toward the rear of the lot.

"Would you like some coffee, Mr. Tallfeather? Or a little wine, perhaps?"

"No, ma'am, but thank you anyway."

"If that's all I can do for you, I'll go back to my soap opera." And she hastened from the room.

Alone, Jason settled into a butternut leather armchair at the end of the enormous bleached oak desk. The tall surrealist wood sculpture standing in one corner, and the muted rainbow colors splashed and splotched on the huge canvas between the built-in wall units, may have been chosen to put the psychiatrist's patients at ease, but their spell didn't work on Jason. He merely fidgeted. After a few minutes, he sauntered over to the bookcase and perused the rows of complex medical titles of expensive leather-bound tomes.

"Depressing," he grunted.

Then the file cabinets caught his attention.

Why not? he rationalized the urge that jittered his fingers. In all likelihood, Dr. Johannsen would show him Manda's case history; if he looked at it now, he'd be prepared to discuss its contents with the doctor when he arrived, thus saving them both time.

Pulling open the drawer labeled *Ga thru Lu,* he quickly located the folder marked 'Lethe, M.' He sat in the doctor's brown leather swivel chair and spread the contents of the folder on the desk's surface.

Jason scanned a copy of Manda's records from the hospital in Paso Robles. Beneath them were Manda's admission and release forms from the local mental health clinic where she had briefly been a patient before she moved into the doctor's home. Next came a sheaf of pages of Dr. Johannsen's engraved stationery.

Jason examined every sheet of paper carefully.

From the medical institutions' records he learned what Manda had already told him. The notes on the doctor's letterhead were something else again. It wasn't the fact that they revealed any as-yet-undisclosed secrets that bothered Jason. The disturbing factor was what they did not reveal.

He saw tabulated columns listing the date, the day of the week, and the hour of what he assumed to be the schedule of Manda's therapy sessions over a period of fourteen months. The final date was almost five months old.

Jason's index finger followed each typed entry across the page to the right-hand side, where he perused the barely legible, cryptic scrawls, comments like *no progress* or *nonproductive* or *no new information.*

"I don't believe this!" Jason exploded, slamming a fist on the desk.

He leaped from the chair, stomped across the carpet to the still-open file drawer. Thumbing at random through the folders, Jason discovered copious notes, pages full of psychological terms he didn't understand. But one thing he did understand.

In every other case history, Johannsen had entered lengthy treatment details, but Manda's file was a complete psychiatric blank.

Jason's mouth clamped shut in a tight thin line. Cheek muscles quivered with the clenching of his jaws. In his eyes, a jet fury blazed. He jerked a pocketknife out of his pants pocket and, feeling absolutely no compunction, used the tip of the thin blade to pick the lock on the deep side drawer of Johannsen's desk.

The front panel dropped forward on hinges to reveal a unique arrangement of stacked sliding shelves filled with cassette tapes, each one tabbed with an individual's name and initial. Jason's questing finger located the *L*'s: Lassiter, W.; Lemmon, D.; Lester, P.; Levy, H., Martin, J. He stopped, then backtracked and double-checked to make sure Manda's tape hadn't been filed in the wrong sequence.

"Damn!"

Since the *L* tapes occupied the back row on that particular shelf, Jason thought perhaps Manda's had dropped down behind the entire sliding unit. He wriggled his long nimble fingers between the cabinet's floor and the bottom shelf of tapes, all the way to the rear panel. There! He'd touched a smooth plastic case. Fingertips hooking behind it, he tugged. He tried a second time, with the same lack of success. Finally, using the point of his pocketknife, he managed to loosen the masking tape holding the container in place. Slowly he eased it out.

The cassette bore no identification, but every nerve and sinew in Jason's tense body attested to what this was. The tape of the sodium pentothal session that Dr. Johannsen had never played back for Manda. Jason inserted it in the recorder on the desk and pressed the play button. While he waited, his heart thundered against his ribs.

The tiny disks rotated quietly for at least five minutes. Jason had almost concluded that his instincts—or his hopes—had tricked him when Dr. Johannsen's treble voice, low and calming, put an end to the expectant silence.

"It's all right, Manda. There is nothing for you to fear . . . Tell me. Where are you?"

"Tangletrees . . . Oh, it's so beautiful!"

"What is beautiful? What do you see?"

"The ocean . . . the surf."

"Tangletrees is a place near the ocean?"

"Yes. A house . . . Carlton's house."

"Carlton is your friend?"

"No . . . He's nicer than I expected."

"Who is?"

"Carlton . . . Carlton Logan."

Ten seconds passed before the doctor posed the next question.

"Can you tell me why you are there? At Tangletrees?"

"Yes. We came to . . . Oh! It's all dark."

"What is dark?"

"The workshop. There's no light . . . But the door's open. . . . There's a flashlight on the floor. I can see the beam . . . shining . . . red . . . Blood! It's blood! . . . Oh, God! Why did we come here? . . . I didn't intend . . ."

After a click, Jason heard only the faint whir of the rewinding tape. One hand gripping the padded chair arm, he listened until with a second click the recorder shut itself off.

He sat dumbfounded, then appalled. Why hadn't the doctor shared with Manda the few facts brought out in the session and helped her to recall more? The unexplained pause in the middle of the tape clearly indicated to Jason that the doctor had recognized the name Carlton Logan. He must have recalled that the jewelry designer had been murdered. Why didn't Dr. Johannsen notify the authorities?

Why indeed?

At last, the puzzle pieces fit . . . and Jason's hand, shaking almost beyond his control, brushed the cold sweat off his forehead.

"Jesus God Almighty." The whispered words composed a prayer, not a curse.

Without taking the time to replace the cassette or Manda's file, or to close the gaping drawers, Jason rushed through the study's private exit onto the arcade. He stopped for a moment, sucking in breaths of the fresh, heavenly air. The room he'd just left, in those last terrible seconds, had smelled to him of fiery, burning brimstone.

Where was the doctor, really? Would he arrive home soon, as he'd informed his housekeeper, or was he at this very minute driving toward Tangletrees?

Jason desperately wanted to sprint along the flagstone walk, but he forced himself to move at a normal pace, lest he attract Mrs. Hendricks's attention.

With uncharacteristic clumsiness, he climbed into the car and started the engine. His heartbeat pounded so loudly in his ears, he barely heard the squealing protest of tires as he sped away from the curb.

He *had* to get to Manda before Johannsen did!

Chapter Twenty

After Emory's ill-tempered departure, Manda wandered restlessly through the house. Would her old records reveal to Jason or Dr. Nils a clue to something she hadn't remembered so far? Optimistic one minute, dejected the next, she finally elected to utilize the seemingly endless hours by transcribing the remainder of Jason's fifth chapter.

The skin on the back of her neck prickled. Someone was watching her. Raising her eyes from the typed page, Manda beheld Jason, his tall broad body filling the office doorway. She began a smile and a cheery greeting. Both disappeared with a gasp. A weakening dread squeezed her heart as somber black eyes looked deeply into hers. His grave, unhappy countenance warned her that smiles and gay lilting words couldn't delay or alter the bad news he'd brought her.

"I can take it." Softly she spoke her determined courage. "I have to, don't I?"

"Yes, I guess you do." He paused, sighed, then went on with a grim forbidding air. "I'm going to say . . . what I have to say only once, so please don't interrupt.

I'll answer your questions later. If I can. All right?"

Manda nodded her bright chestnut head, her gray eyes mirroring the distress she perceived in Jason's.

"I didn't see Dr. Johannsen," he began.

"Then why . . . ? How . . . ?"

His waving hand silenced her surprised stammering.

"No interruptions, remember?" For an instant the flicker of a smile softened the tension on his face, before he dropped tiredly into his swivel chair. "Johannsen hasn't been home since he left here early Sunday morning. Mrs. Hendricks was expecting him today, so she let me wait in his study. I . . . did find your records."

Briefly he explained about the "nothing" file, so different from the other detailed ones, and how, as a result, he felt compelled to search further.

"I broke into the locked drawer of Johannsen's desk." He ignored Manda's squeak of amazement. "And discovered your truth drug session tape."

He hesitated, wishing he could stop the recitation right here. *I can take it,* she'd said. Jason devoutly hoped so. He knew she was brave and possessed emotional stamina, but this—

"Tell me," Manda insisted, her voice tight and uneasy.

Verbatim Jason quoted the taped dialogue, words that had stuck in his brain, poisonous darts piercing his heart's bull's-eye. The *I didn't intend . . .* hung in the silence, vibrating like a discord on a violin string.

In Manda's ghost-white face, her eyes widened and her mouth gaped open. Short rapid breaths moved her small pointed breasts up and down. Fiercely her hands clutched the folds of the green and blue plaid skirt.

Jason, worried and helpless, waited and watched.

At last Manda spoke, her words hushed, grating. "He knew all the time, but he never told me. He could have helped me! He let me go through—I *hate* him!" She gulped the sob rising in her throat. "Why did he do it, Jason? *Why?*"

Jason stood, walked on quick silent feet to her side, gently raised her out of the chair, and pulled her close to his chest. Softly, like a benediction, he kissed the top of her curly head. With her question echoing in his ears and with his heart breaking for her, he told her why.

"Because he . . . murdered Carlton Logan."

One gigantic tremor shook Manda's body, then she took a step backward and looked up into Jason's stricken face.

"I . . . I'm all right, Jason. And don't you feel guilty. You didn't want to tell me. You had to. Please don't be so upset."

She was comforting *him?* Jason had never loved her more than at that moment. Her sensitivity and courage made his heart swell with pride.

"What . . . what will Dr. Nils do now? Where . . . is he?" Manda raked angrily at a traitorous tear that escaped her eye and started down one cheek.

"I thought he might be here. *When* and *if* he returns home, he'll learn from Mrs. Hendricks that I was there. Then he'll discover the desk and file drawers standing open, and he'll break every speed law on the books to get here."

"To . . . to try again to . . . to kill me." She shuddered. How could this . . . this horror be happening to her?

"Oh, no, darling, I don't think so." Jason's fingertip tenderly removed another tear. "When he talks to us and realizes he can't lie his way out of everything, he'll surrender to the authorities. Johannsen's no fool. He'll hire a hotshot defense attorney and get off with a light sentence." He added with some satisfaction, "But he'll never be able to practice medicine again."

Manda nodded her head, accepting Jason's explanation.

"I'm going up to my room now," she decided. "I need to be by myself for a while."

"Of course. But let me or one of the Meechers know where you are every minute."

"You *do* still feel I may be in danger!" The layers of her shock and resentment cracked, exposing a core of pure, dead-black fright.

"I just want you to be careful." He could see that his adoring smile calmed her somewhat. "Don't worry," he added confidently. "Wade and I can overpower Johannsen, should the need arise."

"Emory drove up to Point Lobos."

"He left you alone? He promised me he'd—"

"Jason, I *am* alone." Her bitterness rocked the depths of Jason's soul. "My mother died, and the man who's been pretending for nearly two years to . . . care for me like a father ki—killed my real one."

Her faltering pronouncement concluded, Manda stiffened her backbone, inhaled a single ragged breath, and marched robotlike from the office.

In the privacy of her room, she flung herself on the bed and wept into the pillow to smother her racking sobs. Gradually the warring emotions of despair for herself and loathing for Dr. Nils called a truce, leaving Manda drained of her last ounce of energy. She lay quiet, her treadmilling mind still spinning with what Dr. Nils had done.

After the taped session had disclosed that she'd been here at the time of the murder, Dr. Nils had kept her on a tight rein of rigid supervision. Until she stopped here the night of the fog. She'd slipped the leash and without knowing it, was running free in the last place in the world Dr. Nils wanted her to be. Manda recalled the doctor's orders never to drive the coastal highway alone, and his attempted cover-up of the inn's existence, even after she'd pointed out to him the small, unobtrusive roadside sign.

When, against his wishes, she chose to stay at the inn for a while longer, he sabotaged her car brakes, or had someone do it for him. That incident didn't kill her, nor did it scare her into returning to his home and control. So on the day she drove to Hearst Castle, he made, or paid for, a second attempt on her life.

After she recognized her mother's paintings and called Dr. Nils from Jason's office, he realized that the once-familiar Tangletrees scene was triggering her memory. He rushed up here to learn what she had remembered. Then he encountered Jason's repudiation of his Sandy Springs lie and Manda's anger and distrust. His oh-so-neatly tied plans over the past two years, to keep her from remembering that he was her father's murderer, were unravelling.

The cornered killer turned desperate.

He must have been watching and followed her out into the fog and down the cliffside steps, where he struck her on the head, then carried her to the rocks and left her there, knowing she couldn't swim. No wonder he hadn't answered Jason's urgent knock on his door. He hadn't yet managed to sneak from the beach back into his bedroom.

But what on earth had been his motive for killing Carlton?

Rolling over onto her back, Manda closed her eyes in an effort to recreate what she had seen in the workshop on the last night of her father's life. She tried hard to envision the doctor's face, lighted for only a few seconds by the flashlight beam as he stooped over her father's battered body. Instead, her emotion-flogged brain conjured up a frenetic video close-up of Carlton's face, laughing wildly at first, and then repeating again and again, "You're my daughter! You're my daughter! You're my—"

Manda cried herself to sleep, finding a much deserved respite from the ghastly truths she'd confronted during the past hour and a half.

Chapter Twenty-one

Manda was never sure whether what occurred was a dream, or the instant replay of a surfacing memory at the moment of awakening.

Curtains of mauve, salmon pink, and fading gold folded across the westerly sky as she and Carlton ambled along the beach. It was the Sunday of their second weekend at Tangletrees, and he planned to return to the City early tomorrow. Carlton stopped, bent over to pick up a long straight piece of driftwood, and began to draw lines in the hard-packed sand, identifying them as he made the cuts.

"Here's the path from the house to the cliff, and this is the one that follows the curvature of the cliff all the way to my workshop." He had drawn a square for the small building. "These tiny circles are the Monterey cypress." Next, he depicted the ravine as a funnel, resting upside down on the rim of the embankment. Then, angling off from the tube of the funnel near the cypress grove, Carlton gouged a deep thin triangle, its point almost touching the workshop.

"What's that?" Manda had asked, peering up at the actual area his crude map described. "I don't see anything except bushes and tall dead grass."

Tossing the stick to the ground, Carlton smiled down at her, his hazel eyes full of pride and, strangely, of anxiety.

"I insisted we take this stroll before dark," he told her, "because for some reason I feel I can't postpone telling you."

"Telling me what?" The stern expression on his face alarmed her. "Carlton, you're scaring me. A little."

"I don't mean to, Baby." Sometimes when he evidenced a sentimental streak, he called her Baby, which made Manda feel sublimely cherished.

"It's just that this is very important to me." Carlton paused and expanded his chest with a breath of the salty air. The toe of a brown loafer thoroughly erased the marks in the sand. One freckled hand pointed toward the open mouth of the ravine. "There, under my land, under what will be your land someday, lies a vein of the rarest jade in the world."

Manda stared disbelievingly up at her father's serious face.

"Jade? The beautiful green stone the ancient Chinese carved into statues? Mums showed me a jade dragon once in a Houston art gallery. She said it was very, very expensive."

Carlton laughed with delight at her simplistic remarks. Sobering quickly, he shared with his sole heir the discovery of his treasure.

"I found it purely by accident, after a week of uncommonly heavy rains. The torrential runoff from the hills had loosened the tree roots and grasses, and the ravine wall had crumbled, uncovering a narrow slab of greenish stone. Everything I knew about where jade deposits are located kept me from believing what I saw. I chipped off a piece, about half the size of my thumb, and took it to my appraiser. He confirmed that the sample was jade of a quality similar to that found in Burma.

"I knew if word of my discovery leaked out, speculators and collectors ranging from weekend rockhounds to mining company tycoons would overrun this section of the coast. The wildlife, the beauty, the peace of Tangletrees would be spoiled. I'd have neither the finances nor the power to stop it. Even if the vein proved to be inconsiderable in size, which I suspect, the irreversible damage to the land would already have been done."

"How awful," Manda murmured.

"With no hesitancy and no regret, I decided to cover the jade. I didn't even use any of it for my custom-made jewelry. I put the appraised fragment into a small unmarked envelope in my safe deposit box. It would still be there, except that I wanted my long-lost daughter to have a special, one-of-a-kind gift from her father. So, it now hangs on the charm bracelet I gave you, along with the key and medallion that came from Elaine."

"I'll treasure my bracelet and charms forever."

"I rebuilt the eroded embankment by myself," Carlton continued. "It took days. For ballast I hauled boulders up from the beach and gravel from the meadow behind the house. With a shovel I piled and packed the soil a lot deeper over the jade than it had been before. When I finished the job, I had blistered, bleeding hands and a wrenched back, and the absolute relief of knowing my secret was safe.

"Since we came here, two weeks ago, I've seen how you share my love for the ocean and the shore line. I trust you to take care of it, Samantha. Always. If people knew our secret, they would forever destroy the natural beauty of Tangletrees. No treasure—not even the one hidden here—could compensate for that loss. Remember that, Samantha."

But she had forgotten. Within a few hours, Carlton Logan was dead, and Samantha Joseph remembered nothing.

Manda, wide-awake now in the second blue room she'd slept in at Tangletrees, at last knew why Dr. Nils had killed her father.

The jade. Somehow the doctor had learned of Carlton's find, and the lure of a California vein of the rarest transparent emerald quality had been too much for Dr. Nils to resist. Perhaps he had come here to discuss buying the property, and the two men had quarreled and fought, with the slaying having been accidental. Or even in self-defense. Because, knowing Carlton, Manda understood how he might well have threatened the life of someone who intended to make public the jade's whereabouts.

Manda recalled . . . relived the emotions that had assailed her that terrible night. Astonishment, horror, panic, and a fright that defied description. But what she actually saw or heard in the workshop still remained a blur.

Soon, when she looked into the murderer's face, the phantom would dissolve into the doctor's human form, and she would remember everything.

Manda dreaded it—her heartbeat accelerated at the prospect—but her future couldn't be completely happy until her past freed itself of its mental encumbrances. During the last two weeks, she'd proved she could cope with whatever lay ahead. If her courage needed a boost, Jason would be standing by. He did care for her. How much, of course, constituted the *X* in her happiness equation.

Suddenly her musing took a sharp new turn. She must tell Jason about the jade deposit before Dr. Nils's arrival. Then he would know the motive for the doctor's crime.

Not for a moment did Manda worry that Jason would disclose Carlton's secret. He too nurtured the beauty and isolation of Tangletrees. People who required emergency accommodations, as she had, or those who came back again and again because they appreciated the inn's quiet natural setting, embodied the only customers Jason welcomed. No, he would never allow Tangletrees to be despoiled. He would keep her promise to her father.

Glancing out the window, Manda noticed Emory's car nosing into the space next to hers on the parking lot. He would be seeking her out. If she expected to have a private few words with Jason, she would have to hurry. She rushed down the stairs and glanced into the empty living room. Murmuring voices drifted down the hall. Just before Manda reached the open office doorway, she heard Clive's query.

"What if Manda knew before about the jade underneath the parking lot?"

Her sneaker soles slid to a quick skidding stop.

"If she did, and if she remembers it, I'll think of

something," came Jason's reply.

Manda backed up three slow soundless steps. Then she wheeled around and moved rapidly away from the study. By the time she reached the kitchen, she was running.

Running away from Jason, who had always been aware of the jade and had constructed the parking.lot to conceal its location! No wonder he so desperately wanted to own the inn. He planned to "discover" the vein after the final purchase and become an enormously wealthy man.

Manda was now sure that he'd recognized her from the first, and had offered her a job to keep her here until he delved into her relationship with the prior owner of Tangletrees. The Arizona and Texas searches for her identity were prompted by the same need, to find out how much, if anything, she knew about the jade.

Maybe *Jason* had committed the murder and schemed to make Dr. Nils appear guilty!

Oh, God! Is there NOBODY I can trust?

Manda dashed through the kitchen and outside.

Bess called from the pantry, "What's wrong, Manda? Did something frighten you?"

Manda pretended not to hear. Bess, by her own admission, would do anything on earth for Jason. Would she harm the one person who stood between him and untold wealth?

I must be mad, to be thinking so crazy.

Nothing made sense. Her jigsaw memories were suddenly blown out of proportion, the pieces overlapping and misshapen.

With inhuman effort she focused her sight and

her hopes on Emory, who squatted beside a wheel of his car.

Bess gazed after Manda, then strode briskly down the corridor and entered the office. Without waiting for Jason to finish what he was saying to her husband, she demanded, "What have you two done to scare Manda out of her wits?"

"Where did you see her?" Jason wanted to know, instantly alert.

"Tearing through my kitchen as though Satan himself was after her."

"When?"

"Just before I came in here."

"She came from this direction?"

"I heard her footsteps all the way down the hall. Didn't you?"

"We were talking about the jade," Jason suddenly recalled. "I should have told her about it. Damn! Don't you see? Now she's afraid of *me!*"

He raced from the room, leaving Bess and Clive staring at one another.

While Manda hurried along the path to the parking lot, she heard the hum of a car's engine. Through a gap between the trees on the hill, she caught a fleeting glimpse of Dr. Nils's silvery Continental.

She walked faster. Whether the man who had tried three times to kill her was Dr. Nils or Jason, Emory would protect her.

Brandishing a tire iron, Emory banged violently on

the already badly dented hubcap which stubbornly refused to budge. Spitting out a continuous stream of curses, he didn't hear Manda's approach.

A near-hysterical laugh rose in her throat, but it died there. This seemed to be her afternoon for sneaking up on people. First Jason and Clive, and now Emory.

He sensed her presence and looked up. His eyes were wild and glassy, his face a hideous, unfamiliar mask of frustration and rage.

No. It was hideous, but not unfamiliar.

Manda had seen that same, exact face once before. Not in the daylight, but eerily illuminated from below, by a flashlight's beam.

The picture in her memory was clear, real, mesmerizing.

She had stepped inside a small squarish building containing vises and odd-looking power tools bolted to work benches. The blond man who had stared up at her with crazed blue eyes, his mouth contorted in an ugly grimace, was bending over another man's inert rag doll body. His upraised hand had clutched not a tire iron, but a huge fire engine red mallet. Even in the dim glow of the flashlight, Manda could see that the mallet was covered with a darker shade of red. Blood red. The darker shade of death.

Emory had murdered her father!

Manda, paralyzed by shock and revulsion, simply stood there, looking down at Emory's upturned malevolent countenance.

Finally he spoke. "So you know." Slowly he straightened up.

Time after time, Emory had warned her that someday her readable honest face would get her into serious trouble. *Well, now it has,* she thought.

Horror gripped her. She turned to flee, but Emory grabbed her arm. He viciously twisted it behind her back, and she cried out from the excruciating pain.

Jason had plummeted out the kitchen door, excitedly calling Manda's name. At her outcry, he halted momentarily.

"That's right, Tallfeather," Emory shouted. "You stop right there." With his free hand, he raised the tire iron in a threatening gesture above Manda's head. "Last time, the driftwood didn't do the job, but this iron will crush her skull like an egg."

"The way . . . you killed . . . Carlton . . . with the hammer?" Manda grunted after each few words, whenever Emory tugged on her wrenched arm.

Aware that she might goad Emory into hitting her, she was nevertheless driven by a need, greater than her fear, to know everything that had happened that night two years ago in the workshop.

"That's right, Baby," he snarled. "See, Baby? Now I can call you Baby whenever I please."

He let the tire iron drop, and it clanged like a bell when it hit the cement.

Jason, when he saw the tire iron fall, took two running strides along the path before he noticed the gun.

Emory had pulled a pistol from beneath the elastic waistband of his cream-colored jeans, where it had been hidden under his loose shirt tail.

Jason stopped again. He heard Clive's alarmed intake of breath behind him as he, too, spied the weapon in Wade's hand.

"Go back and call the sheriff," Jason ordered quietly.

"And an ambulance. And stay inside with Bess."

From out of the corner of his eye, Jason watched as Dr. Johannsen braked his car several feet short of the turn-in to the parking lot. The man had done some reprehensible things, but he hadn't beat Carlton Logan to death.

Emory Wade had done it.

That had to be the reason for what was happening to Manda. Somehow, within the last few minutes, she had suddenly remembered *seeing* him do it, so now—Emory was holding her captive and insanely yelling "Baby!" at the top of his lungs.

If he, Jason, had told Manda earlier about the jade, the overheard conversation between him and Clive wouldn't have sent her flying to Wade for help. And straight into mortal danger.

The police would never arrive in time!

And Dr. Johannsen had left his car and disappeared up the wooded slope. Was the doctor running away from the violence, or hoping to enlist the aid of some passerby on the highway?

In either case, Jason knew it was up to him, and him alone, to save Manda from that screeching lunatic.

Wade, beginning to move again, had apparently decided upon a plan of action.

Chapter Twenty-two

Manda bit her lip to keep from screaming. Each time Emory shouted "Baby!" in her ear, he re-tightened his brutal grip on her arm. Trying to forget the agony in her shoulder and elbow, she concentrated on learning the reason for his heinous crime.

"Tell me why," she managed to say quickly between jerks on her arm.

"Baby! Baby! Baby!"

Emory had gone stark raving mad. Or had he always been mentally flawed? Maybe Dr. Nils could explain it to her. If she lived through this.

She blinked away the tears that blurred her vision, and over her shoulder watched with a kind of detached astonishment as Dr. Nils got out of his car and hurried away through the trees.

Emory, still restraining her with the hammerlock, propelled her ahead of him as he shuffled across the expanse of concrete. Twice her feet slipped out from under her, when he kicked her heels because she wouldn't move fast enough, and she would have fallen except that he held her up by her tormented arm. The racking pain nauseated her. She took deep breaths with her mouth open, and the sickness eased a bit.

Although she continued to stumble as Emory's thighs bumped hers from behind to shove her along, her traction improved slightly when they reached the dirt path. After a few more cruel, lifting pulls on her arm, she worked out a sort of rhythm, taking a quick mincing step at the moment he tensed to make another stride. Wait, step, wait, step. It was awkward, but at least his repugnant body didn't touch hers as closely with every step.

He'd stopped screaming. Now and then he chortled to himself.

Softly, with as much normalcy as she could muster, she asked him, "Emory, why did you kill my father?"

"I didn't *know* he was your father!" His defensive tone was the whine of a pouting child.

"Of course, you didn't," she appeased him. "But why did you—ah—hurt him?"

"He wouldn't tell me where the treasure was," he whimpered.

The jade. That damnable jade! If she got out of this alive, she never wanted to hear the word *jade* again.

"How did you know about the j—the treasure?" She missed a step and knew a blessed relief when he didn't wrest her arm. Briefly, his mind had focused on something other than the pleasure of causing her pain.

"I heard you and him talking about it," Emory said. "On the beach. I couldn't hear much, though. Later that night, in the shed, I kept asking him and asking him, 'Where's the treasure? Where's the treasure?' He wouldn't tell me, so I hit him. And then I hit him some more."

He sounded *proud!* Of bludgeoning to death a human being he didn't even know. Emory's conscience, if ever he had one, was as dead as Carlton.

"You didn't know about the treasure before you came here?" she asked, bewildered anew. Then why had he come?

"I knew he had jewels!" Again the petulant little-boy voice.

"You knew he had jewels?" What was he talking about?

Emory took her along the pathway that followed the cliff's rim, toward the spot where jagged boulders came right up to the embankment, where this morning they'd sat together. Would he shove her over the edge, or shoot her?

"I read an article in a lapidary journal," he said. "It was about this famous jewelry designer. It told how he made some of the rings and necklaces himself. It claimed he sold them for thousands of dollars apiece." He went on in a singsong fashion. "It said he had a workshop near his isolated weekend house. It told how he was rich, and he had lots of jewels."

"So you found out where his hideaway was," she prompted.

"No. I found out where he lived, and I followed him from there to here. I wanted to be rich."

He stopped suddenly and relaxed the hammerlock. She moaned when the blood rushed agonizingly back into her shoulder. At the sound he grabbed the wrist of the throbbing arm and turned her to face him.

He bore little resemblance to the Emory she had known. This evil, demented person lasciviously delighted in his wickedness.

"You were here that whole weekend?" Manda asked in stunned amazement.

"Camping out in my car up in the woods. I watched you with my binoculars. You walked on the beach and sat in the living room in front of the fire. The first time you both left the house, I went inside and searched everywhere. Not one ruby or diamond. I couldn't even find a wall safe. And you never wore any jewelry except that cheap charm bracelet."

"It is not cheap!" she protested.

In retaliation he almost jerked her tortured arm out of the shoulder socket. "You shut up!"

He pointed the gun at her. The hole in the barrel looked like a huge black pipe into which she might be sucked to disappear forever.

"*You* know where the treasure is," he said, "and you're going to show me. Then we'll get married, and I'll own half of it. Later on, I'm going to kill you, and then I'll have your half."

"You've already tried to kill me three times," she whispered.

And next time he would really do it. She wished he would hurry up and get it over with, because she couldn't stand much more of this pain and terror.

"I had to get you away from this place," he said. "I messed up your brakes to scare you away, but it didn't work. I borrowed a buddy's car and followed you and pushed the loosened urn off the railing. You dodged, damn you, you *dodged!* Then I had to take the car back. Next thing I knew, you started to remember things. You told the doc about it on the phone. I listened in. If you kept on remembering, you'd know I ki—how I hurt the man with the jewels. I put you out on those rocks and drove home to wait for someone to call me and tell me that you'd drowned. But *you* called, and I told you I'd been watching the late-late movie." His cackling laugh was spine-chilling. "I tried to stop you from remembering. But now you know. And you have to marry me, so I'll be rich."

"I *won't* marry you!" she shrieked. "Never, never, *never!*"

"Yes, you will, Baby." The weapon must have been getting heavy, because his gun hand dropped to his side. The leer on his face scared her more, if possible, than the pistol had. "And maybe, if you perform all of your wifely duties in a way that pleases me, maybe I'll let you live a little while."

Manda had only the vaguest notion of what his perverted list of wifely duties included, but the malicious, lewd expression on his face horrified her. She would rather die this instant than give herself to him.

"The treasure," Emory reminded her, his voice like warped rusty metal. "Tell me where it is, Manda Baby. Now. Or you're dead."

He slung her around, and she was able to see the path along which he'd dragged her.

Jason was closing the gap between him and them. He raised a silencing finger to his lips. Manda's gray eyes, looking past Emory's shoulder, suddenly widened and brightened at the chance, however slight, of being extricated from this nightmare.

Emory saw the hopefulness flicker across her reflective features. He flung her to the ground, stamped one foot hard on her still-benumbed hand to prevent her escape, and wheeled to confront Jason.

She heard the click as Emory cocked the pistol. He

leveled it at Jason, and a wave of inestimable despair washed over her. At that range Emory couldn't possibly miss.

Jason had to live! If he died, her life forever afterward would be a worthless nothing.

"Don't shoot him!" she begged. "Oh, Emory, please don't! I'll tell you where the treasure is. I'll marry you. You can have everything, do anything you want to me. Only please, *please,* don't hurt Jason! I promise, Emory. I'll marry you!" Her pleas changed to sobs.

"No, Manda, darling, no!" Jason yelled, and continued his slow, steady approach.

Manda, huddled dejectedly on the grassy verge of the path, struggled to pull her bruised hand from beneath Emory's shoe. If she could trip him, throw his mark off when he pulled the trigger . . . But her efforts were in vain. Tears blinded her, rolled down her colorless cheeks. She felt like some writhing insect being crushed underfoot.

A gunshot cracked.

She fainted.

Manda's first conscious sensation involved a strange kind of jiggling, floating movement. Opening her eyes, she recognized, a couple of inches from her nose, the hammered silver buttons of Jason's royal blue sweater. Jason wasn't dead! She was in his arms, being carried . . . she didn't care where. As long as he was all right, nothing else mattered.

She had promised, and she would marry Emory. It would be sheer hell, but at least she could take comfort in the knowledge that, even if she never saw Jason's beloved face again, somewhere on earth he would be alive.

Manda sighed. Total memory recall had been a painful, wearying experience and now, finally, she truly belonged to herself.

Until she belonged to Emory. Her whole body shuddered at the repulsive thought.

Jason felt her shaking against his chest. Smiling down into her wan sad face, he hugged her close, leaned his head over, and tenderly kissed her forehead.

"You don't have to be afraid anymore," he murmured. "Ahead are only happy days."

"Emory . . . I promised," she said in a high wavering voice. "I have to marry—"

"Emory is dead, Manda, darling."

"Oh." All she could feel was relief. At length she asked, "How—how did he—? Did you get his gun and shoot him?"

Jason grinned and shook his head. "I'm not the hero. Dr. Johannsen saved us both."

"But . . . He ran away."

"That's what I thought, too, at first."

They'd reached the inn. Bess hovered over her, patting her arm, crooning encouraging syllables of nonsense, and in general obstructing Jason's progress as he carried Manda through the house to the living room and gently deposited her on the sofa.

"Clive?" Jason inquired of Bess.

"He stayed with the bod—with them." She gave Jason a quizzical glance.

"I've already told Manda about Emory."

"You said them." Manda had immediately picked

up on the word. "Is Dr. Nils dead, too?"

"According to Clive, he's still breathing," Bess replied. "I warned him not to move the doctor before the ambulance team arrives."

"He was shot?"

"Oh, no, Manda." Bess patted Manda's shoulder, then again looked questioningly at Jason, who nodded permission for her to continue. "While Mr. Wade was dragging you along the path, the doctor ran through the woods to outflank you. Just as Mr. Wade pulled the trigger to . . . to shoot Jason, the doctor came from the side, and hit Mr. Wade so hard that they both fell over the edge together."

"Oh, my God," Manda murmured.

"Wade landed on the rocks," Jason told her. "Dr. Johannsen tumbled down the face of the cliff, which broke some of his fall."

"I hope—" She stopped when she heard the distant siren. "The ambulance?"

"No, my darling." Jason kept saying that wonderful word! "That will be the sheriff. Clive called them when Wade pulled out the gun. A little bit later, Bess phoned for the ambulance. I'm sure it'll be here shortly."

"Do I have to talk to the police today?" she begged, tears of exhaustion forming in her eyes. In the last week and a half, she'd had more than enough of talking to policemen.

"You certainly do not," Bess replied crisply. "I'm a nurse, and I forbid it. You've been through a trying ordeal. You're practically in shock."

"Don't overdo it, Bess," Jason chuckled. "Just be firm about her needing several hours' rest. I'll handle everything else."

"Humph!" she grunted in agreement.

Manda adored the big homely woman.

She closed her eyes and snuggled under the soft fuzzy afghan Jason spread over her. As he tucked the edges of the coverlet around the swells of her breasts and hips, she quivered rapturously at his touch. This time he kissed her on the lips.

Chapter Twenty-three

At mid-afternoon the following day, Jason came home.

He'd phoned from the hospital around midnight, to inform Bess that Dr. Johannsen's hip operation had gone well. The doctor had sustained several fractured ribs, a broken arm, a crushed hip, and a multitude of cuts, some requiring stitches. Nevertheless he'd been lucky. The surgeon thought a slight limp would be his only permanent damage.

Jason spent the early morning hours dozing in a chair in the patient's private room. Without a doubt he owed the man his life, because Wade's shot would have found its mark if the doctor hadn't tackled the crazed gunman at the instant of firing.

Jason had kept a vigil beside Dr. Johannsen's bed for another reason. Before the ambulance sped away from Tangletrees, the injured man had mumbled, "Tell Manda . . . tell Manda . . ." and lapsed into unconsciousness. Jason was waiting to hear first-hand the doctor's message for Manda. Regardless of the mishandling of Manda's therapy, Jason understood her deep concern over the doctor's injuries. She could never discount the man's taking her into his home when she had been ill and alone in the world.

Manda had been waiting impatiently for Jason's return from the hospital.

The same sheriff's deputy who had investigated her near-drowning had returned soon after breakfast to speak with her about the events leading up to Emory's death. He didn't tarry long. Jason had filled him in the evening before about the accident itself. Mostly, Deputy Watson wanted background information on Emory. The name and address of his next of kin, whether or not he had a police record and, if so, where. She knew none of those facts. It struck her that Emory—of his own choice—had been as lost and unknown to everyone as her amnesia had compelled her to be.

Manda was leaning against the terrace railing, watching a pelican dive into a cresting wave and flap away with a dripping fish in its pouchy beak, when she heard Jason's footsteps behind her.

Her heart vaulted into her throat as he spun her around and took her in his arms. Savoring his prolonged hungry kiss, she clung to him in ecstasy.

Their lips parted, and Jason thought he'd never forget the wonderment on her adoring ingenuous face.

"I love you, Manda," he said huskily. "I have, almost from the moment you stepped inside this house that foggy twilight almost two weeks ago. But . . . that's part of the problem—"

"Problem?" Suddenly she was smitten with dread. What could be wrong now, after Jason had just told her that he loved her?